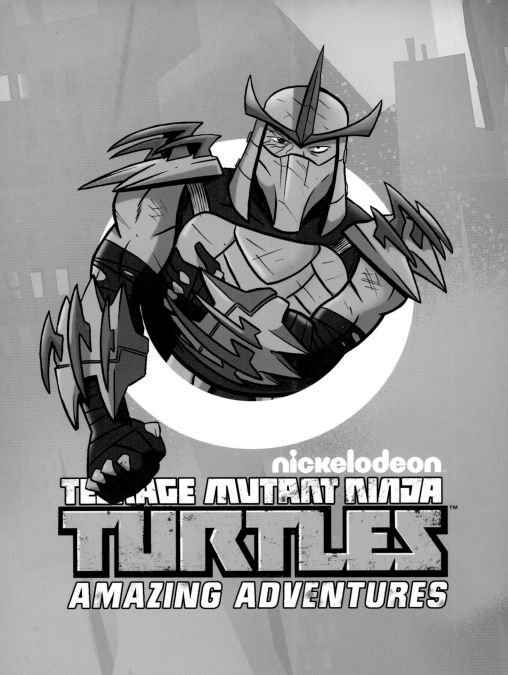

nickelodeon

TEENAGE MUTANT NINJA
TURTLES™
AMAZING ADVENTURES

The Meeting of the Mutanimals
Story by **Matthew K. Manning**
Art by **Chad Thomas**
Colors by **Heather Breckel**

Volcano Time
By **James Kochalka**

Zine-Age Mutant Ninja Turtle
By **Caleb Goellner, Chad Thomas**, and **Noah Van Sciver**

Special thanks to Joan Hilty & Linda Lee for their invaluable assistance.

ISBN: 978-1-63140-779-6

nickelodeon™

For international rights, contact licensing@idwpublishing.com

19 18 17 16   1 2 3 4

Ted Adams, CEO & Publisher
Greg Goldstein, President & COO
Robbie Robbins, EVP/Sr. Graphic Artist
Chris Ryall, Chief Creative Officer/Editor-in-Chief
Laurie Windrow, Senior Vice President of Sales & Marketing
Matthew Ruzicka, CPA, Chief Financial Officer
Dirk Wood, VP of Marketing
Lorelei Bunjes, VP of Digital Services
Jeff Webber, VP of Licensing, Digital and Subsidiary Rights
Jerry Bennington, VP of New Product Development

www.IDWPUBLISHING.com

Facebook: facebook.com/idwpublishing
Twitter: @idwpublishing
YouTube: youtube.com/idwpublishing
Tumblr: tumblr.idwpublishing.com
Instagram: instagram.com/idwpublishing

Zodiac
Story by **Landry Q. Walker**
Art by **Chad Thomas**
Colors by **Heather Breckel**

Freaks and Frogs
By **Ben Costa**

Donnie Finds A Relic
By **Sina Grace**

Series Edits by **Bobby Curnow**
Cover by **Jon Sommariva**
Collection Edits by **Justin Eisinger** and **Alonzo Simon**
Letters and Collection Design by **Shawn Lee**
Publisher: **Ted Adams**

Art by **Jon Sommariva**

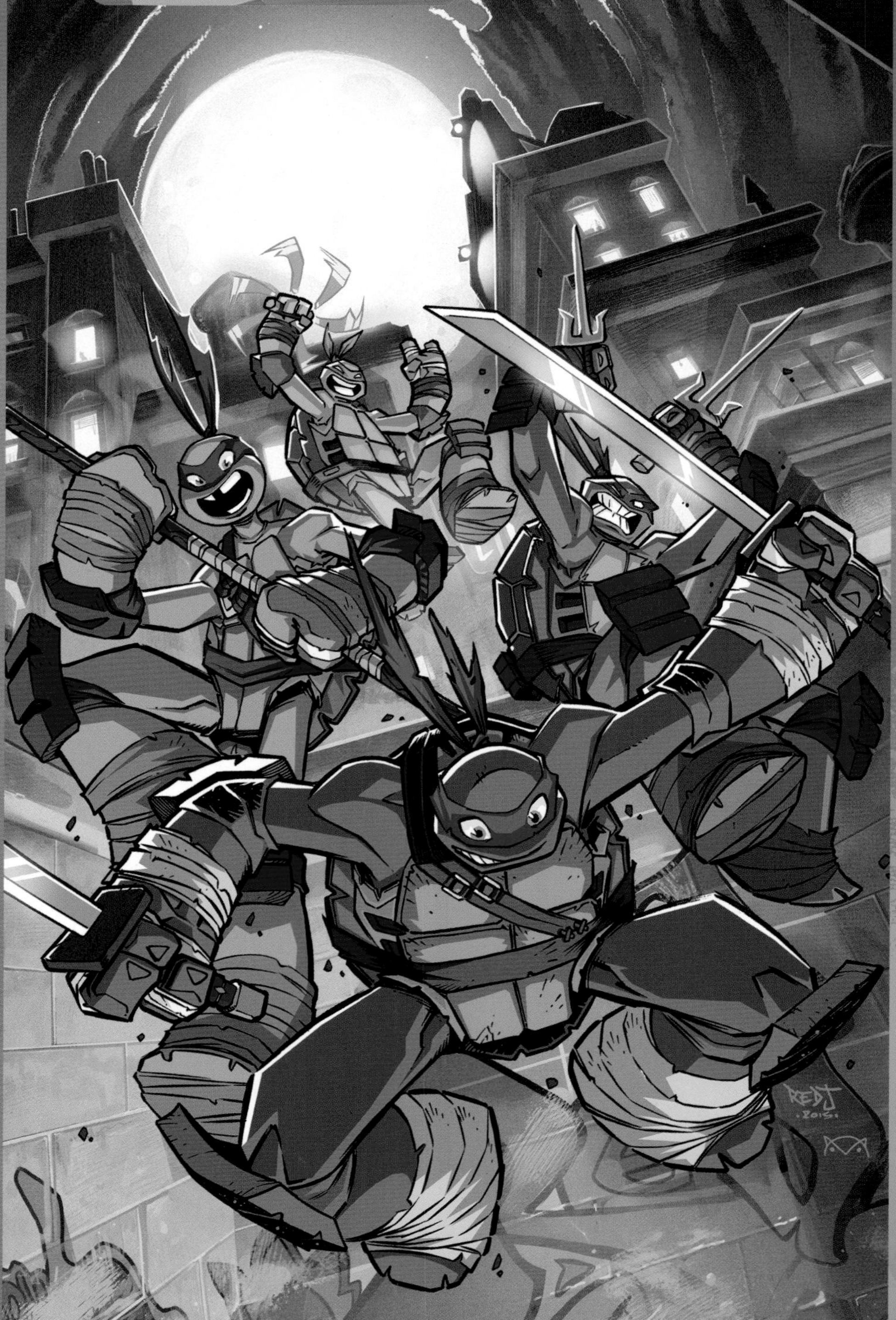

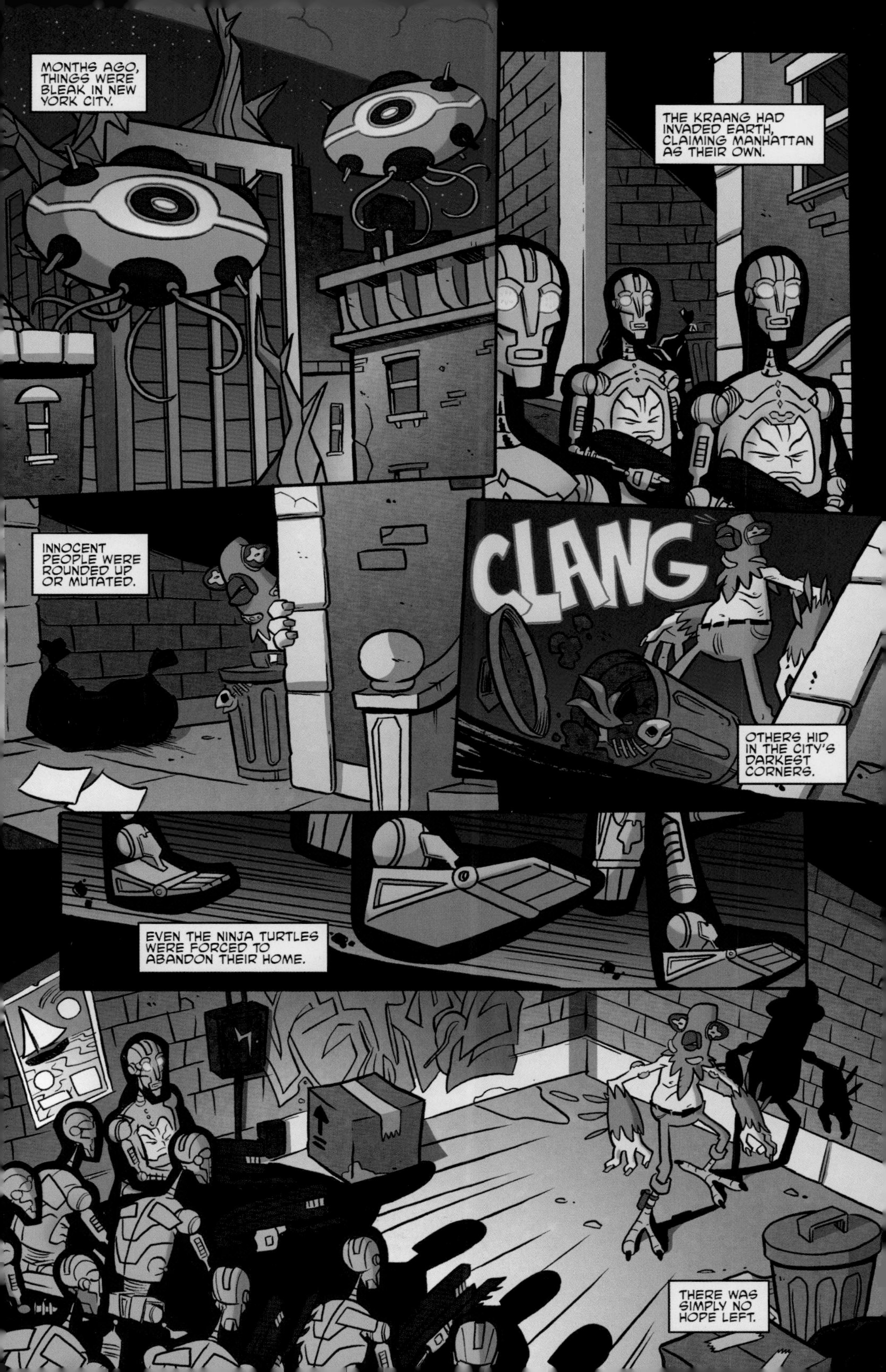
MONTHS AGO, THINGS WERE BLEAK IN NEW YORK CITY.
THE KRAANG HAD INVADED EARTH, CLAIMING MANHATTAN AS THEIR OWN.
INNOCENT PEOPLE WERE ROUNDED UP OR MUTATED.
CLANG
OTHERS HID IN THE CITY'S DARKEST CORNERS.
EVEN THE NINJA TURTLES WERE FORCED TO ABANDON THEIR HOME.
THERE WAS SIMPLY NO HOPE LEFT.

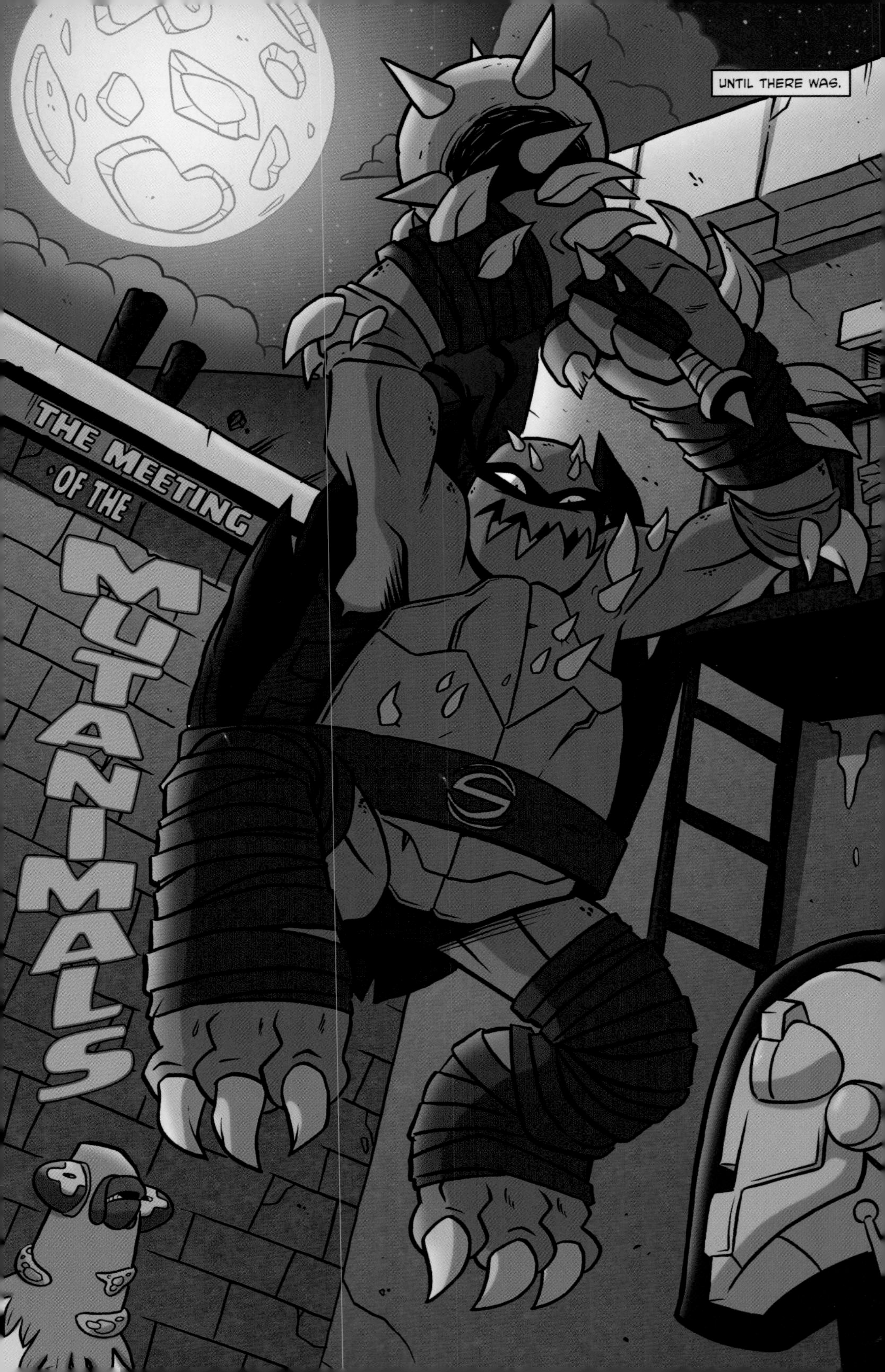
UNTIL THERE WAS.
THE MEETING OF THE MUTANIMALS

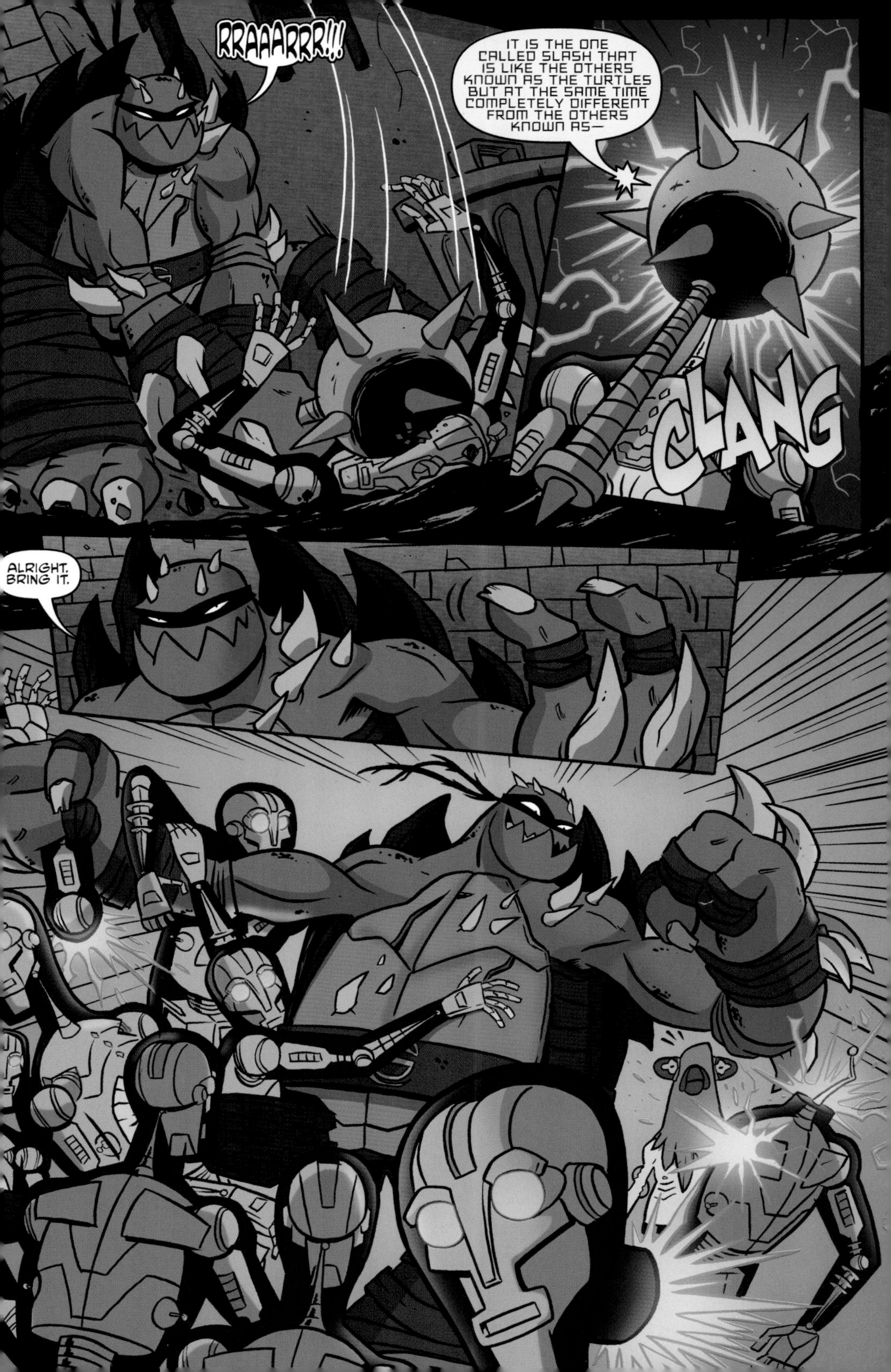
RRAAARRR!!!
IT IS THE ONE CALLED SLASH THAT IS LIKE THE OTHERS KNOWN AS THE TURTLES BUT AT THE SAME TIME COMPLETELY DIFFERENT FROM THE OTHERS KNOWN AS—
CLANG
ALRIGHT. BRING IT.

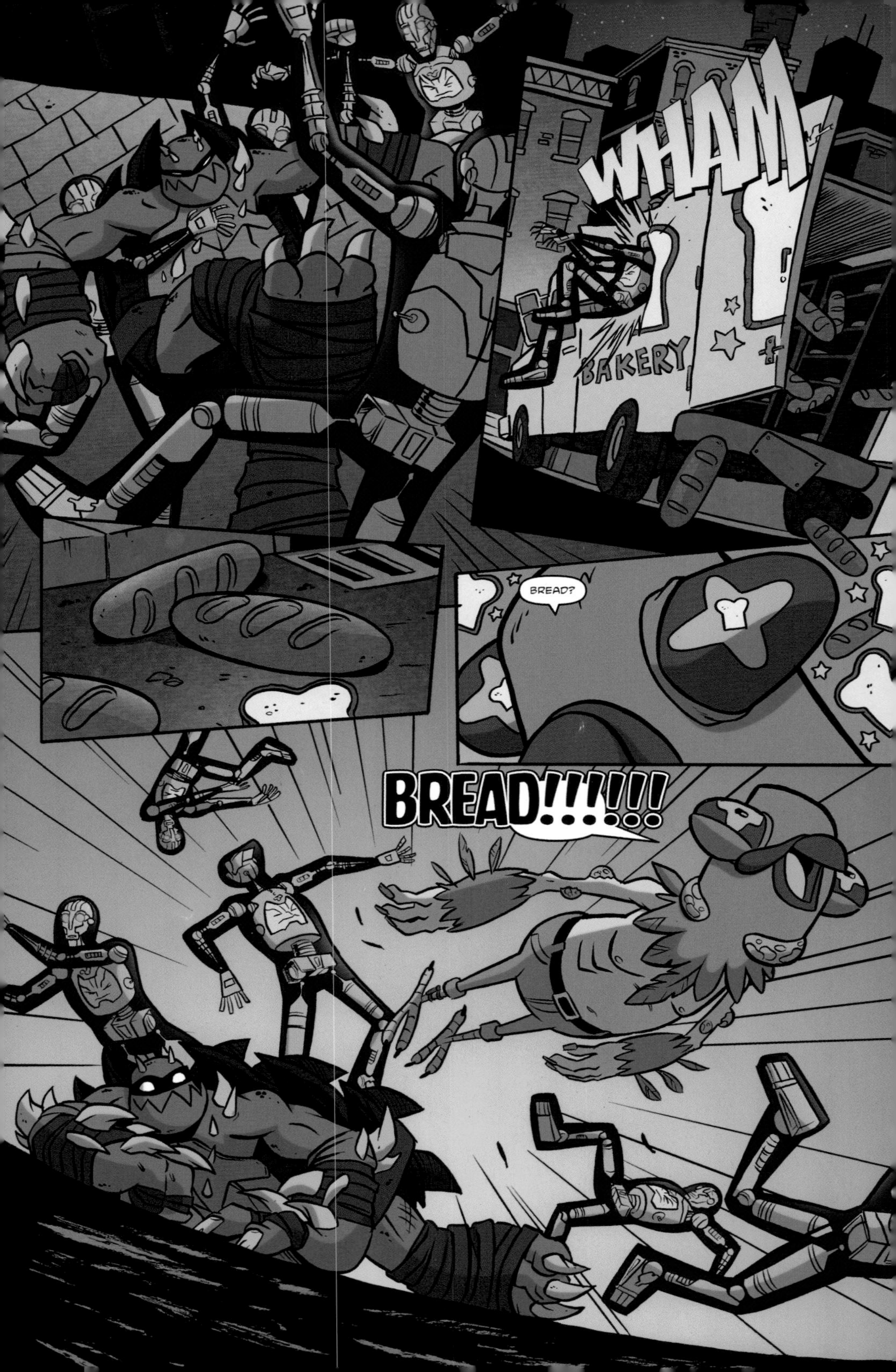
WHAM
BAKERY
BREAD?
BREAD!!!!!!!

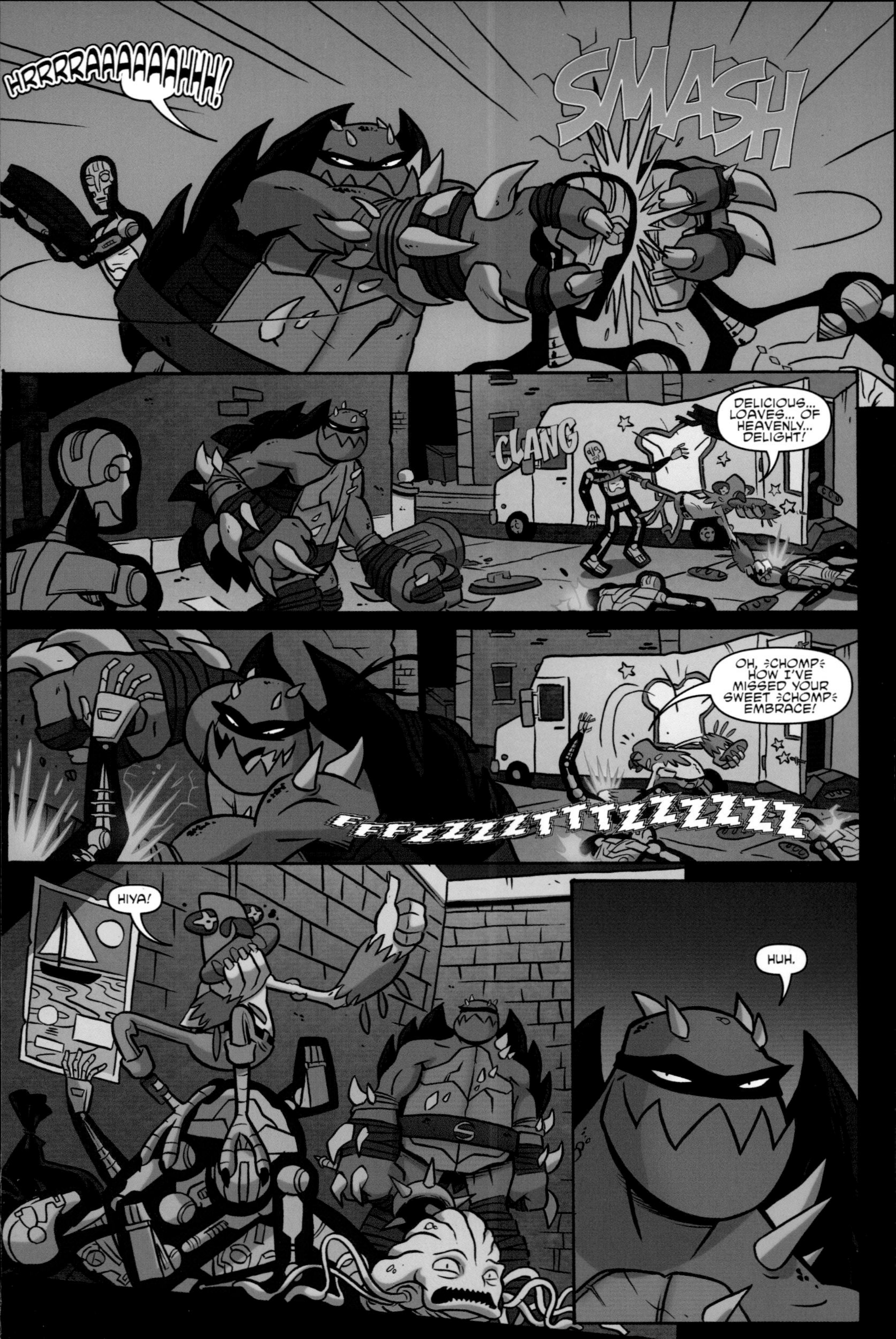
HRRRRAAAAAAAHHH!
SMASH
CLANG
DELICIOUS... LOAVES... OF HEAVENLY... DELIGHT!
OH, *CHOMP* HOW I'VE MISSED YOUR SWEET *CHOMP* EMBRACE!
FFFZZZZZZTTTTZZZZZZZZ
HIYA!
HUH.

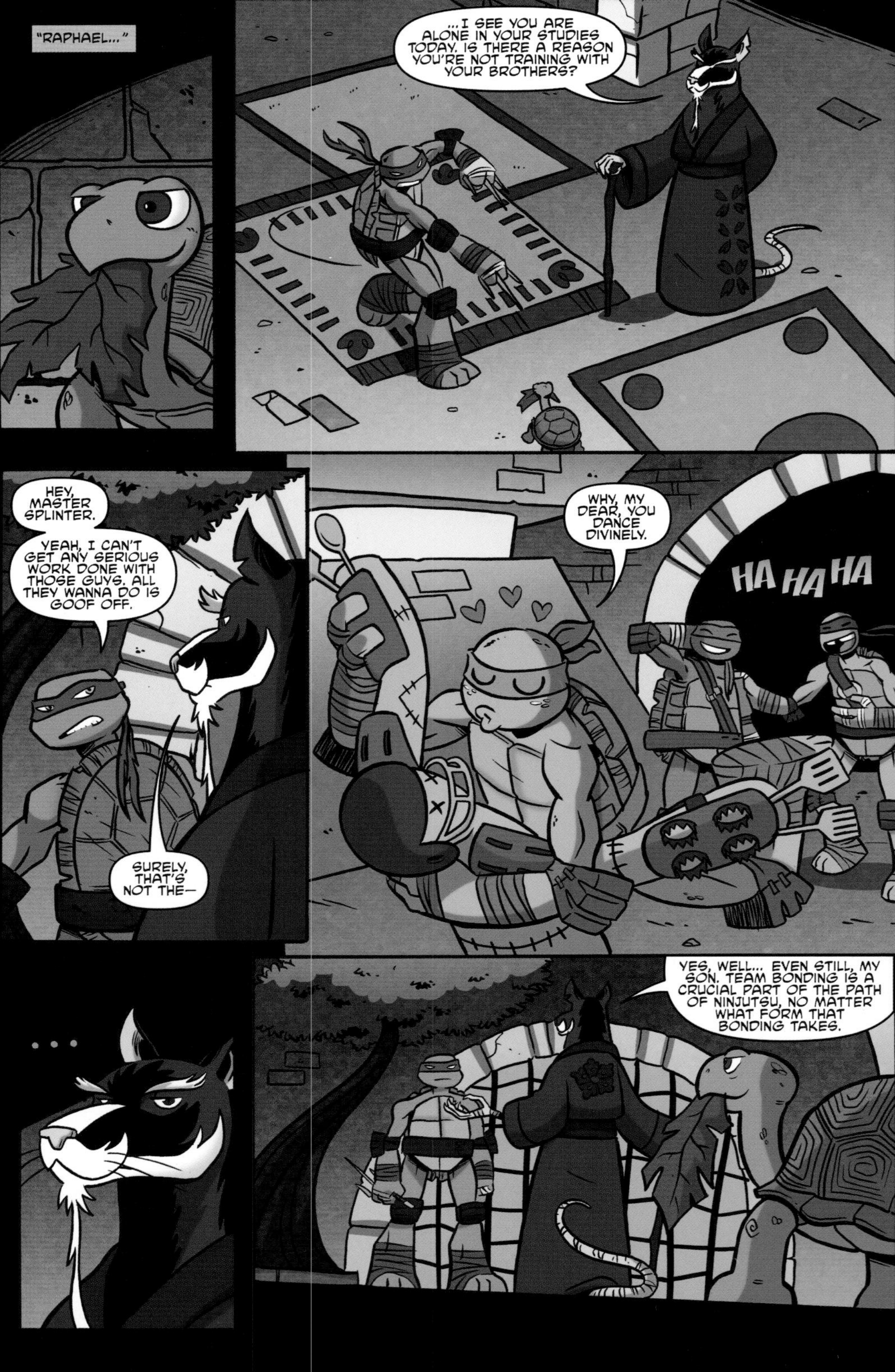
"RAPHAEL..."
...I SEE YOU ARE ALONE IN YOUR STUDIES TODAY. IS THERE A REASON YOU'RE NOT TRAINING WITH YOUR BROTHERS?
HEY, MASTER SPLINTER.
YEAH, I CAN'T GET ANY SERIOUS WORK DONE WITH THOSE GUYS. ALL THEY WANNA DO IS GOOF OFF.
SURELY, THAT'S NOT THE—
WHY, MY DEAR, YOU DANCE DIVINELY.
HA HA HA
...
YES, WELL... EVEN STILL, MY SON. TEAM BONDING IS A CRUCIAL PART OF THE PATH OF NINJUTSU, NO MATTER WHAT FORM THAT BONDING TAKES.

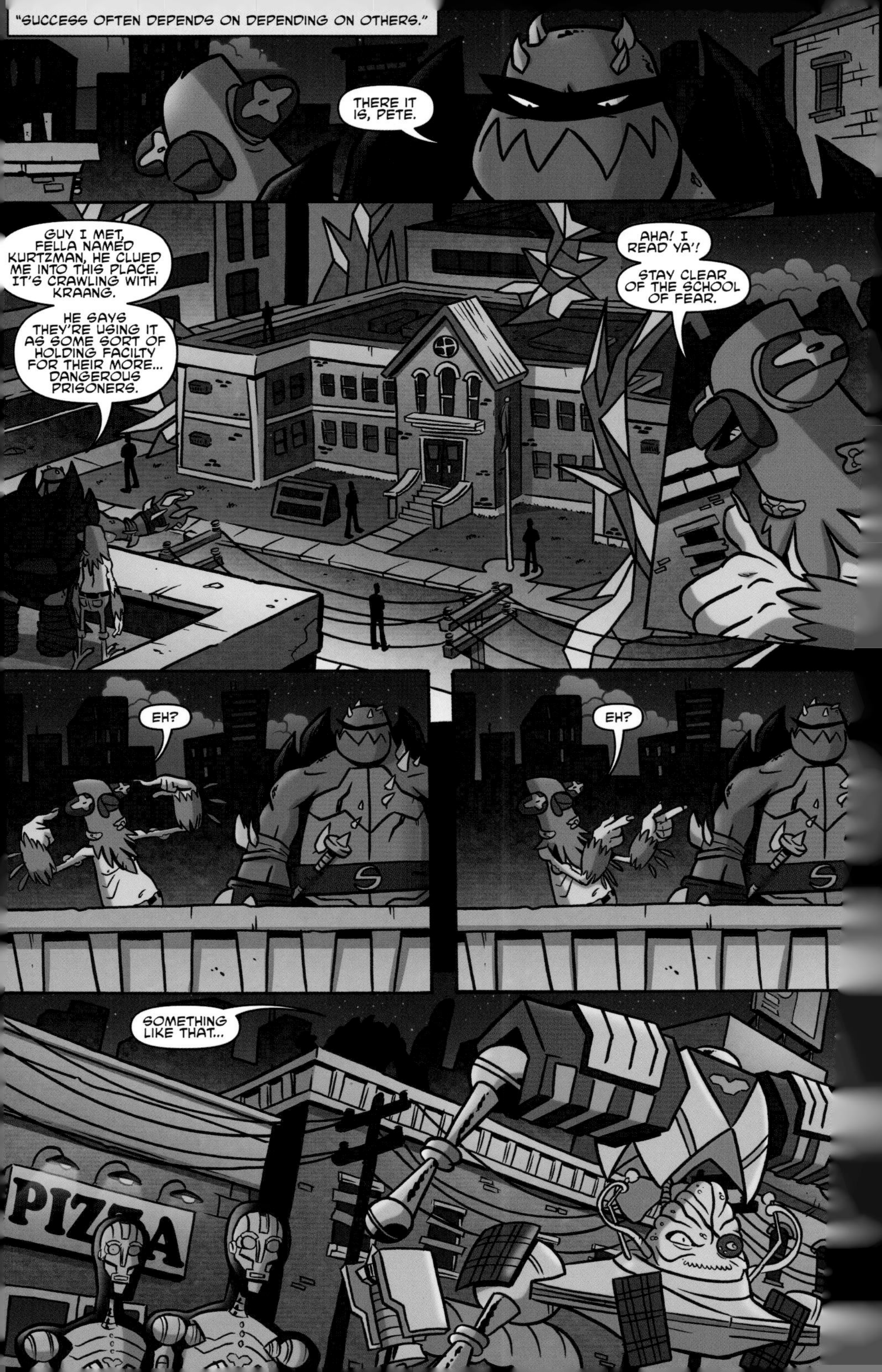
"SUCCESS OFTEN DEPENDS ON DEPENDING ON OTHERS."
THERE IT IS, PETE.
GUY I MET, FELLA NAMED KURTZMAN, HE CLUED ME INTO THIS PLACE. IT'S CRAWLING WITH KRAANG.
HE SAYS THEY'RE USING IT AS SOME SORT OF HOLDING FACILTY FOR THEIR MORE... DANGEROUS PRISONERS.
AHA! I READ YA'!
STAY CLEAR OF THE SCHOOL OF FEAR.
EH?
EH?
SOMETHING LIKE THAT...
PIZZA

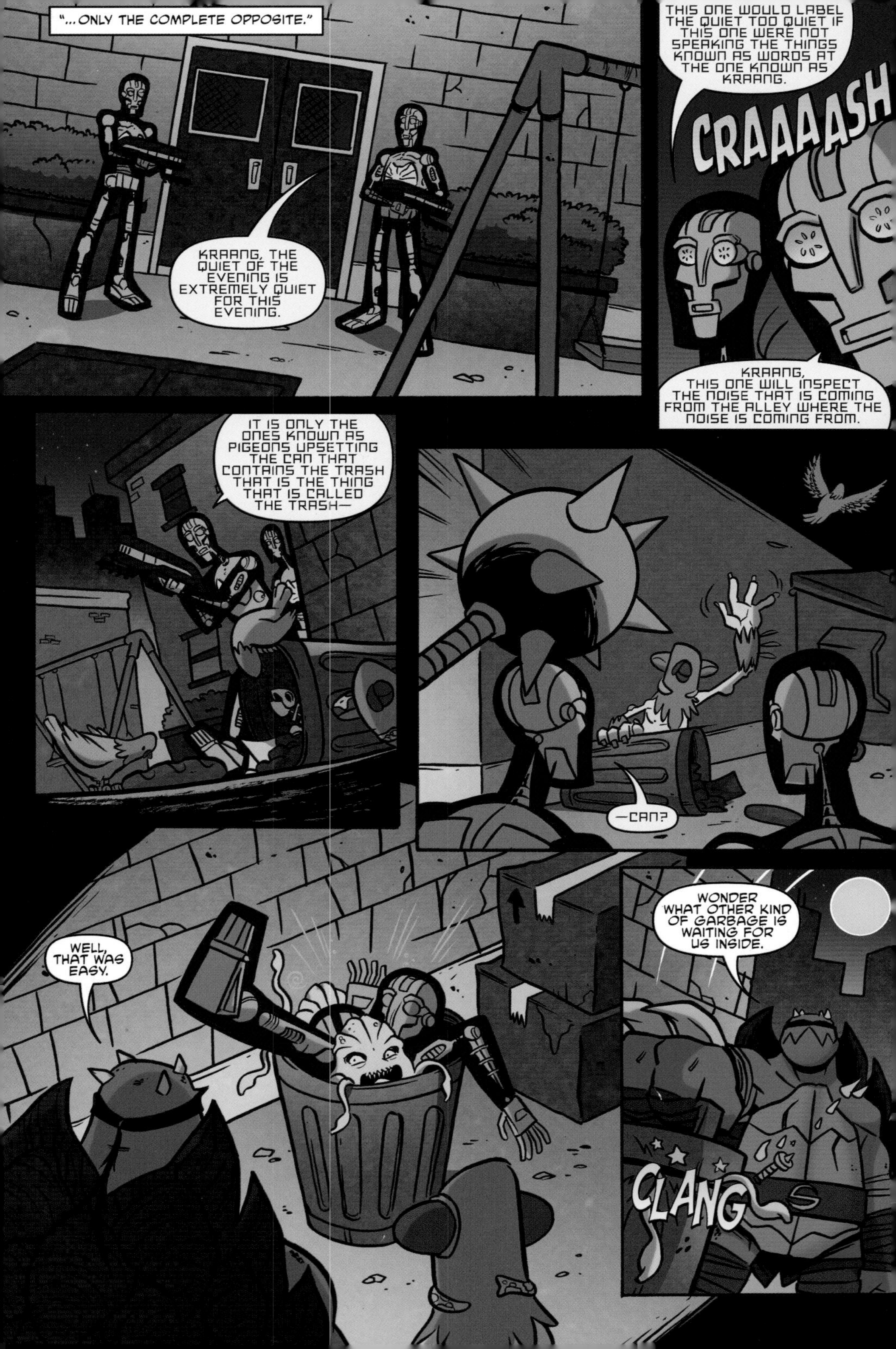
"...ONLY THE COMPLETE OPPOSITE."
KRAANG, THE QUIET OF THE EVENING IS EXTREMELY QUIET FOR THIS EVENING.
THIS ONE WOULD LABEL THE QUIET TOO QUIET IF THIS ONE WERE NOT SPEAKING THE THINGS KNOWN AS WORDS AT THE ONE KNOWN AS KRAANG.
CRAAAASH
KRAANG, THIS ONE WILL INSPECT THE NOISE THAT IS COMING FROM THE ALLEY WHERE THE NOISE IS COMING FROM.
IT IS ONLY THE ONES KNOWN AS PIGEONS UPSETTING THE CAN THAT CONTAINS THE TRASH THAT IS THE THING THAT IS CALLED THE TRASH—
—CAN?
WELL, THAT WAS EASY.
WONDER WHAT OTHER KIND OF GARBAGE IS WAITING FOR US INSIDE.
CLANG

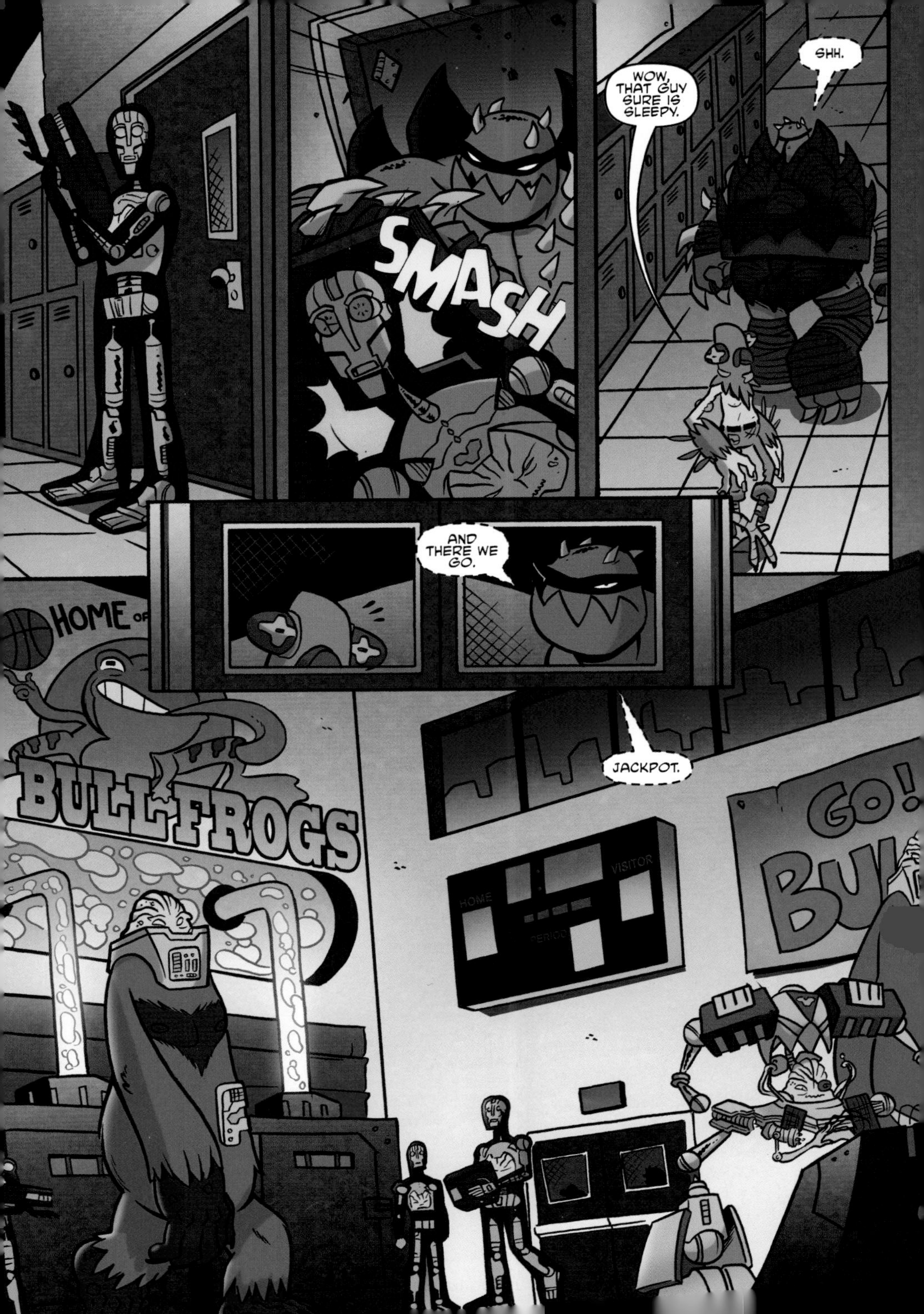
SMASH
WOW, THAT GUY SURE IS SLEEPY.
SHH.
AND THERE WE GO.
HOME OF
BULLFROGS
JACKPOT.
GO!
HOME
VISITOR
PERIOD

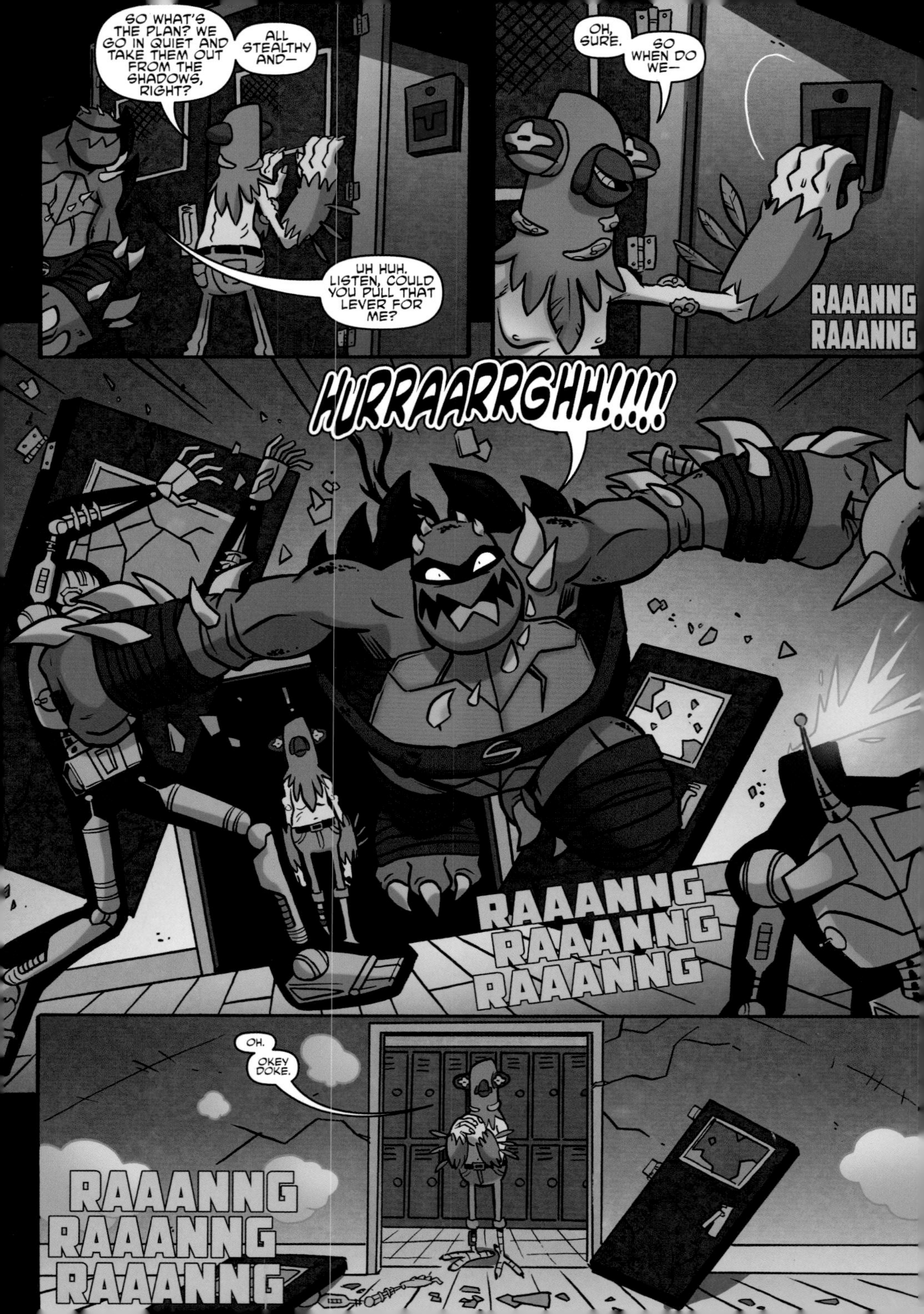
SO WHAT'S THE PLAN? WE GO IN QUIET AND TAKE THEM OUT FROM THE SHADOWS, RIGHT?
ALL STEALTHY AND—
UH HUH. LISTEN, COULD YOU PULL THAT LEVER FOR ME?
OH, SURE.
SO WHEN DO WE—
RAAANNG
RAAANNG
HURRAARRGHH!!!!!
RAAANNG
RAAANNG
RAAANNG
OH.
OKEY DOKE.
RAAANNG
RAAANNG
RAAANNG

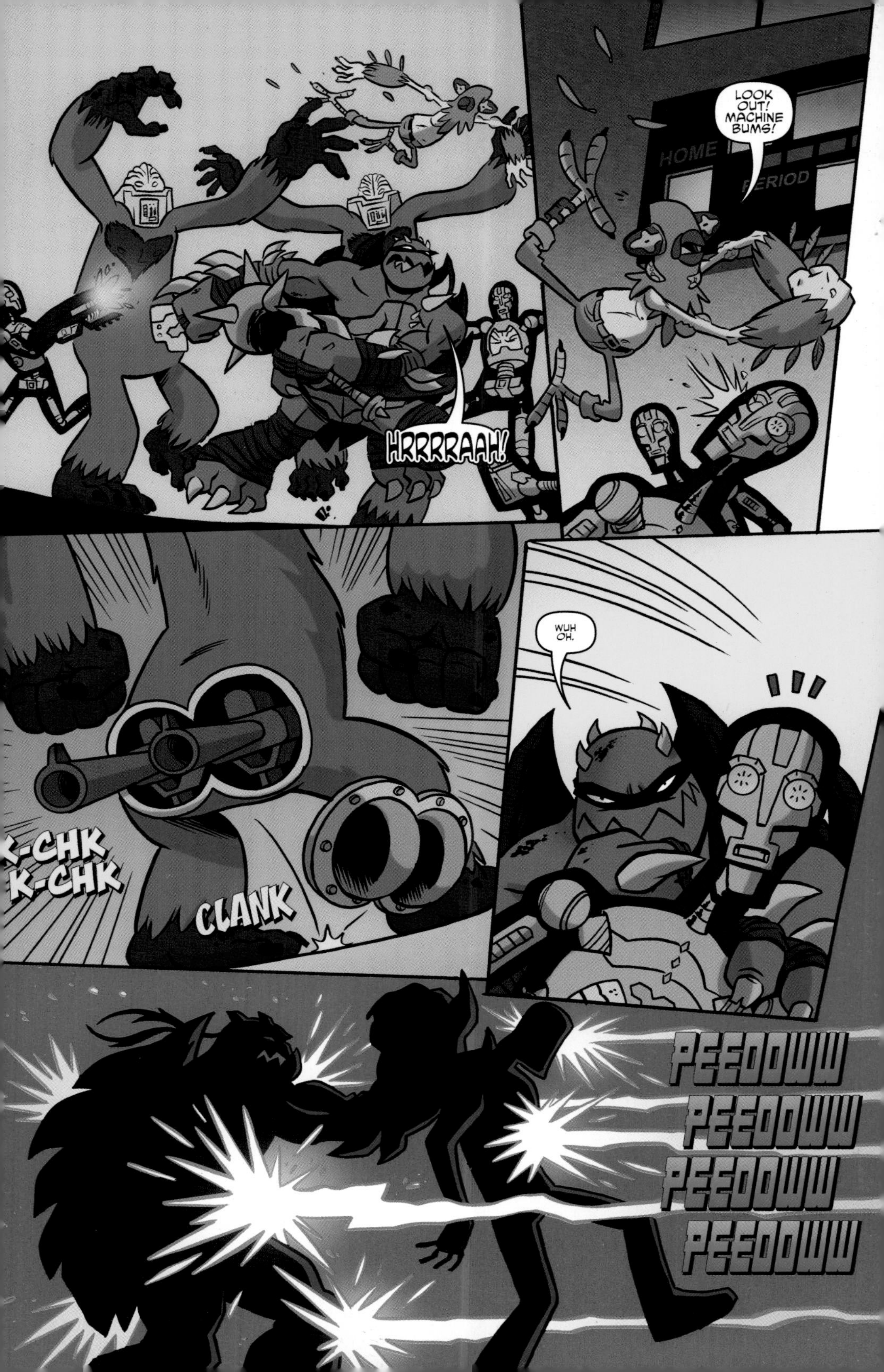

LOOK OUT! MACHINE BUMS!
HOME
PERIOD
HRRRRAAH!
K-CHK
K-CHK
CLANK
WUH OH.
PEEOOWW
PEEOOWW
PEEOOWW
PEEOOWW

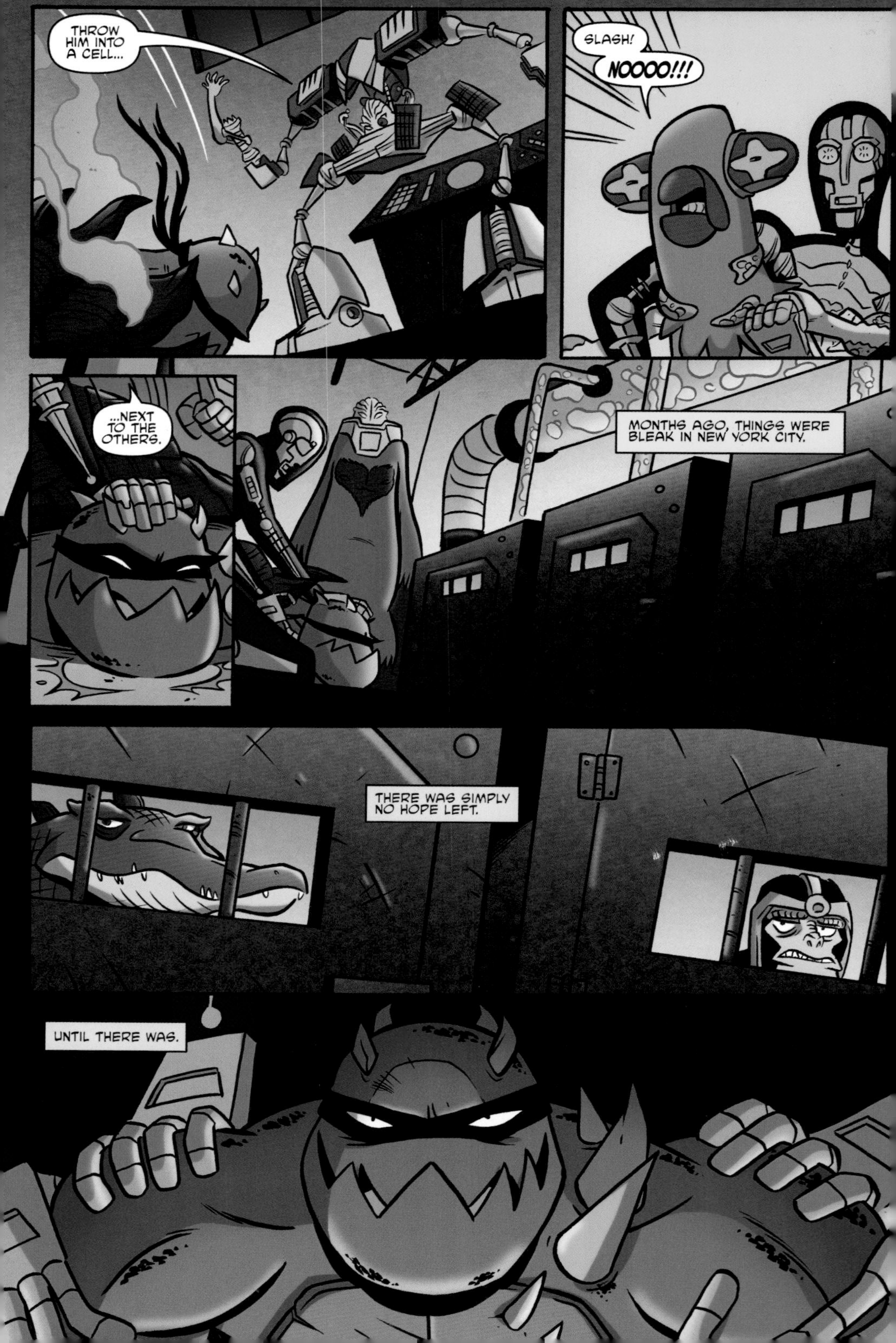
THROW HIM INTO A CELL...
SLASH!
NOOOO!!!
...NEXT TO THE OTHERS.
MONTHS AGO, THINGS WERE BLEAK IN NEW YORK CITY.
THERE WAS SIMPLY NO HOPE LEFT.
UNTIL THERE WAS.

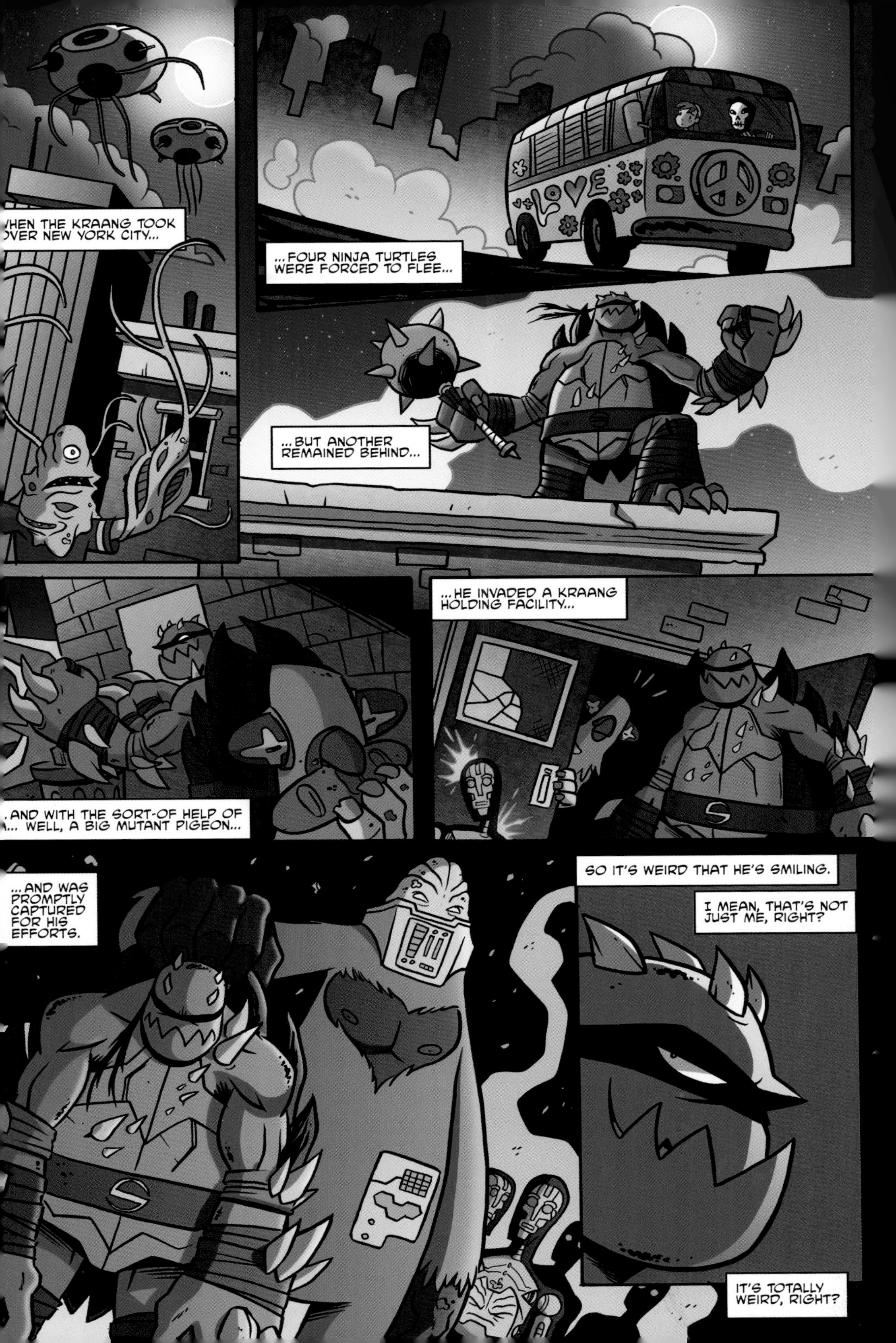

WHEN THE KRAANG TOOK OVER NEW YORK CITY...
...FOUR NINJA TURTLES WERE FORCED TO FLEE...
LOVE
...BUT ANOTHER REMAINED BEHIND...
...AND WITH THE SORT-OF HELP OF A... WELL, A BIG MUTANT PIGEON...
...HE INVADED A KRAANG HOLDING FACILITY...
...AND WAS PROMPTLY CAPTURED FOR HIS EFFORTS.
SO IT'S WEIRD THAT HE'S SMILING.
I MEAN, THAT'S NOT JUST ME, RIGHT?
IT'S TOTALLY WEIRD, RIGHT?

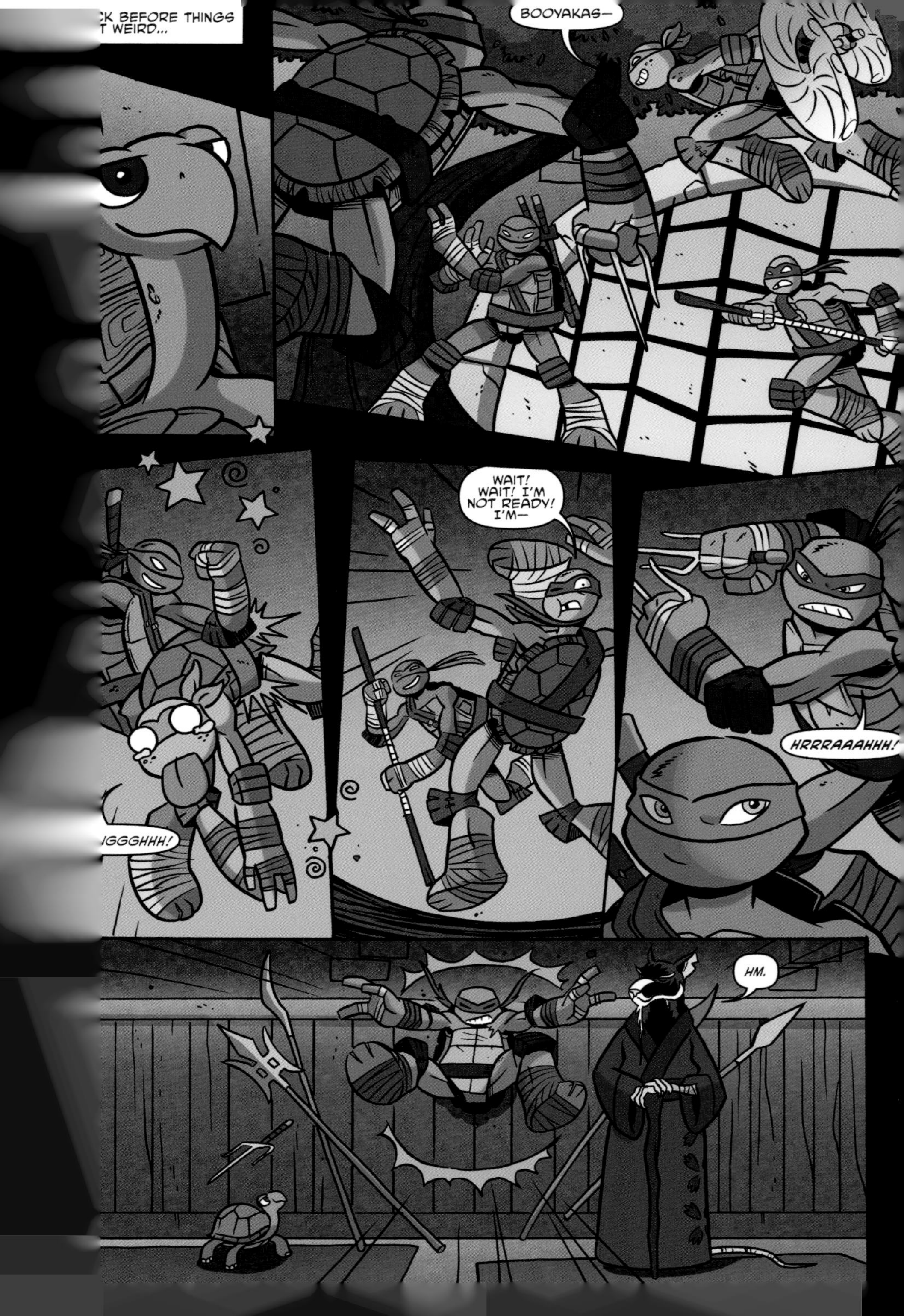

CK BEFORE THINGS
T WEIRD...
BOOYAKAS—
IGGGHHH!
WAIT! WAIT! I'M NOT READY! I'M—
HRRRAAAHHH!
HM.

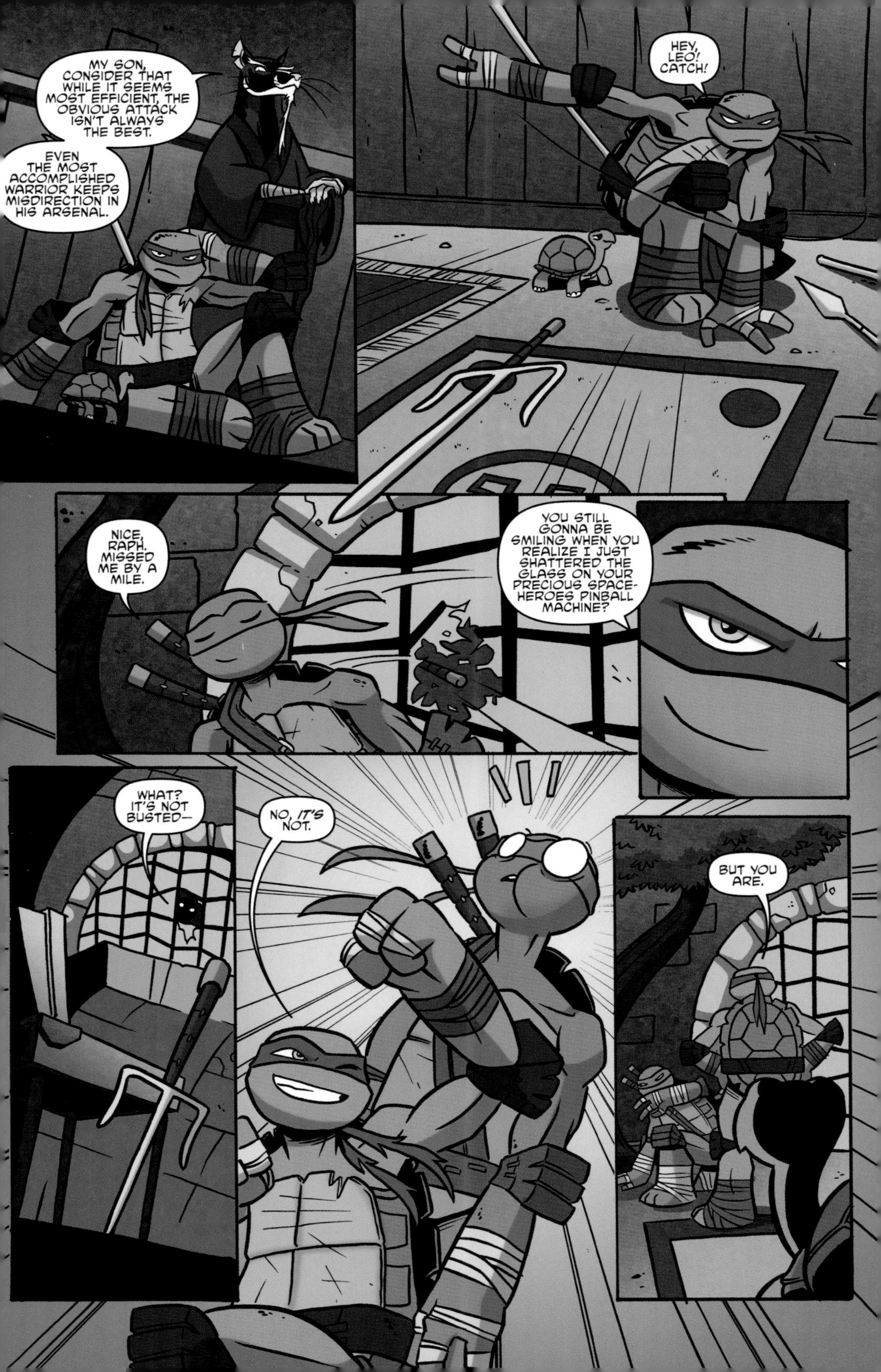
MY SON, CONSIDER THAT WHILE IT SEEMS MOST EFFICIENT, THE OBVIOUS ATTACK ISN'T ALWAYS THE BEST.
EVEN THE MOST ACCOMPLISHED WARRIOR KEEPS MISDIRECTION IN HIS ARSENAL.
HEY, LEO! CATCH!
NICE, RAPH. MISSED ME BY A MILE.
YOU STILL GONNA BE SMILING WHEN YOU REALIZE I JUST SHATTERED THE GLASS ON YOUR PRECIOUS SPACE-HEROES PINBALL MACHINE?
WHAT? IT'S NOT BUSTED—
NO, IT'S NOT.
BUT YOU ARE.

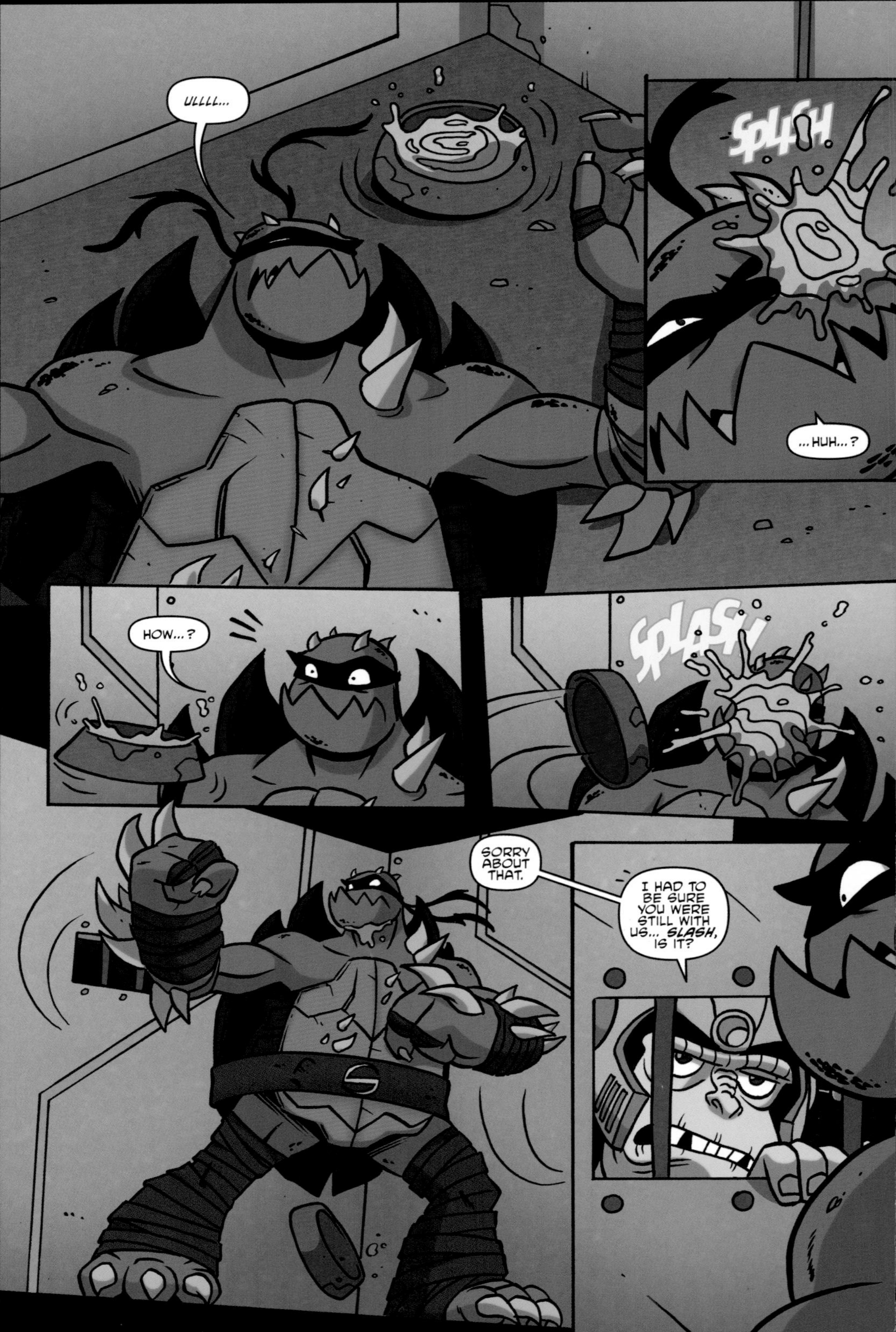

ULLLL...
SPLASH
...HUH...?
HOW...?
SPLASH
SORRY ABOUT THAT.
I HAD TO BE SURE YOU WERE STILL WITH US... SLASH, IS IT?

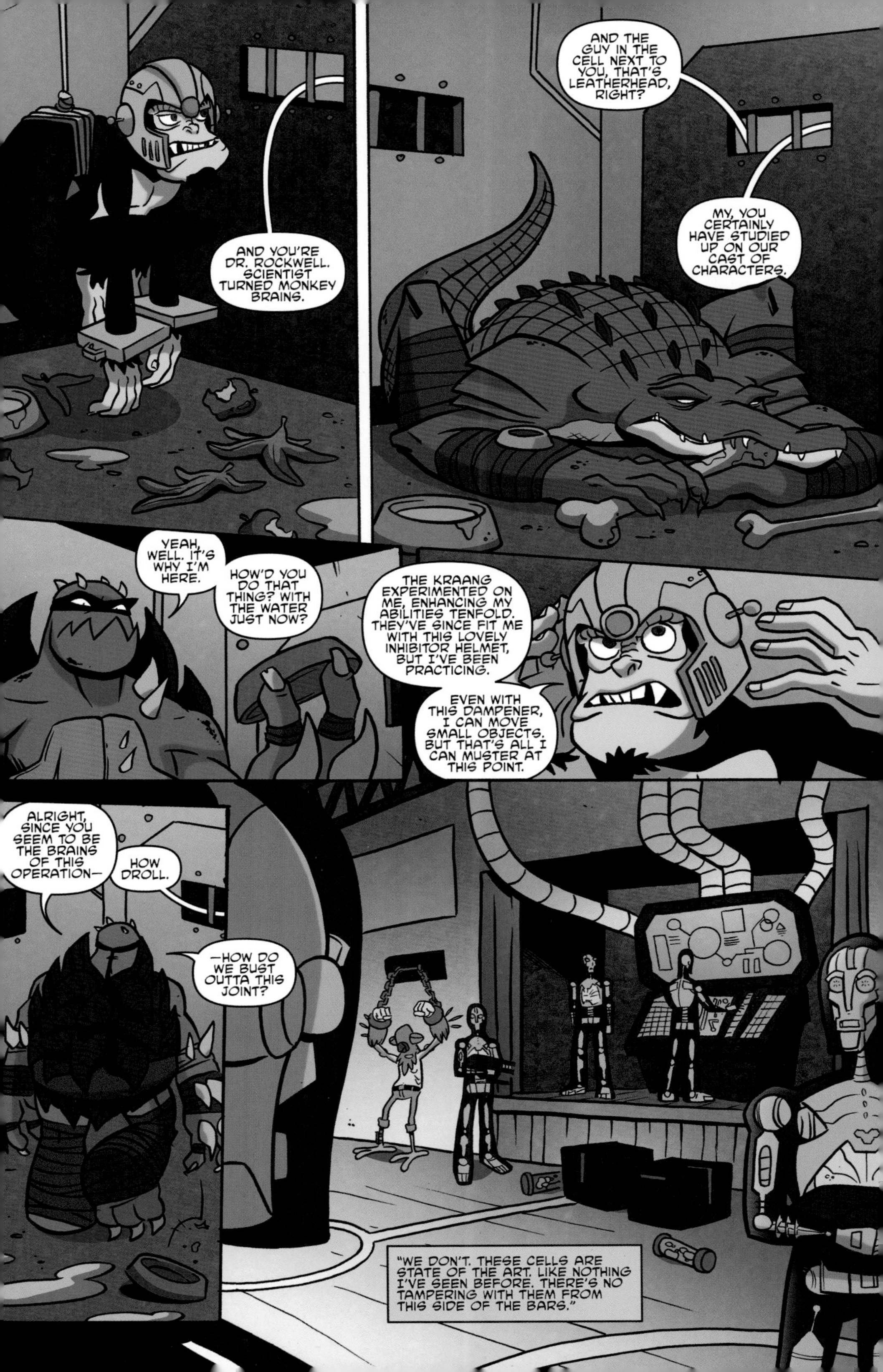
AND YOU'RE DR. ROCKWELL. SCIENTIST TURNED MONKEY BRAINS.
AND THE GUY IN THE CELL NEXT TO YOU, THAT'S LEATHERHEAD, RIGHT?
MY, YOU CERTAINLY HAVE STUDIED UP ON OUR CAST OF CHARACTERS.
YEAH, WELL. IT'S WHY I'M HERE.
HOW'D YOU DO THAT THING? WITH THE WATER JUST NOW?
THE KRAANG EXPERIMENTED ON ME, ENHANCING MY ABILITIES TENFOLD. THEY'VE SINCE FIT ME WITH THIS LOVELY INHIBITOR HELMET, BUT I'VE BEEN PRACTICING.
EVEN WITH THIS DAMPENER, I CAN MOVE SMALL OBJECTS. BUT THAT'S ALL I CAN MUSTER AT THIS POINT.
ALRIGHT, SINCE YOU SEEM TO BE THE BRAINS OF THIS OPERATION—
HOW DROLL.
—HOW DO WE BUST OUTTA THIS JOINT?
"WE DON'T. THESE CELLS ARE STATE OF THE ART. LIKE NOTHING I'VE SEEN BEFORE. THERE'S NO TAMPERING WITH THEM FROM THIS SIDE OF THE BARS."

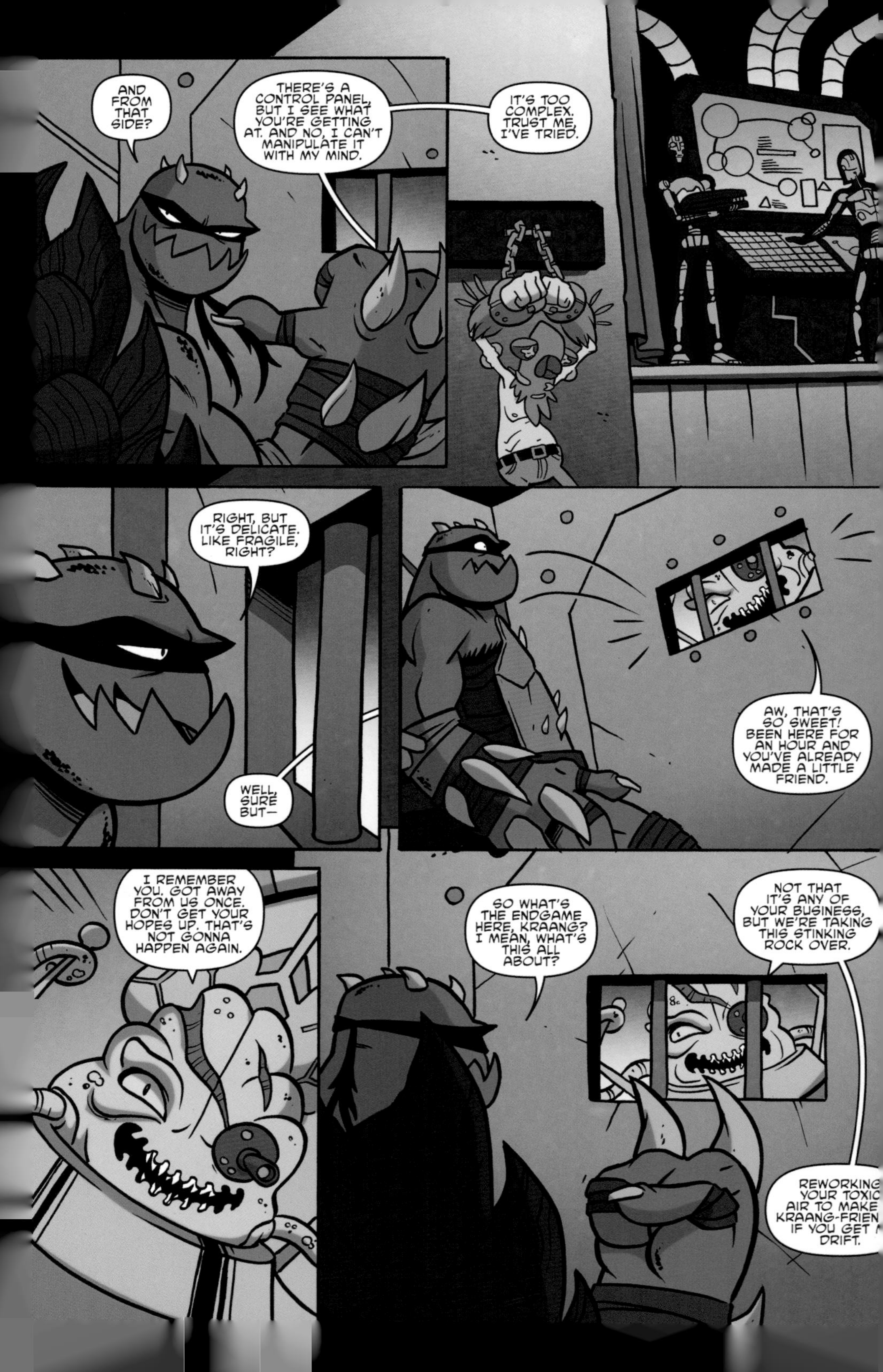
AND FROM THAT SIDE?
THERE'S A CONTROL PANEL, BUT I SEE WHAT YOU'RE GETTING AT. AND NO, I CAN'T MANIPULATE IT WITH MY MIND.
IT'S TOO COMPLEX. TRUST ME, I'VE TRIED.
RIGHT, BUT IT'S DELICATE. LIKE FRAGILE, RIGHT?
WELL, SURE BUT—
AW, THAT'S SO SWEET! BEEN HERE FOR AN HOUR AND YOU'VE ALREADY MADE A LITTLE FRIEND.
I REMEMBER YOU. GOT AWAY FROM US ONCE. DON'T GET YOUR HOPES UP. THAT'S NOT GONNA HAPPEN AGAIN.
SO WHAT'S THE ENDGAME HERE, KRAANG? I MEAN, WHAT'S THIS ALL ABOUT?
NOT THAT IT'S ANY OF YOUR BUSINESS, BUT WE'RE TAKING THIS STINKING ROCK OVER.
REWORKING YOUR TOXIC AIR TO MAKE

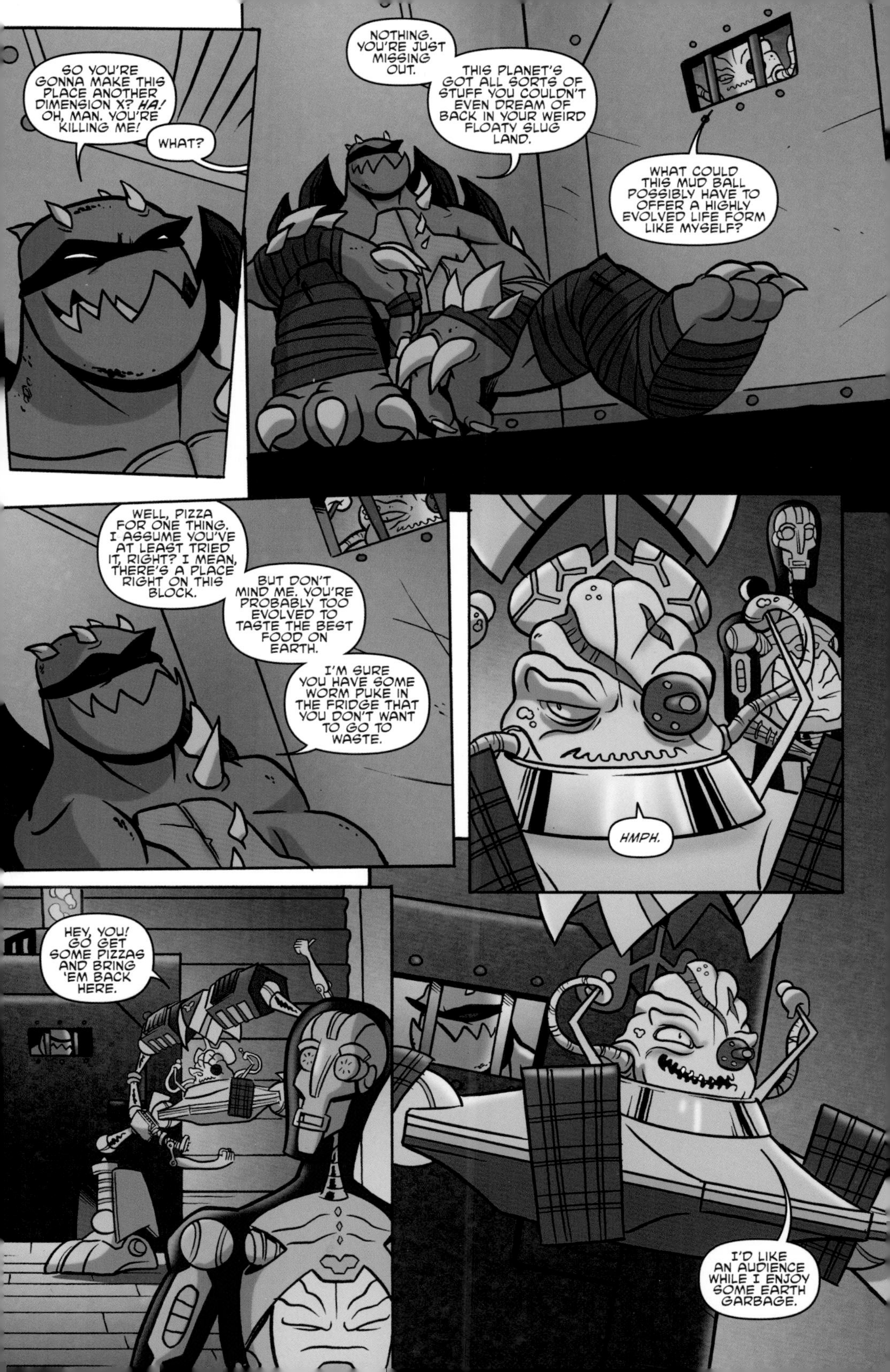
SO YOU'RE GONNA MAKE THIS PLACE ANOTHER DIMENSION X? HA! OH, MAN. YOU'RE KILLING ME!
WHAT?
NOTHING. YOU'RE JUST MISSING OUT.
THIS PLANET'S GOT ALL SORTS OF STUFF YOU COULDN'T EVEN DREAM OF BACK IN YOUR WEIRD FLOATY SLUG LAND.
WHAT COULD THIS MUD BALL POSSIBLY HAVE TO OFFER A HIGHLY EVOLVED LIFE FORM LIKE MYSELF?
WELL, PIZZA FOR ONE THING. I ASSUME YOU'VE AT LEAST TRIED IT, RIGHT? I MEAN, THERE'S A PLACE RIGHT ON THIS BLOCK.
BUT DON'T MIND ME. YOU'RE PROBABLY TOO EVOLVED TO TASTE THE BEST FOOD ON EARTH.
I'M SURE YOU HAVE SOME WORM PUKE IN THE FRIDGE THAT YOU DON'T WANT TO GO TO WASTE.
HMPH.
HEY, YOU! GO GET SOME PIZZAS AND BRING 'EM BACK HERE.
I'D LIKE AN AUDIENCE WHILE I ENJOY SOME EARTH GARBAGE.

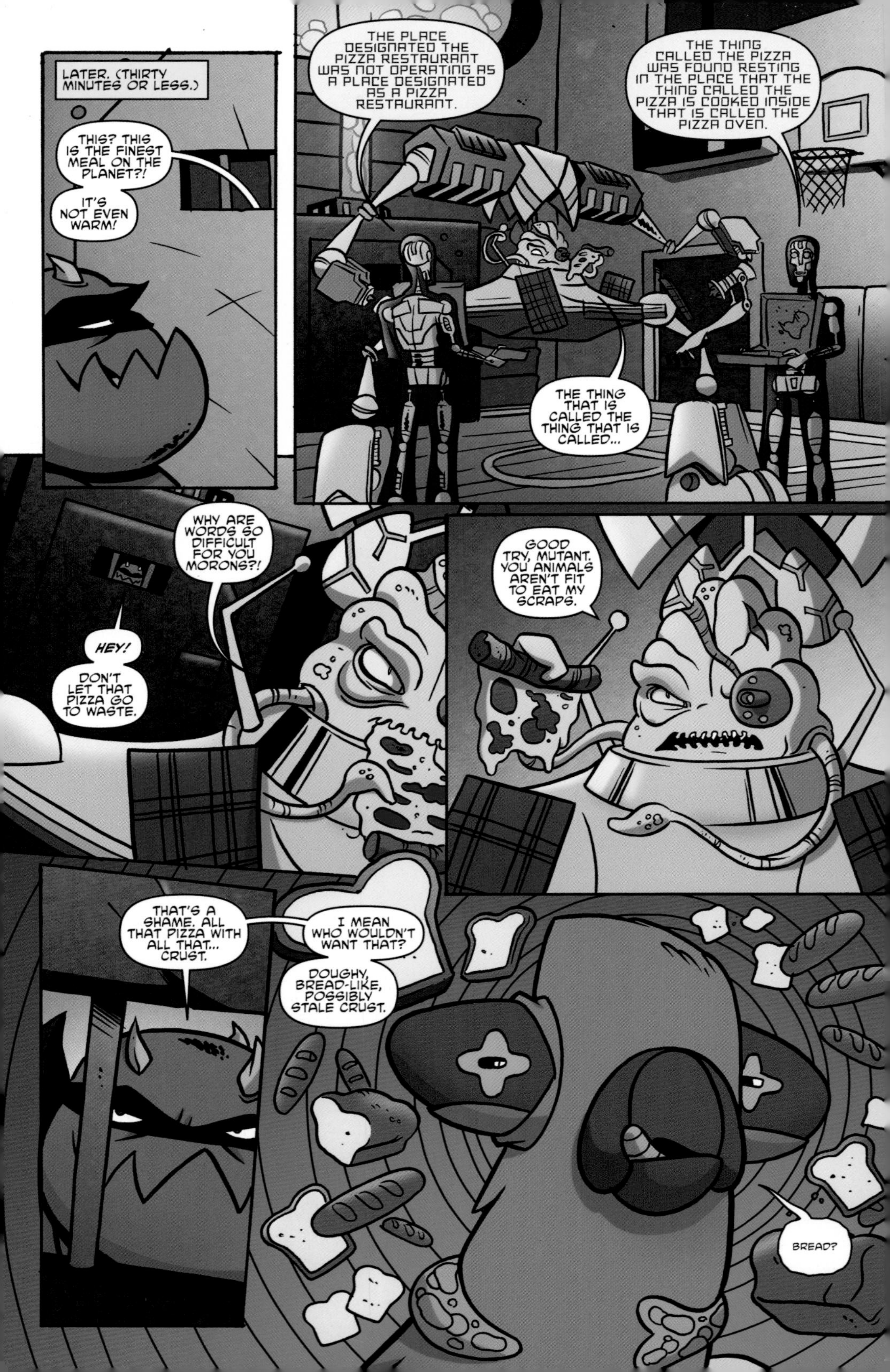
LATER. (THIRTY MINUTES OR LESS.)
THIS? THIS IS THE FINEST MEAL ON THE PLANET?!
IT'S NOT EVEN WARM!
THE PLACE DESIGNATED THE PIZZA RESTAURANT WAS NOT OPERATING AS A PLACE DESIGNATED AS A PIZZA RESTAURANT.
THE THING CALLED THE PIZZA WAS FOUND RESTING IN THE PLACE THAT THE THING CALLED THE PIZZA IS COOKED INSIDE THAT IS CALLED THE PIZZA OVEN.
THE THING THAT IS CALLED THE THING THAT IS CALLED...
WHY ARE WORDS SO DIFFICULT FOR YOU MORONS?!
HEY!
DON'T LET THAT PIZZA GO TO WASTE.
GOOD TRY, MUTANT. YOU ANIMALS AREN'T FIT TO EAT MY SCRAPS.
THAT'S A SHAME. ALL THAT PIZZA WITH ALL THAT... CRUST.
I MEAN WHO WOULDN'T WANT THAT?
DOUGHY, BREAD-LIKE, POSSIBLY STALE CRUST.
BREAD?

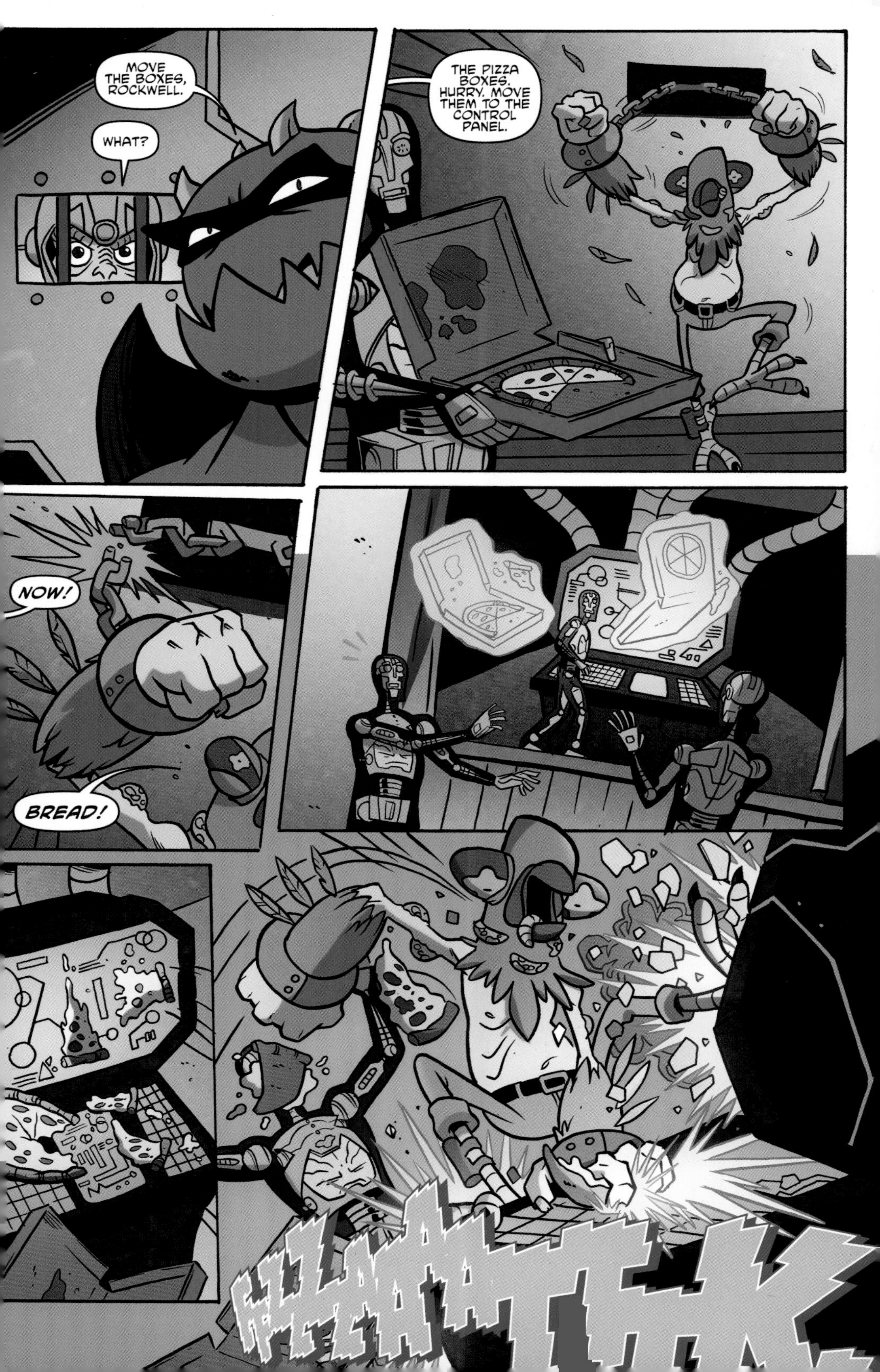
MOVE THE BOXES, ROCKWELL.
WHAT?
THE PIZZA BOXES. HURRY. MOVE THEM TO THE CONTROL PANEL.
NOW!
BREAD!

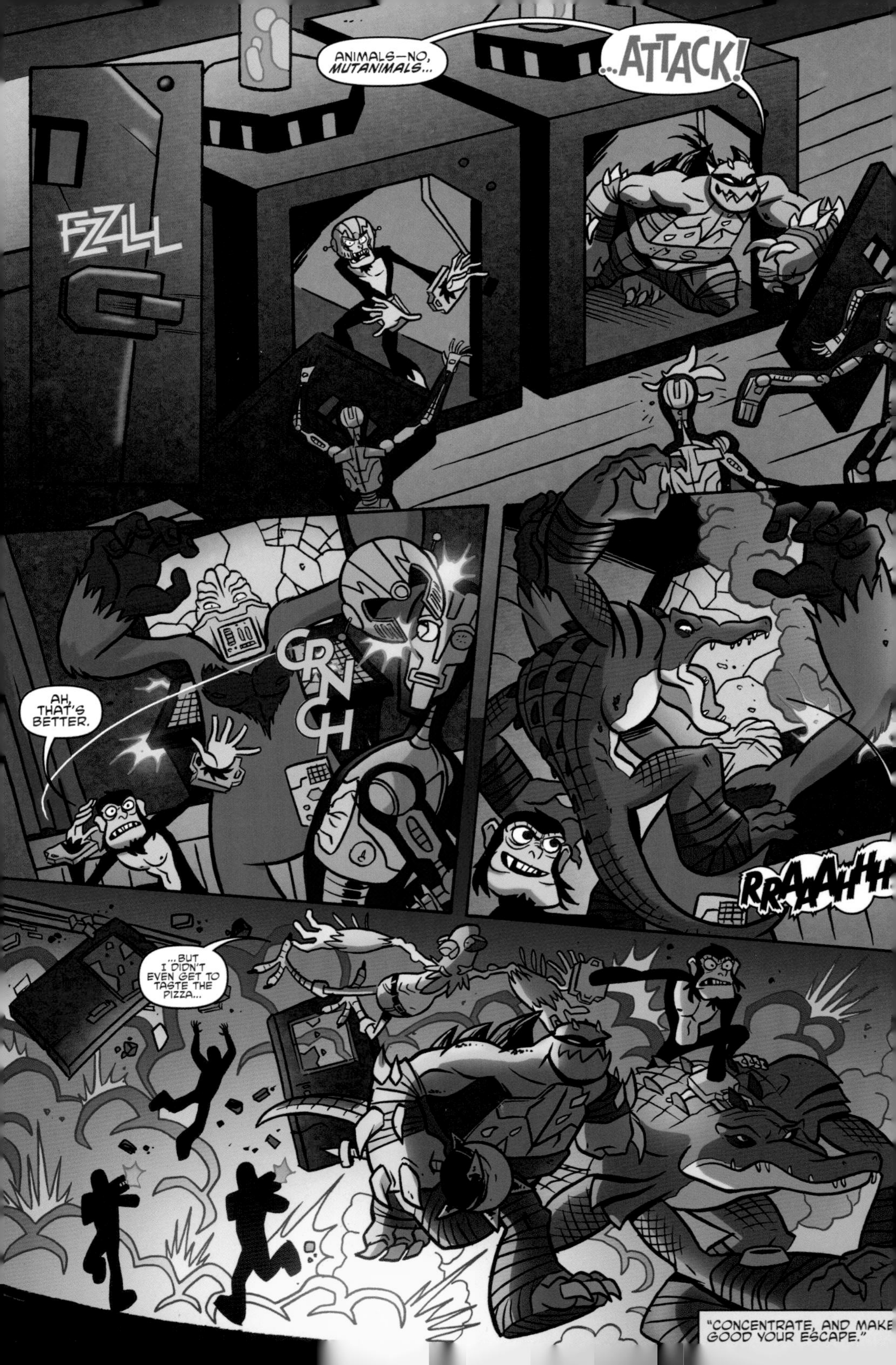

ANIMALS—NO, MUTANIMALS...
...ATTACK!
FZZLLL
AH, THAT'S BETTER.
CRNCH
RRAAAHHH
...BUT I DIDN'T EVEN GET TO TASTE THE PIZZA...
"CONCENTRATE, AND MAKE GOOD YOUR ESCAPE."

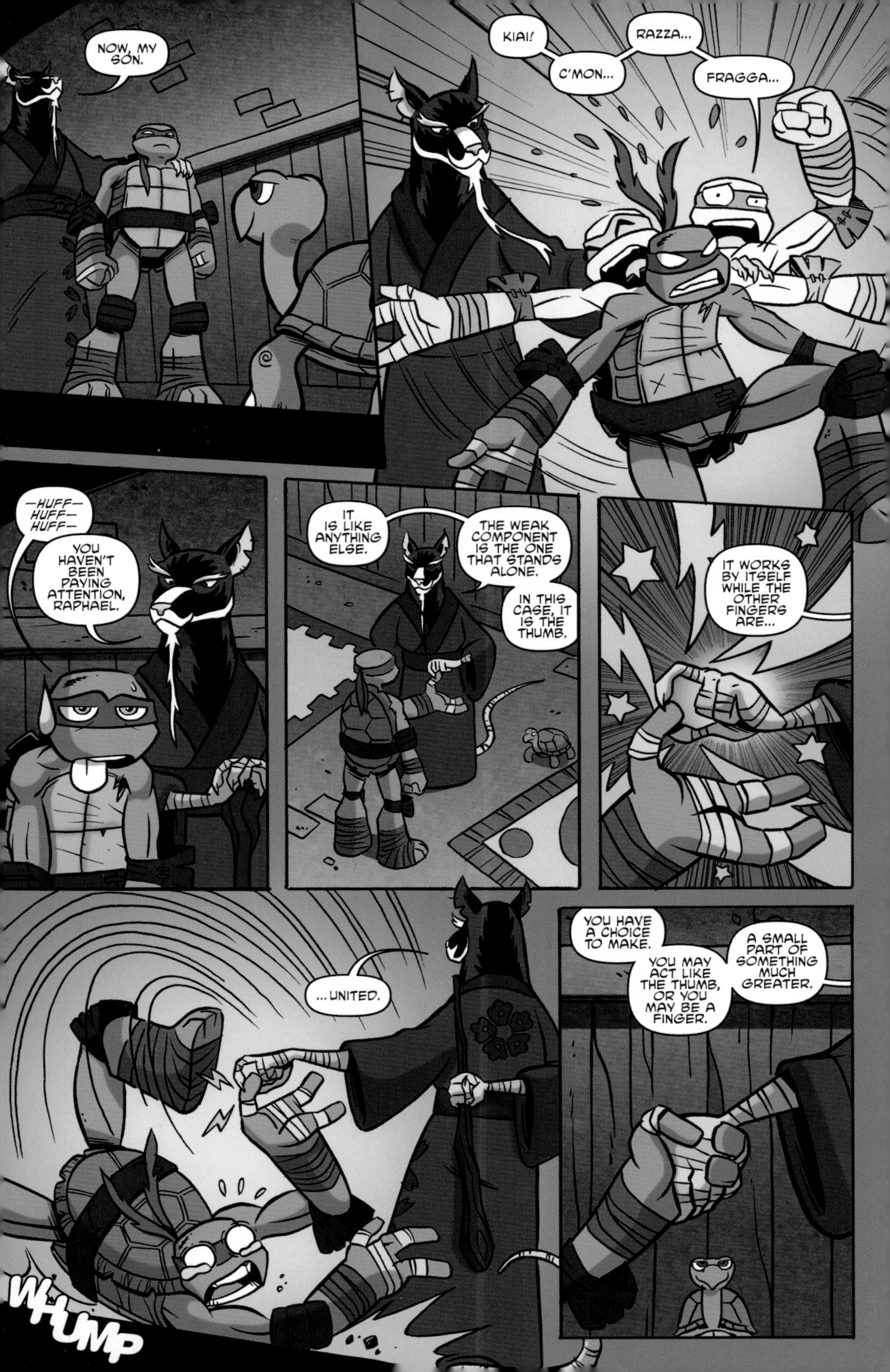
NOW, MY SON.
KIAI!
C'MON...
RAZZA...
FRAGGA...
—HUFF— HUFF— HUFF—
YOU HAVEN'T BEEN PAYING ATTENTION, RAPHAEL.
IT IS LIKE ANYTHING ELSE.
THE WEAK COMPONENT IS THE ONE THAT STANDS ALONE.
IN THIS CASE, IT IS THE THUMB.
IT WORKS BY ITSELF WHILE THE OTHER FINGERS ARE...
...UNITED.
WHUMP
YOU HAVE A CHOICE TO MAKE.
YOU MAY ACT LIKE THE THUMB, OR YOU MAY BE A FINGER.
A SMALL PART OF SOMETHING MUCH GREATER.

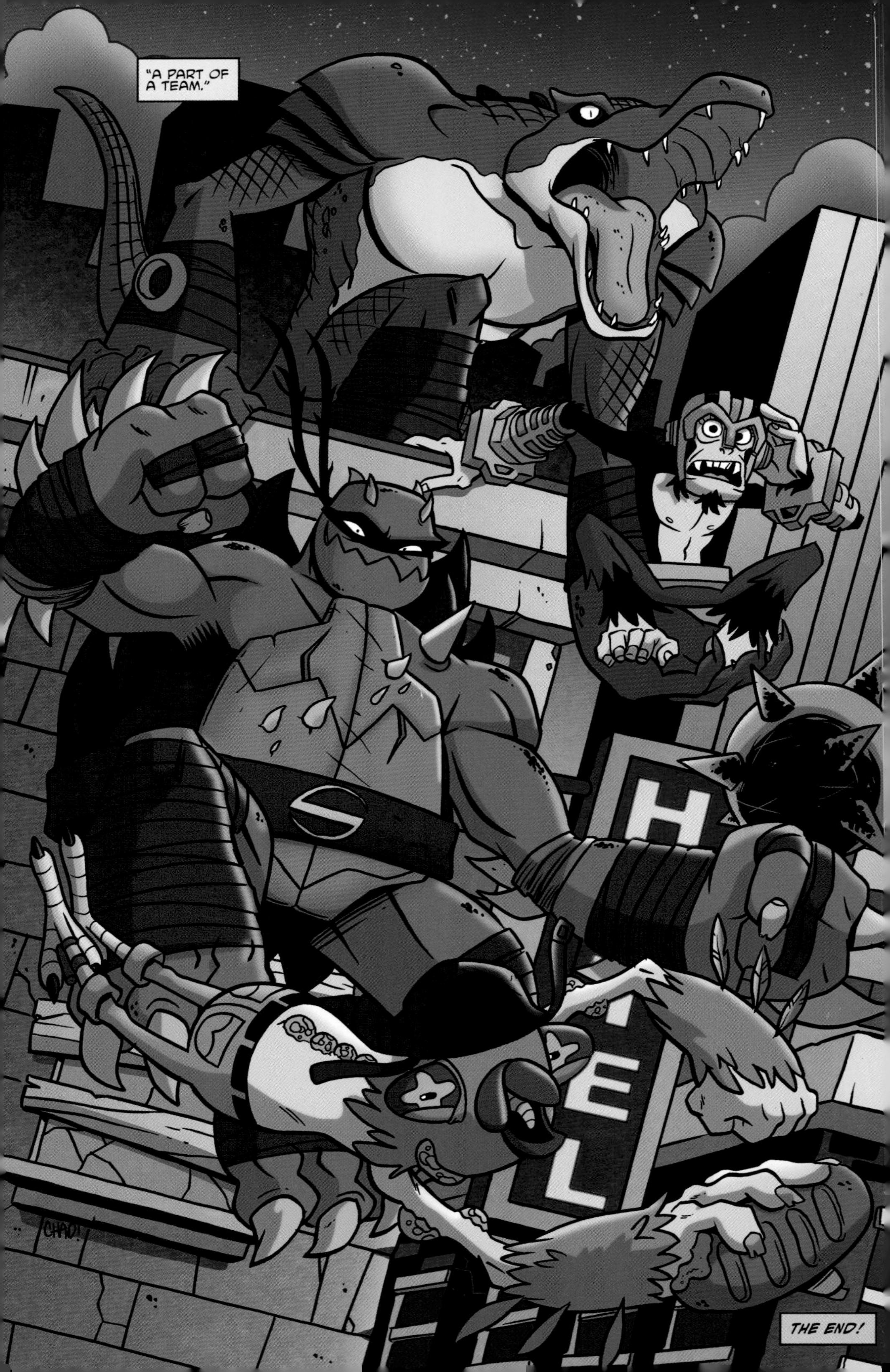
"A PART OF A TEAM."
HOTEL
CHAD!
THE END!

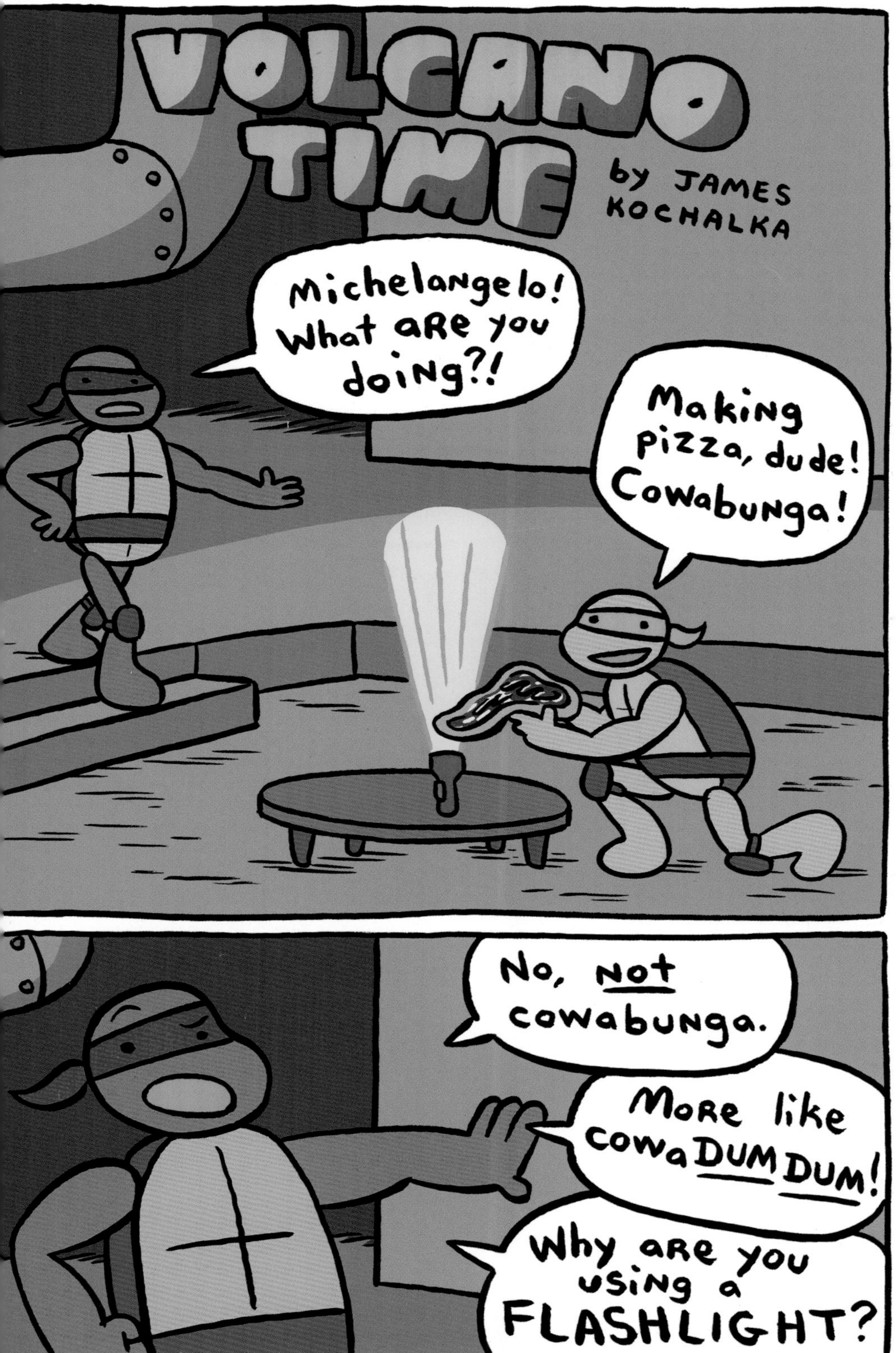
VOLCANO TIME
by JAMES KOCHALKA
Michelangelo! What ARE you doing?!
Making pizza, dude! Cowabunga!
No, NOT cowabunga.
More like cowaDUMDUM!
Why are you using a FLASHLIGHT?

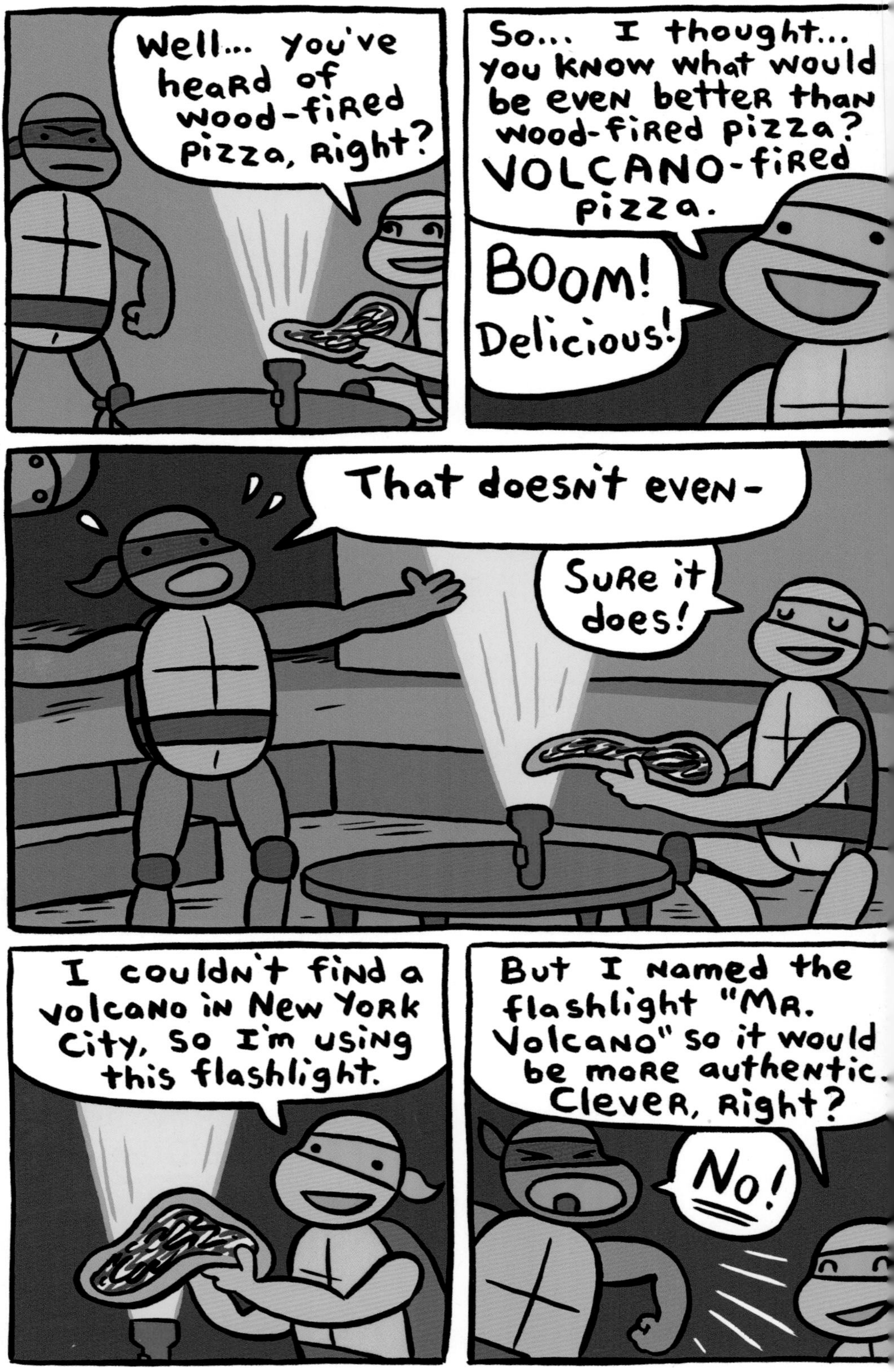
Well... you've heard of wood-fired pizza, right?
So... I thought... you know what would be even better than wood-fired pizza? VOLCANO-fired pizza.
BOOM! Delicious!
That doesn't even-
Sure it does!
I couldn't find a volcano in New York City, so I'm using this flashlight.
But I named the flashlight "Mr. Volcano" so it would be more authentic. Clever, right?
No!

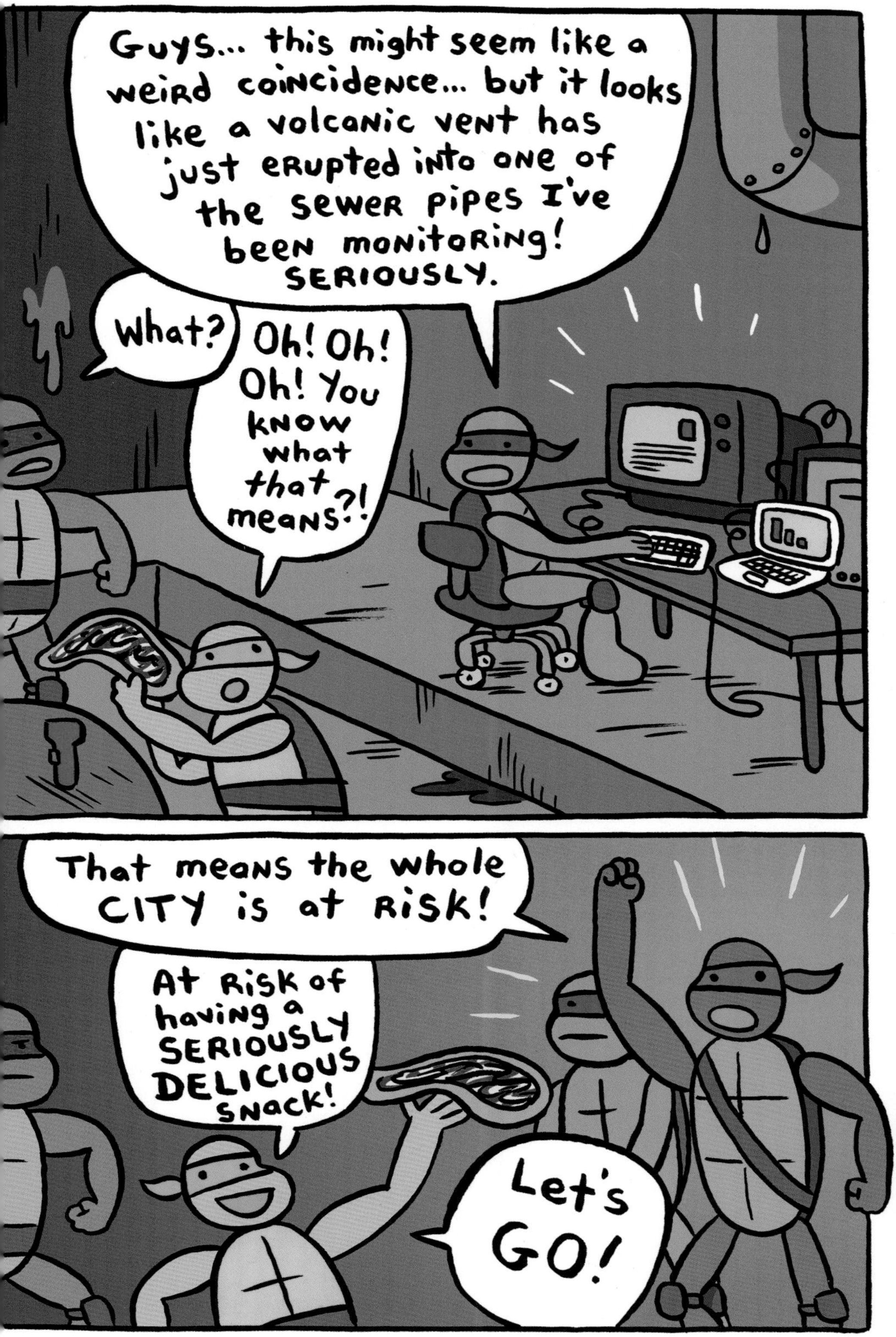

Guys... this might seem like a weird coincidence... but it looks like a volcanic vent has just erupted into one of the sewer pipes I've been monitoring! SERIOUSLY.
What?
Oh! Oh! Oh! You know what that means?!
That means the whole CITY is at RISK!
At RISK of having a SERIOUSLY DELICIOUS SNACK!
Let's GO!

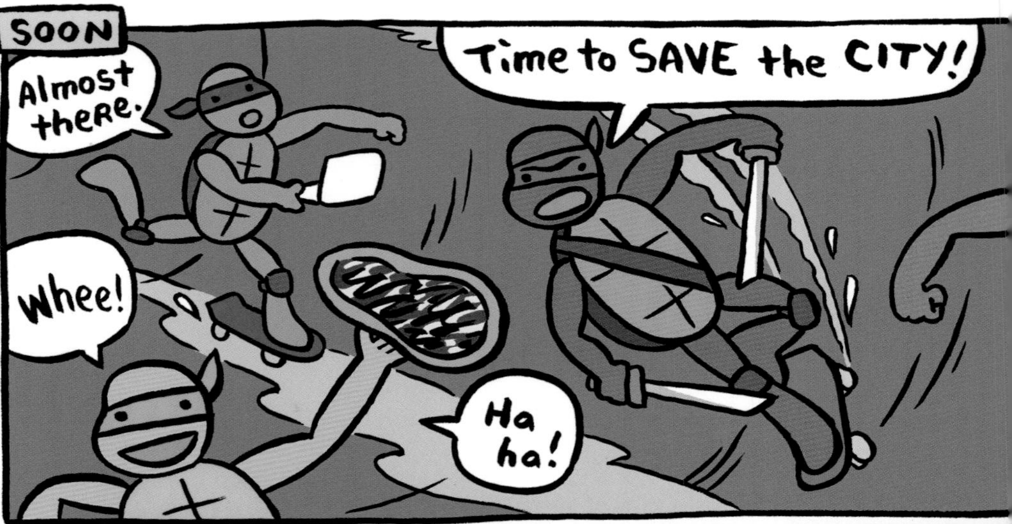
SOON
Almost there.
Time to SAVE the CITY!
Whee!
Ha ha!

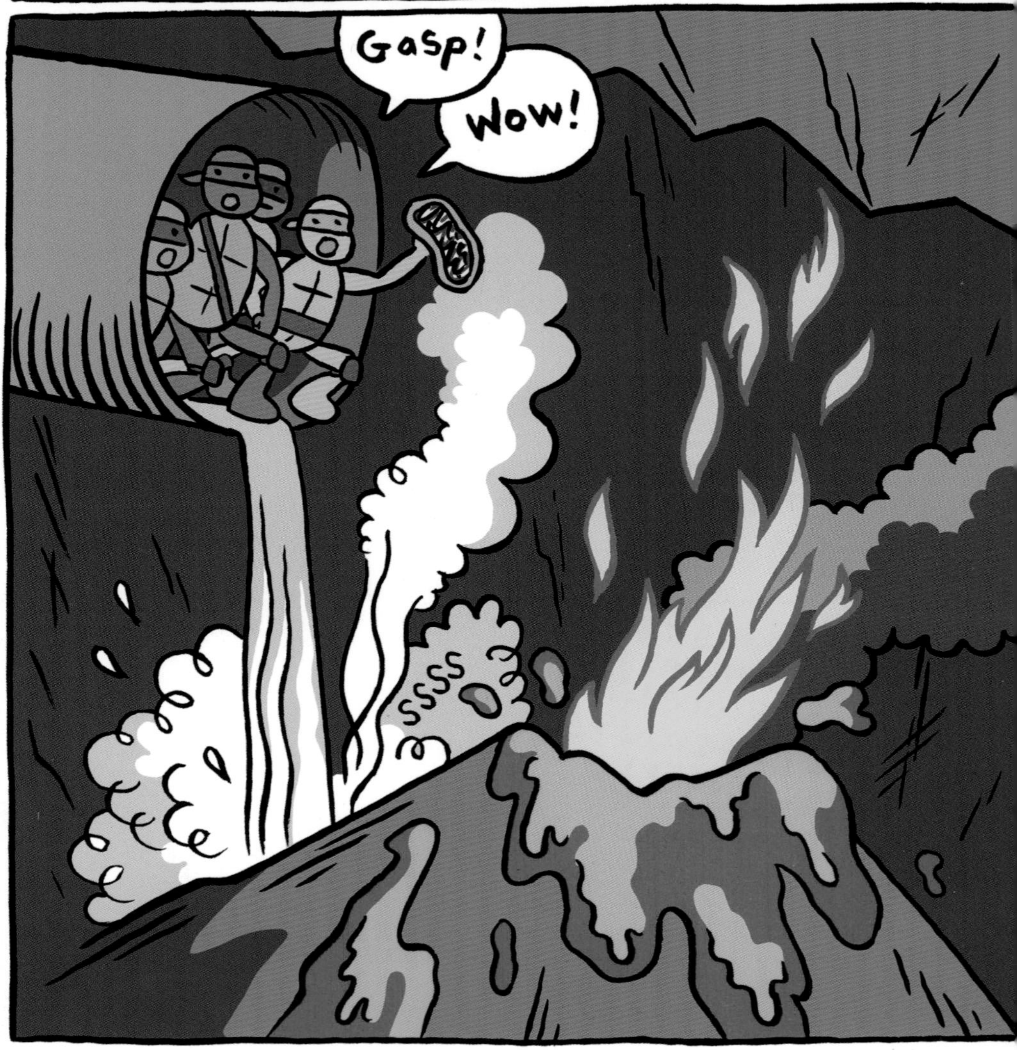
Gasp!
Wow!
SSSSS

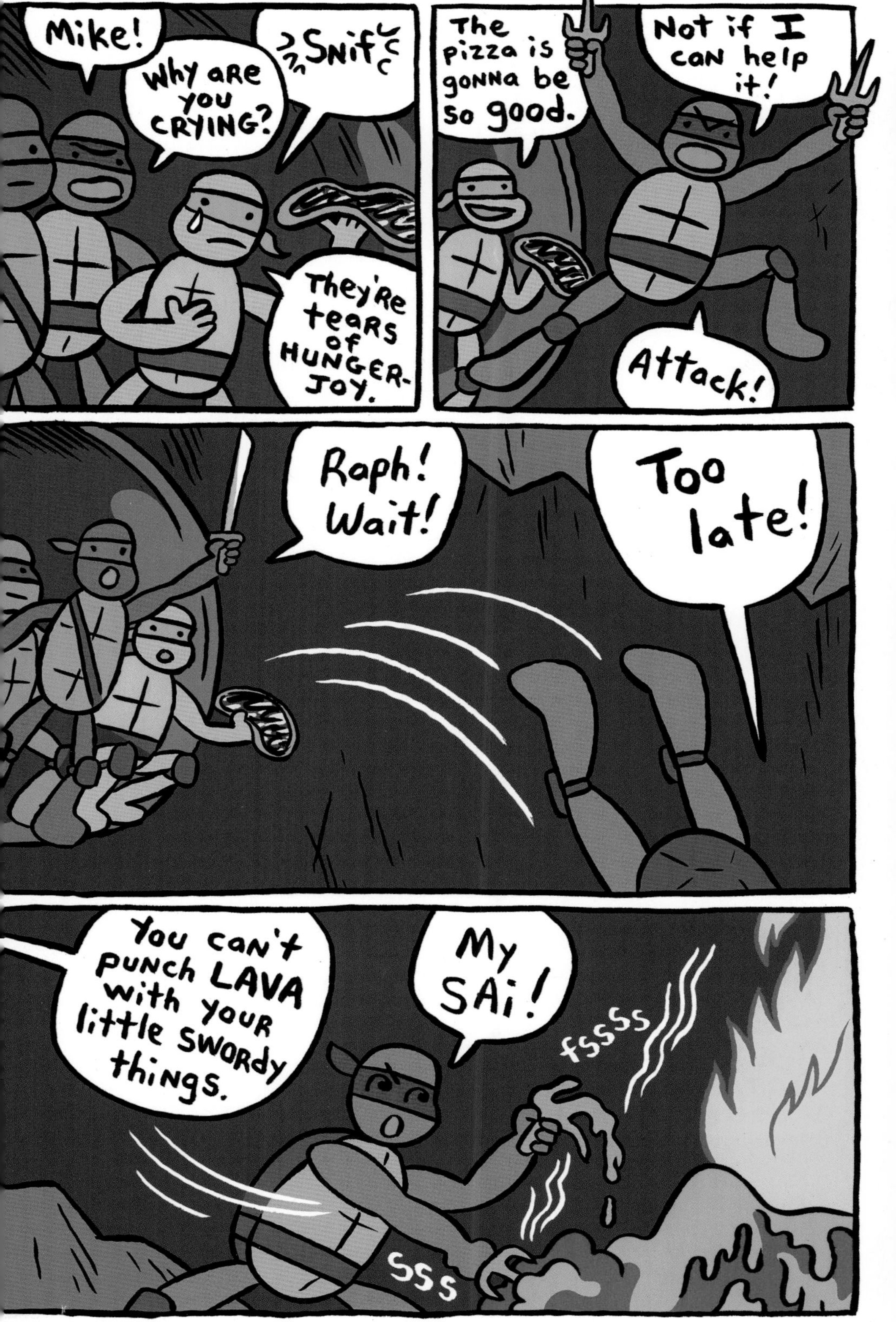
Mike!
Why are you CRYING?
Snif
They're tears of HUNGER-JOY.
The pizza is gonna be so good.
Not if I can help it!
Attack!
Raph! Wait!
Too late!
You can't punch LAVA with your little swordy things.
My SAi!
fssss
sss

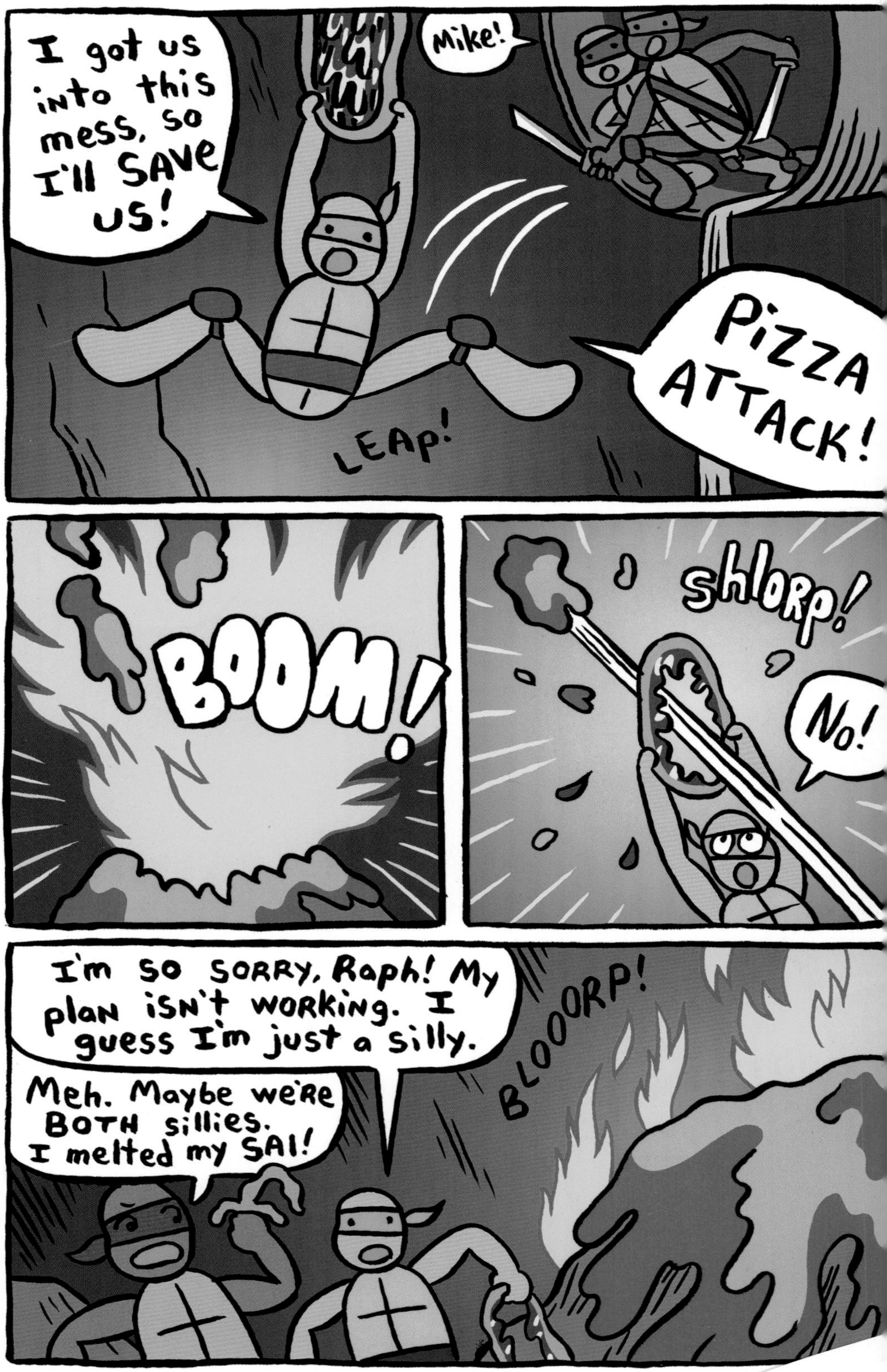
I got us into this mess, so I'll SAVE us!
Mike!
PIZZA ATTACK!
LEAP!
BOOM!
shlorp!
No!
I'm so SORRY, Raph! My plan isn't working. I guess I'm just a silly.
Meh. Maybe we're BOTH sillies. I melted my SAI!
BLOOORP!

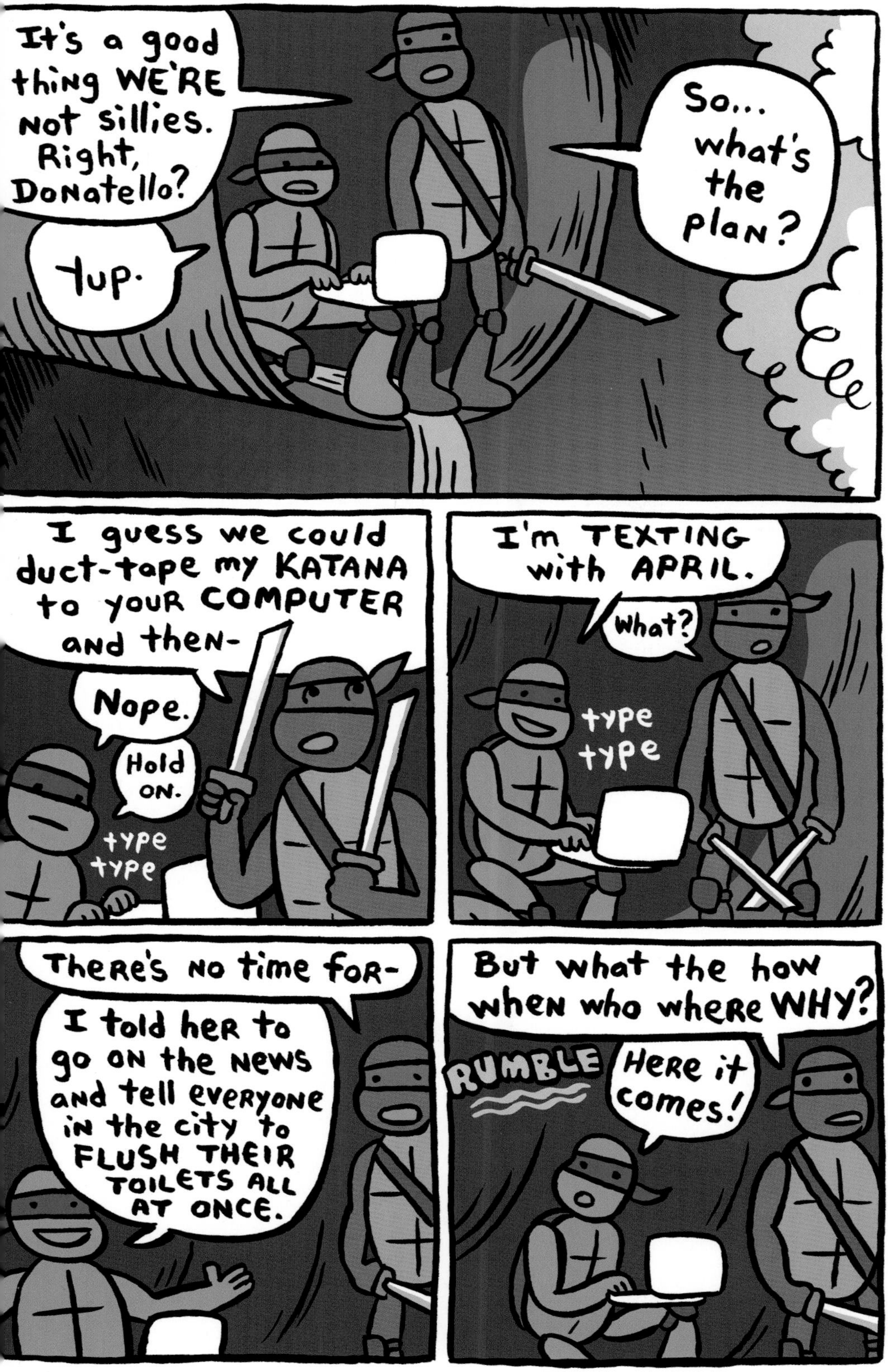
It's a good thing WE'RE not sillies. Right, Donatello?
Yup.
So... what's the plan?
I guess we could duct-tape my KATANA to your COMPUTER and then-
Nope.
Hold on.
type type
I'm TEXTING with APRIL.
What?
type type
There's no time for-
I told her to go on the news and tell everyone in the city to FLUSH THEIR TOILETS ALL AT ONCE.
But what the how when who where WHY?
RUMBLE
Here it comes!

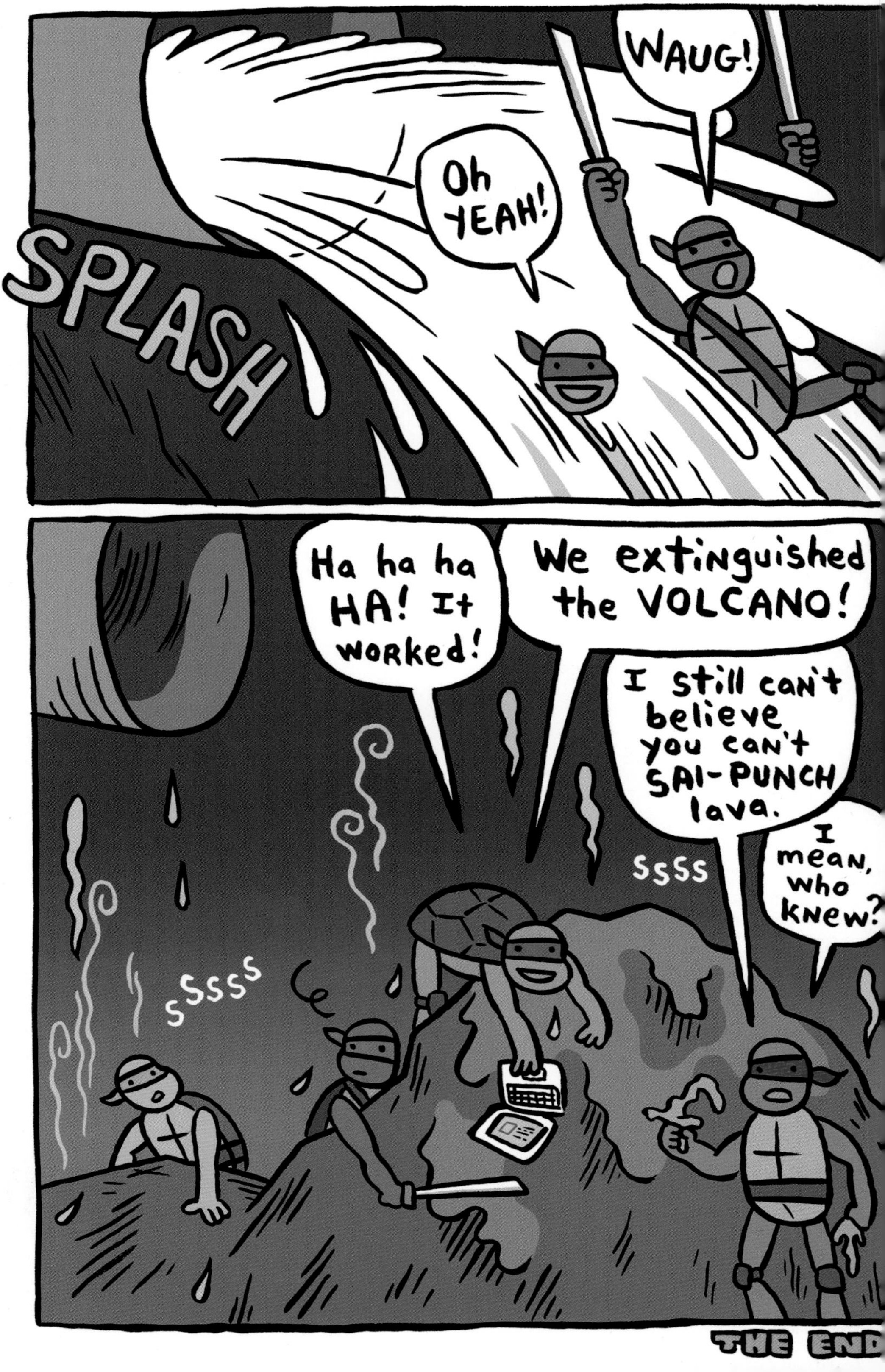
WAUG!
Oh YEAH!
SPLASH
Ha ha ha HA! It worked!
We extinguished the VOLCANO!
I still can't believe you can't SAI-PUNCH lava.
I mean, who knew?
SSSS
sSSSS
THE END

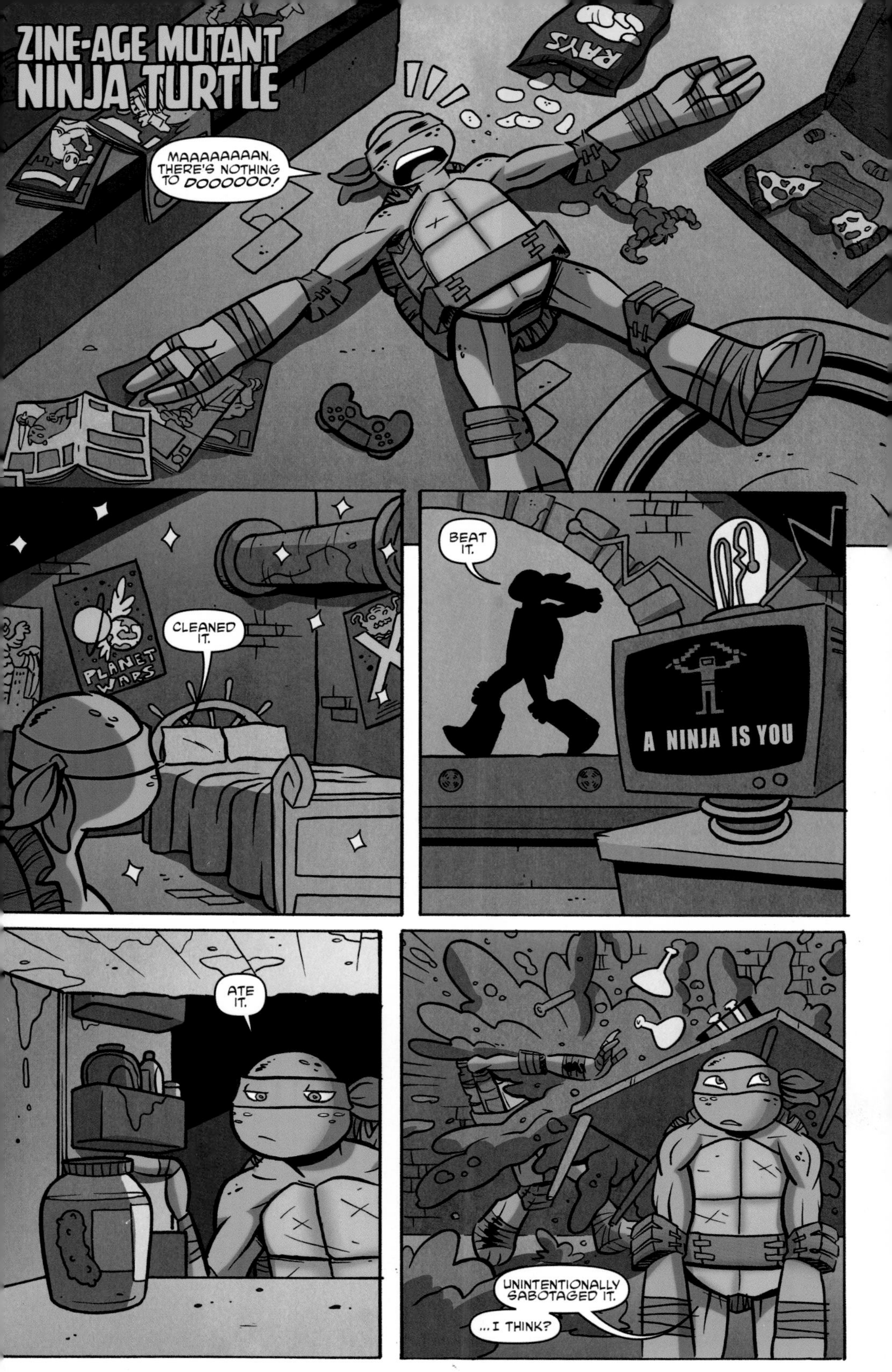
ZINE-AGE MUTANT NINJA TURTLE
RAYS
MAAAAAAAAN. THERE'S NOTHING TO DOOOOOO!
CLEANED IT.
PLANET WARS
BEAT IT.
A NINJA IS YOU
ATE IT.
UNINTENTIONALLY SABOTAGED IT.
...I THINK?

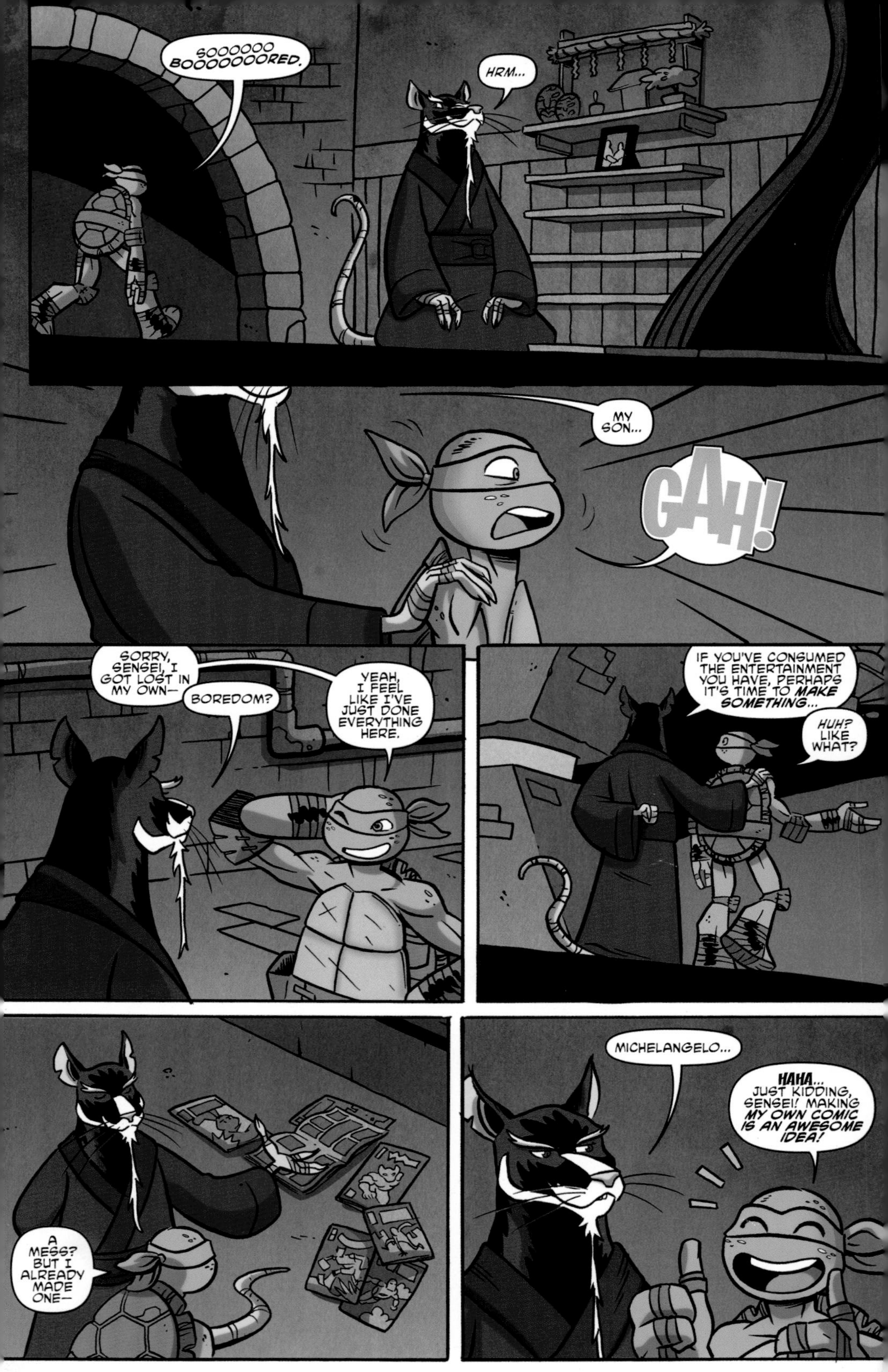
SOOOOOO BOOOOOOORED.
HRM...
MY SON...
GAH!
SORRY, SENSEI, I GOT LOST IN MY OWN—
BOREDOM?
YEAH, I FEEL LIKE I'VE JUST DONE EVERYTHING HERE.
IF YOU'VE CONSUMED THE ENTERTAINMENT YOU HAVE, PERHAPS IT'S TIME TO MAKE SOMETHING...
HUH? LIKE WHAT?
A MESS? BUT I ALREADY MADE ONE—
MICHELANGELO...
HAHA... JUST KIDDING, SENSEI! MAKING MY OWN COMIC IS AN AWESOME IDEA!

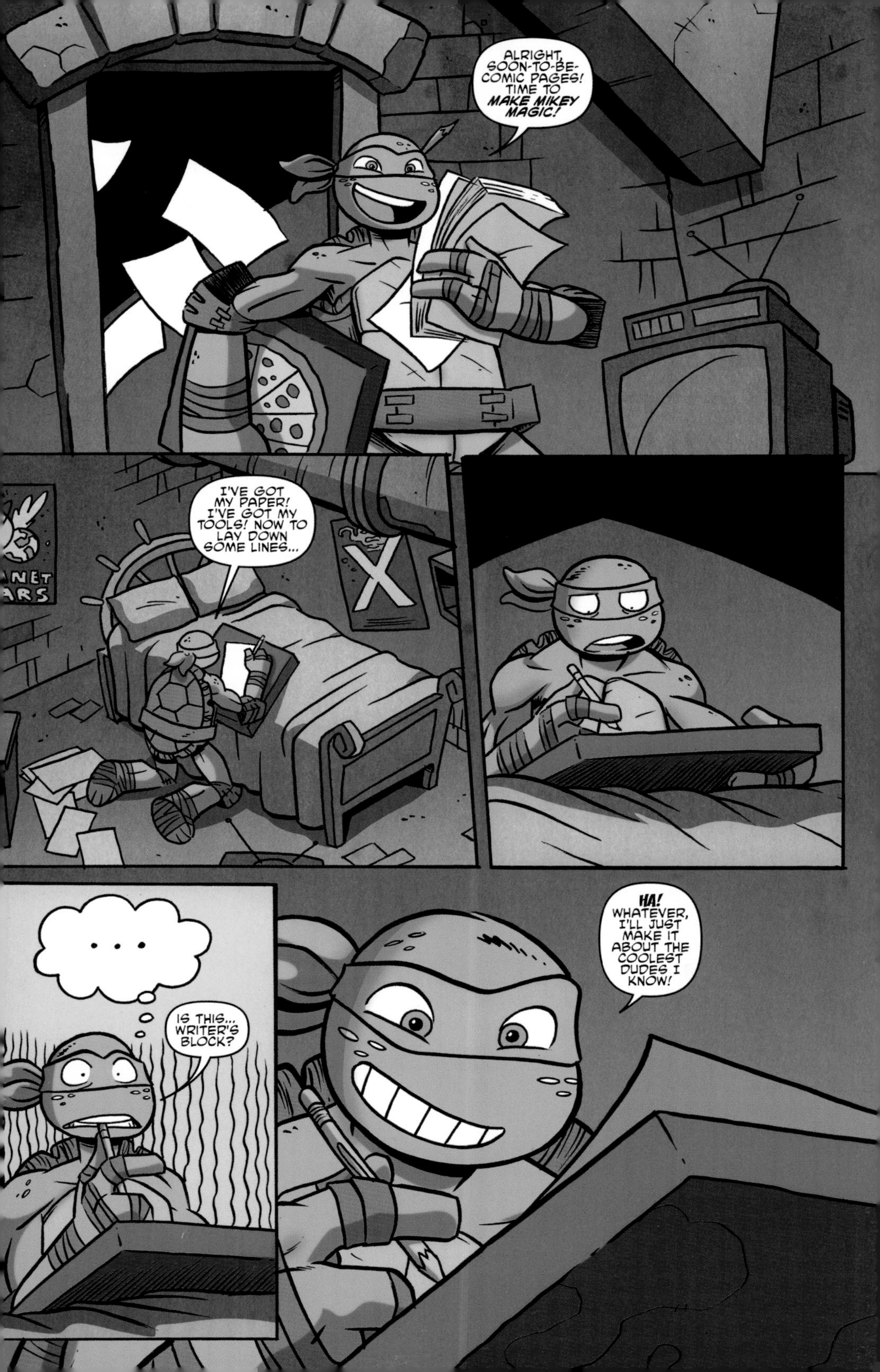

ALRIGHT, SOON-TO-BE-COMIC PAGES! TIME TO MAKE MIKEY MAGIC!
I'VE GOT MY PAPER! I'VE GOT MY TOOLS! NOW TO LAY DOWN SOME LINES...
NET
ARS
X
...
IS THIS... WRITER'S BLOCK?
HA! WHATEVER, I'LL JUST MAKE IT ABOUT THE COOLEST DUDES I KNOW!

I don't remember getting zapped, but I do remember the rest of my night. Believe it or not, getting zapped wasn't what hurt the most—

Mikey! How many fingers am I holding up?

Haaa... is that a trick question?

We'd been on patrol all night, but things were dead. It was up to me to liven things up.

It always is.

It's been a slow night, but stay vigilant.

You never know when—

Guys! over here!

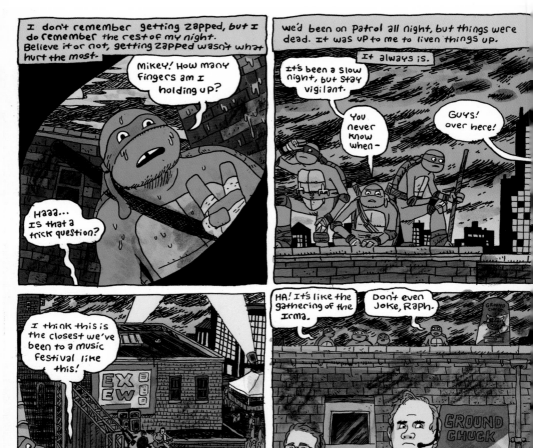

I think this is the closest we've been to a music festival like this!

EX EW

HA! It's like the gathering of the Irma.

Don't even joke, Raph.

GROUND CHUCK

SECURITY

ECURITY

I guess if the Foot is taking tonight off...

Yeah!

GROUND CHUCK

ENERGY DRINK

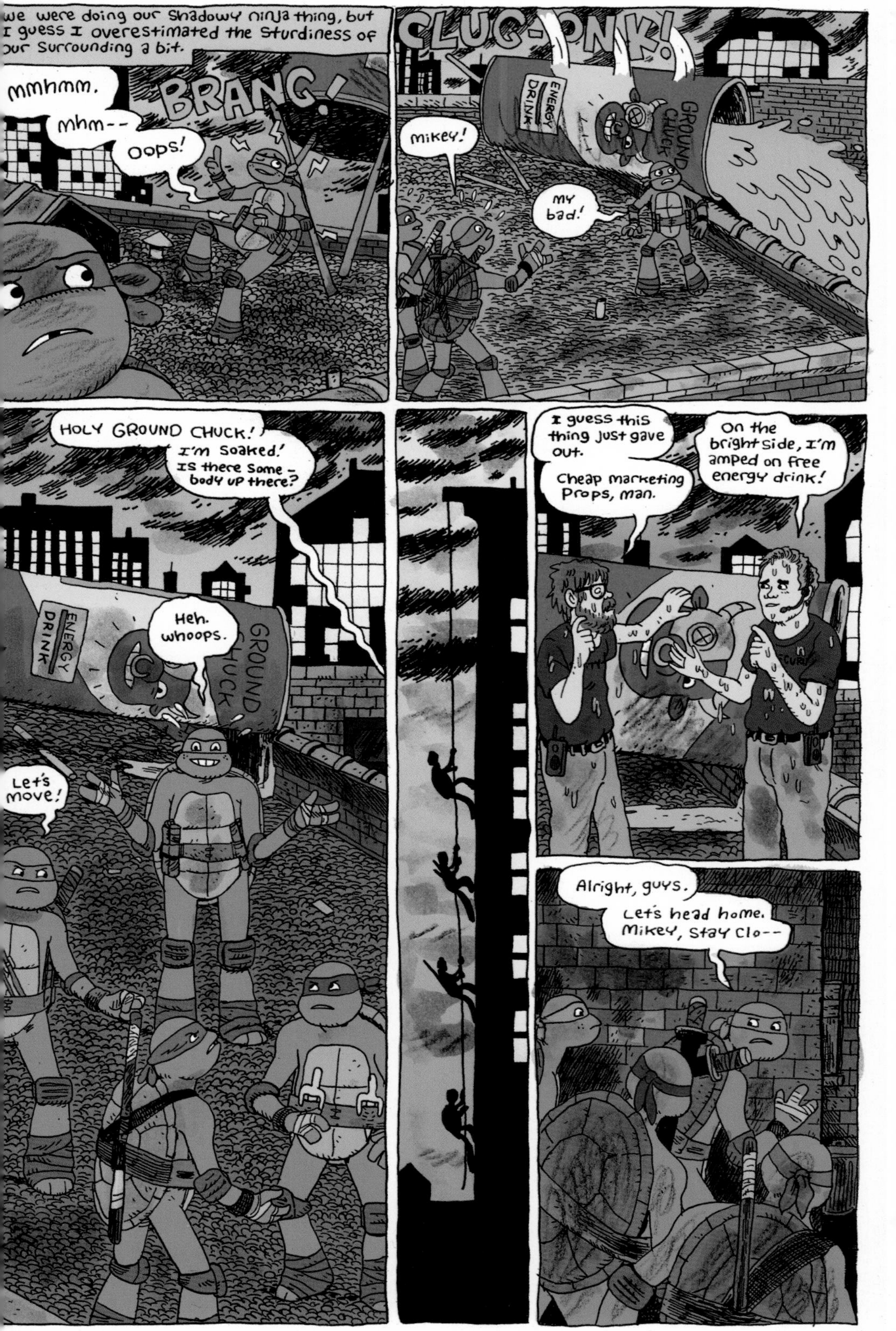
we were doing our shadowy ninja thing, but I guess I overestimated the sturdiness of our surrounding a bit.
mmhmm.
mhm--
BRANG!
Oops!
CLUG-ONK!
ENERGY DRINK
GROUND CHUCK
Mikey!
My bad!
HOLY GROUND CHUCK!
I'm soaked! Is there some-body up there?
ENERGY DRINK
GROUND CHUCK
Heh. whoops.
Let's move!
I guess this thing just gave out.
Cheap marketing props, man.
On the bright side, I'm amped on free energy drink!
Alright, guys.
Let's head home. Mikey, stay clo--

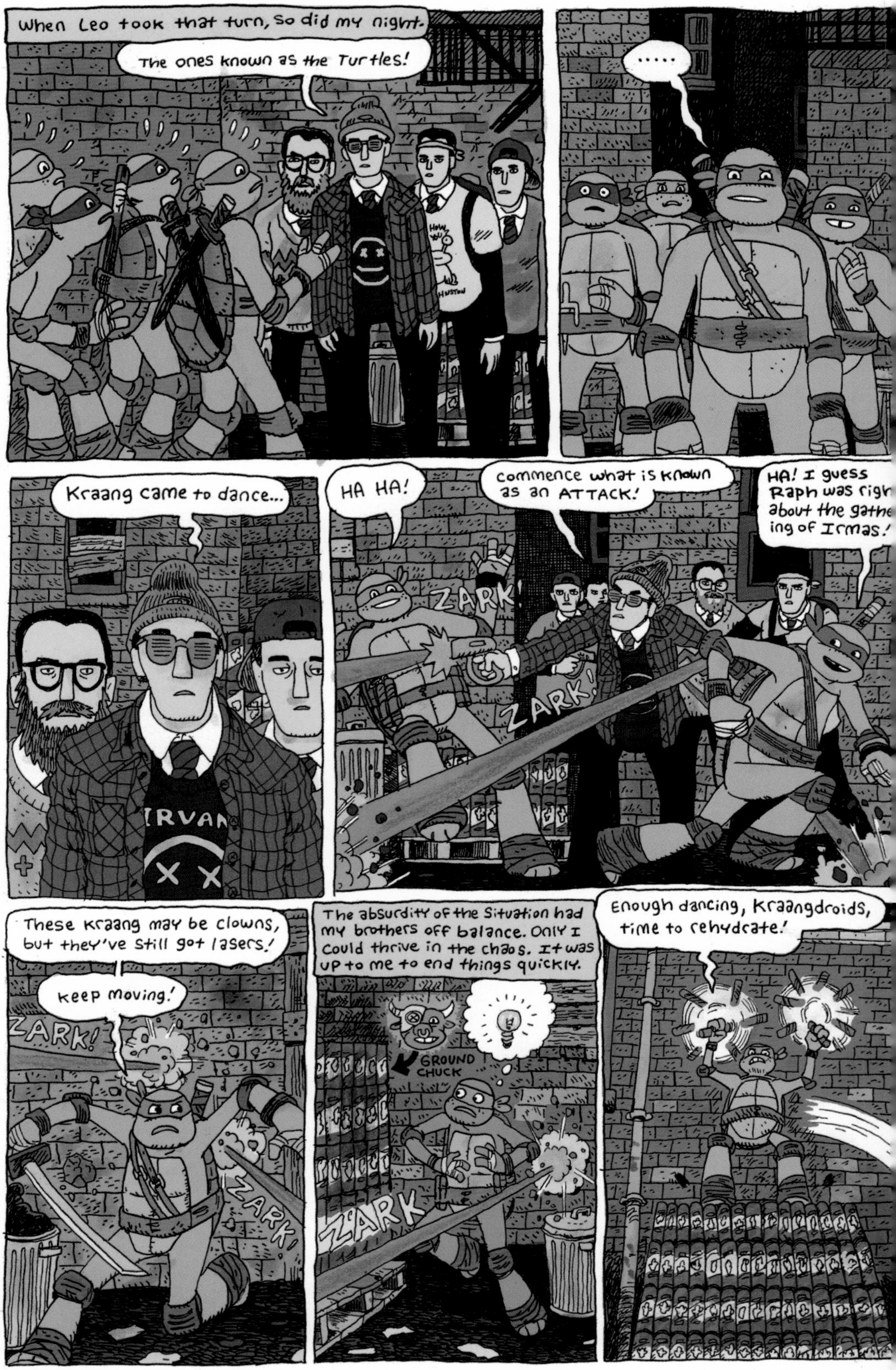
When Leo took that turn, so did my night.
The ones known as the Turtles!
.....
Kraang came to dance...
HA HA!
ZARK!
commence what is known as an ATTACK!
ZARK!
HA! I guess Raph was righ about the gathe ing of Irmas!
These Kraang may be clowns, but they've still got lasers!
Keep moving!
ZARK!
ZARK
The absurdity of the situation had my brothers off balance. Only I could thrive in the chaos. It was up to me to end things quickly.
GROUND CHUCK
ZARK
Enough dancing, Kraangdroids, time to rehydrate!

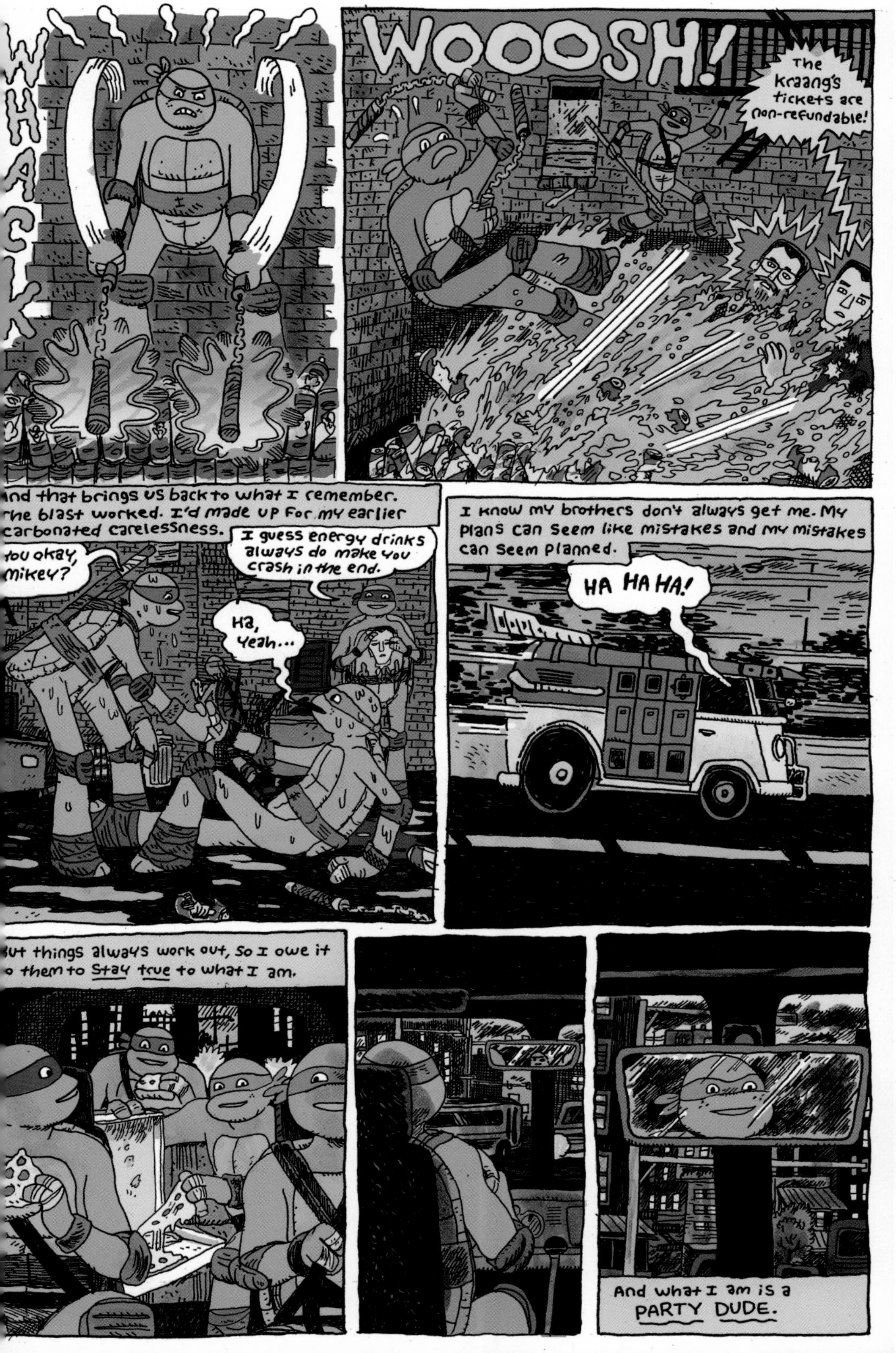
WHACK
WOOOSH!
The kraang's tickets are non-refundable!
nd that brings us back to what I remember. he blast worked. I'd made up for my earlier carbonated carelessness.
ou okay, mikey?
I guess energy drinks always do make you crash in the end.
Ha, yeah...
I know my brothers don't always get me. My plans can seem like mistakes and my mistakes can seem planned.
HA HA HA!
ut things always work out, so I owe it o them to stay true to what I am.
And what I am is a PARTY DUDE.

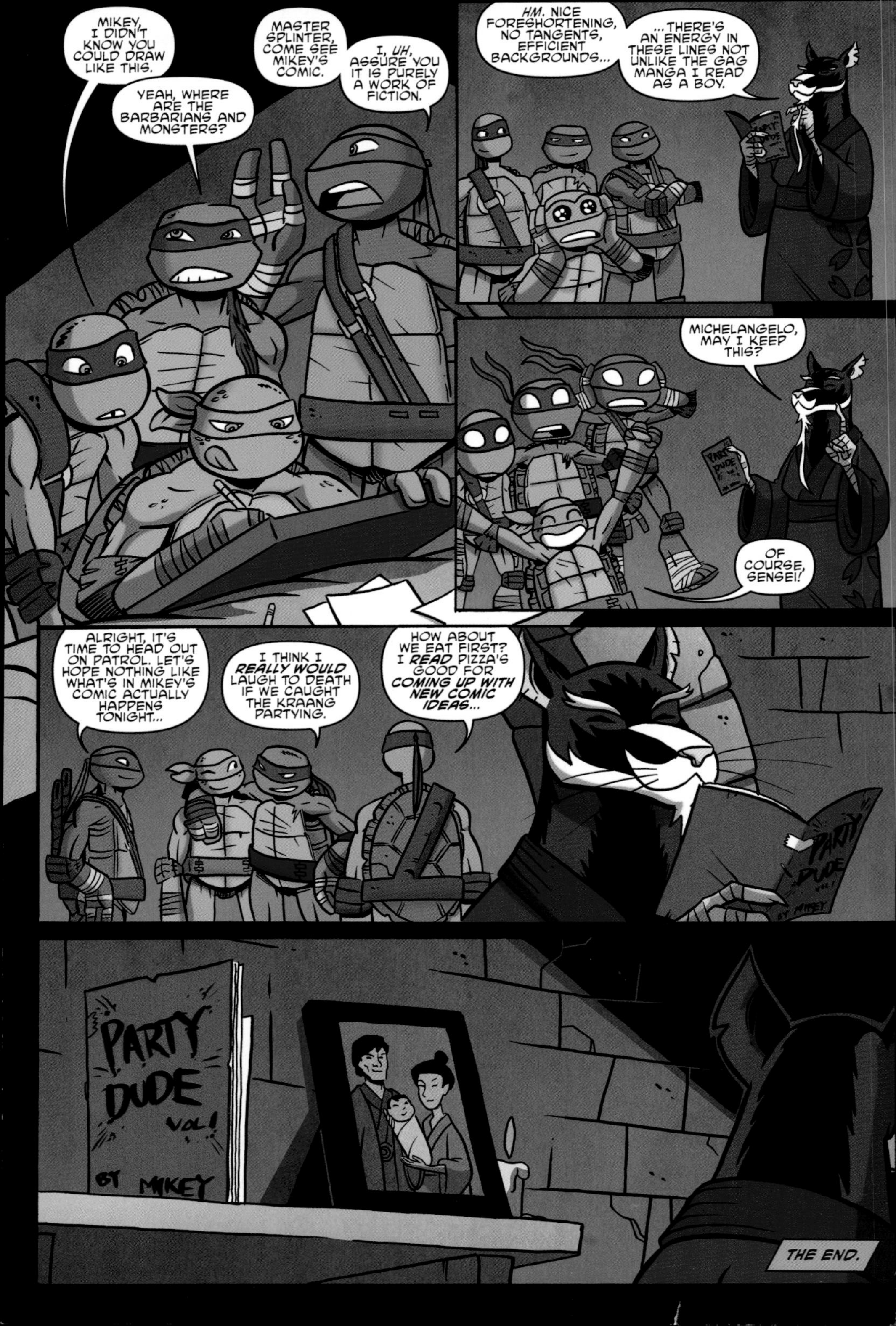

MIKEY, I DIDN'T KNOW YOU COULD DRAW LIKE THIS.
YEAH, WHERE ARE THE BARBARIANS AND MONSTERS?
MASTER SPLINTER, COME SEE MIKEY'S COMIC.
I, *UH*, ASSURE YOU IT IS PURELY A WORK OF FICTION.
HM. NICE FORESHORTENING, NO TANGENTS, EFFICIENT BACKGROUNDS...
...THERE'S AN ENERGY IN THESE LINES NOT UNLIKE THE GAG MANGA I READ AS A BOY.
MICHELANGELO, MAY I KEEP THIS?
OF COURSE, SENSEI!
ALRIGHT, IT'S TIME TO HEAD OUT ON PATROL. LET'S HOPE NOTHING LIKE WHAT'S IN MIKEY'S COMIC ACTUALLY HAPPENS TONIGHT...
I THINK I ***REALLY WOULD*** LAUGH TO DEATH IF WE CAUGHT THE KRAANG PARTYING.
HOW ABOUT WE EAT FIRST? I *READ* PIZZA'S GOOD FOR ***COMING UP WITH NEW COMIC IDEAS...***
PARTY DUDE
BY MIKEY
PARTY DUDE VOL. I
BY MIKEY
THE END.

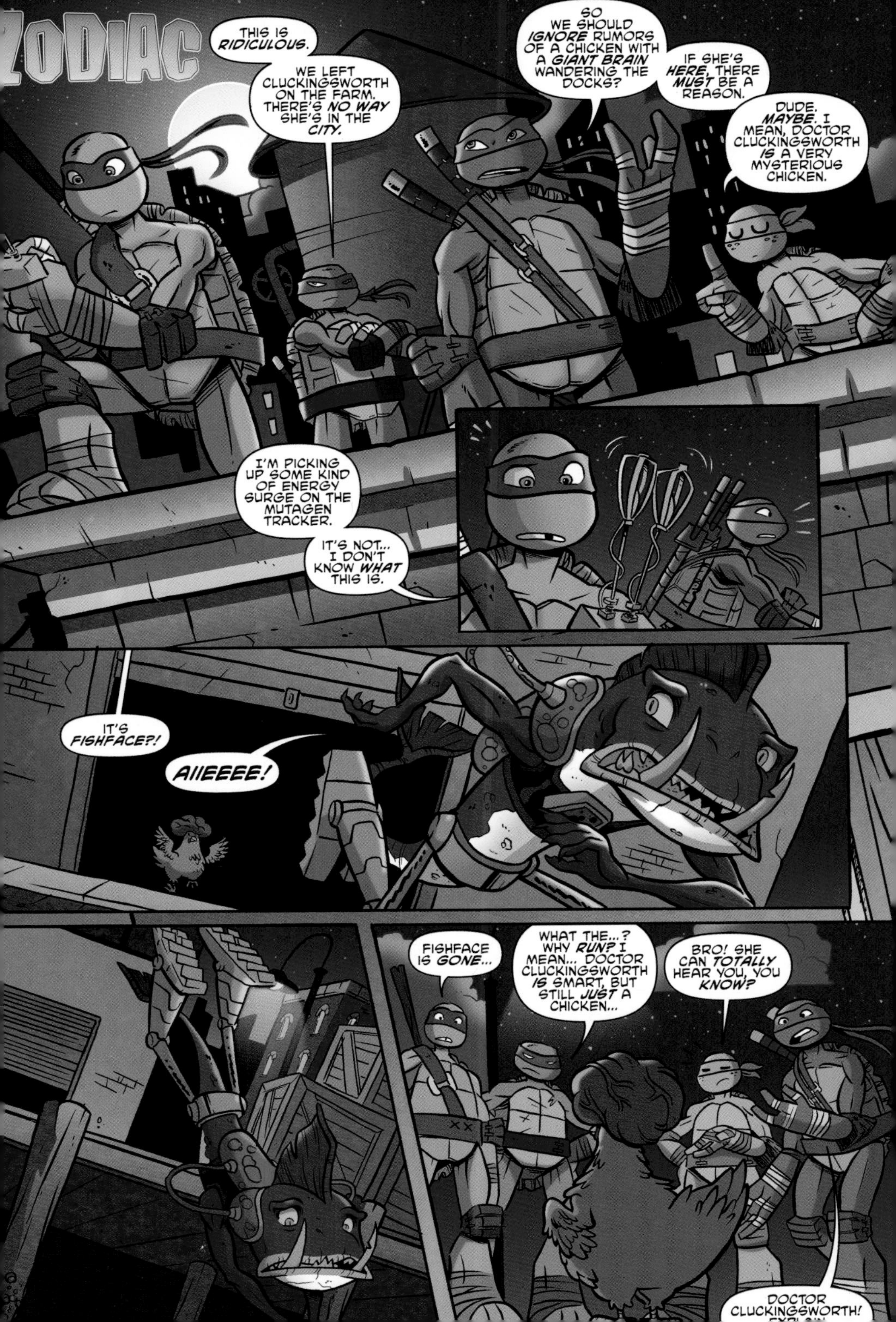
ZODIAC
THIS IS *RIDICULOUS*.
WE LEFT CLUCKINGSWORTH ON THE FARM. THERE'S *NO WAY* SHE'S IN THE *CITY*.
SO WE SHOULD *IGNORE* RUMORS OF A CHICKEN WITH A *GIANT BRAIN* WANDERING THE DOCKS?
IF SHE'S *HERE*, THERE *MUST* BE A REASON.
DUDE. *MAYBE*. I MEAN, DOCTOR CLUCKINGSWORTH *IS* A VERY MYSTERIOUS CHICKEN.
I'M PICKING UP SOME KIND OF ENERGY SURGE ON THE MUTAGEN TRACKER.
IT'S NOT... I DON'T KNOW *WHAT* THIS IS.
IT'S *FISHFACE?!*
AIIEEEE!
FISHFACE IS *GONE*...
WHAT THE...? WHY *RUN?* I MEAN... DOCTOR CLUCKINGSWORTH *IS* SMART, BUT STILL *JUST* A CHICKEN...
BRO! SHE CAN *TOTALLY* HEAR YOU, YOU *KNOW?*
DOCTOR CLUCKINGSWORTH!

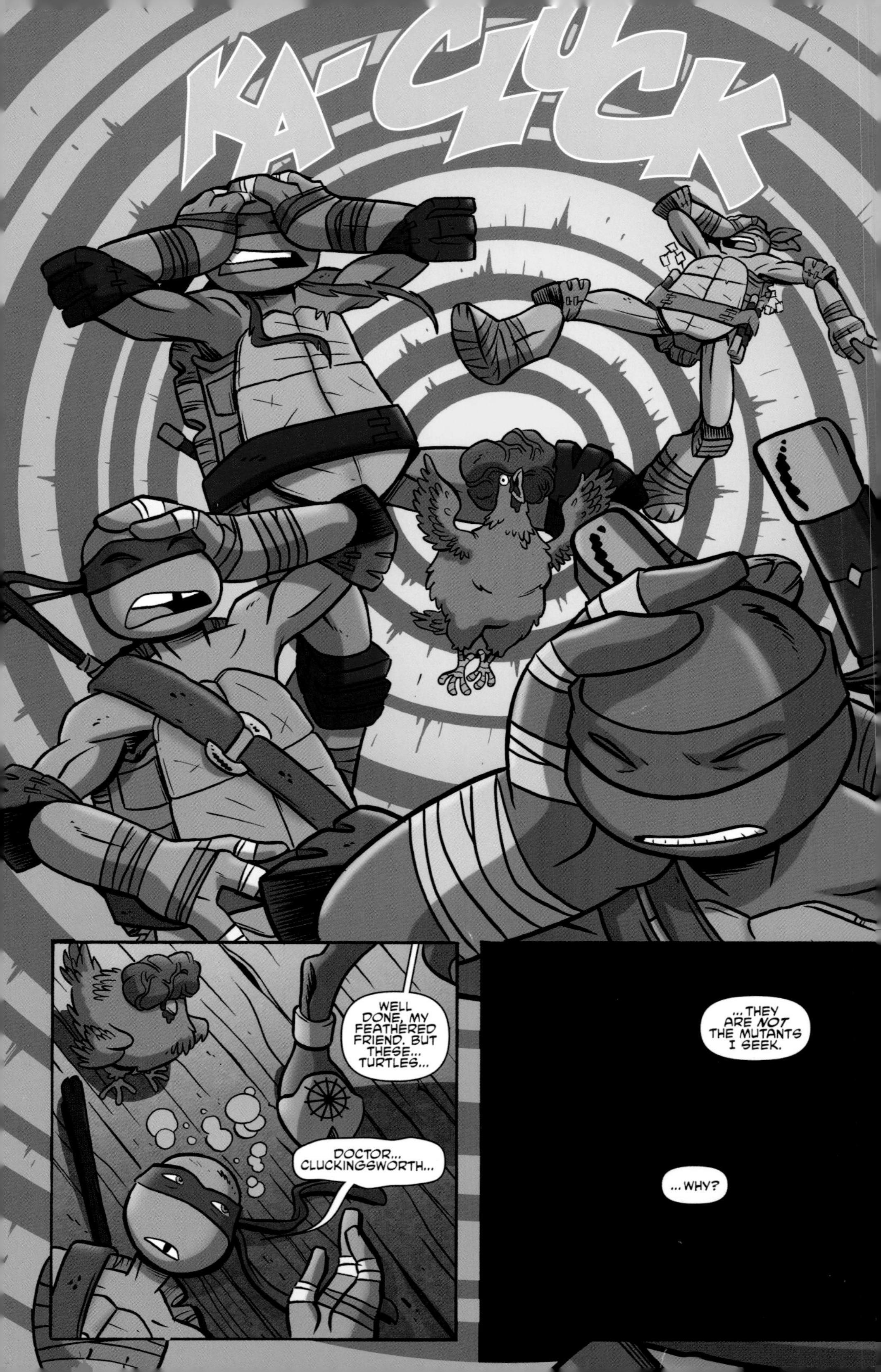
KA-CLUCK
WELL DONE, MY FEATHERED FRIEND. BUT THESE... TURTLES...
DOCTOR... CLUCKINGSWORTH...
...THEY ARE *NOT* THE MUTANTS I SEEK.
...WHY?

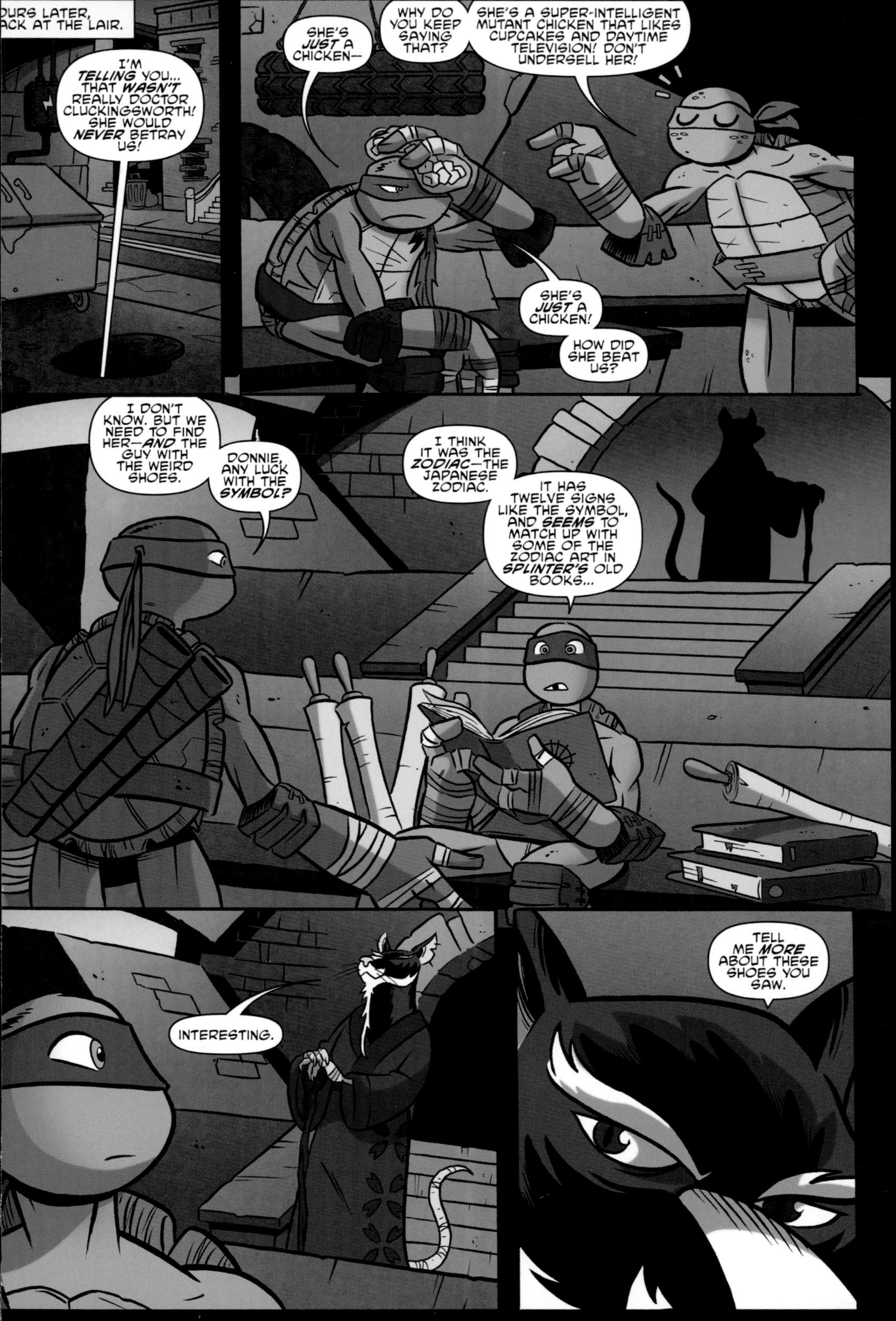

...OURS LATER, ...ACK AT THE LAIR.
I'M TELLING YOU... THAT WASN'T REALLY DOCTOR CLUCKINGSWORTH! SHE WOULD NEVER BETRAY US!
SHE'S JUST A CHICKEN—
WHY DO YOU KEEP SAYING THAT?
SHE'S A SUPER-INTELLIGENT MUTANT CHICKEN THAT LIKES CUPCAKES AND DAYTIME TELEVISION! DON'T UNDERSELL HER!
SHE'S JUST A CHICKEN!
HOW DID SHE BEAT US?
I DON'T KNOW. BUT WE NEED TO FIND HER—AND THE GUY WITH THE WEIRD SHOES.
DONNIE, ANY LUCK WITH THE SYMBOL?
I THINK IT WAS THE ZODIAC—THE JAPANESE ZODIAC.
IT HAS TWELVE SIGNS LIKE THE SYMBOL, AND SEEMS TO MATCH UP WITH SOME OF THE ZODIAC ART IN SPLINTER'S OLD BOOKS...
INTERESTING.
TELL ME MORE ABOUT THESE SHOES YOU SAW.

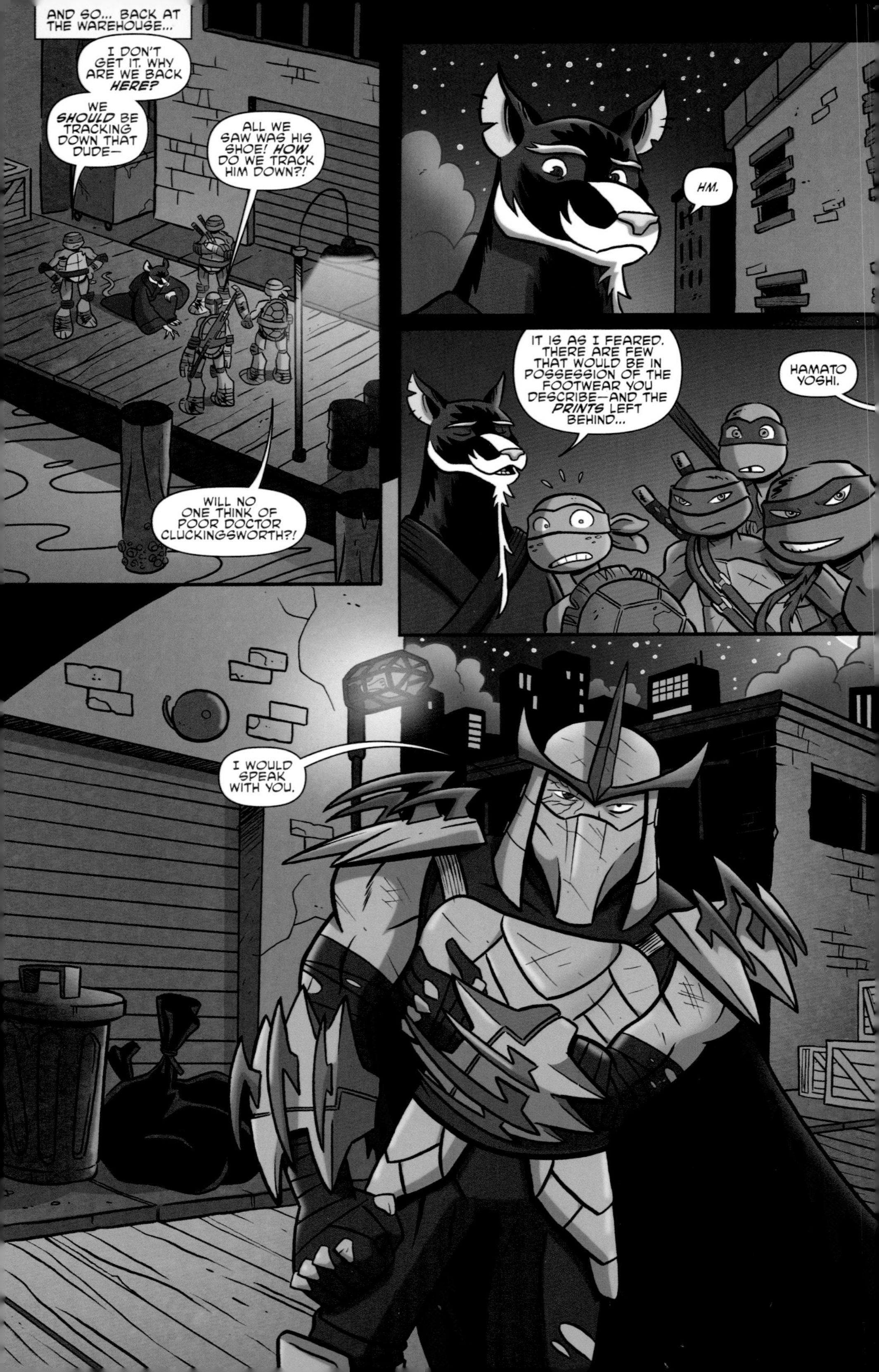
AND SO... BACK AT THE WAREHOUSE...
I DON'T GET IT. WHY ARE WE BACK HERE?
WE SHOULD BE TRACKING DOWN THAT DUDE—
ALL WE SAW WAS HIS SHOE! HOW DO WE TRACK HIM DOWN?!
WILL NO ONE THINK OF POOR DOCTOR CLUCKINGSWORTH?!
HM.
IT IS AS I FEARED. THERE ARE FEW THAT WOULD BE IN POSSESSION OF THE FOOTWEAR YOU DESCRIBE—AND THE PRINTS LEFT BEHIND...
HAMATO YOSHI.
I WOULD SPEAK WITH YOU.

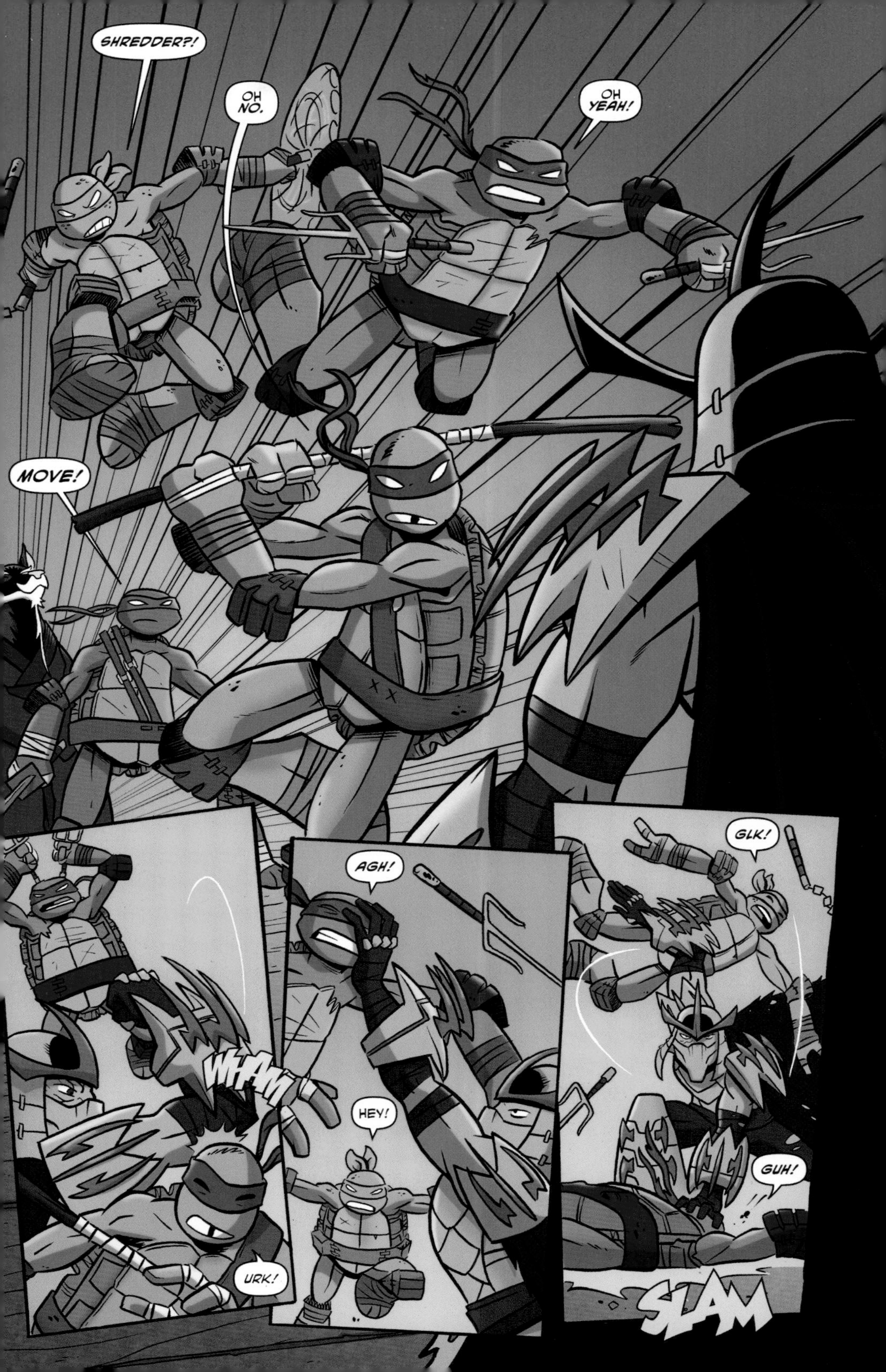
SHREDDER?!
OH NO.
OH YEAH!
MOVE!
WHAM
URK!
AGH!
HEY!
GLK!
GUH!
SLAM

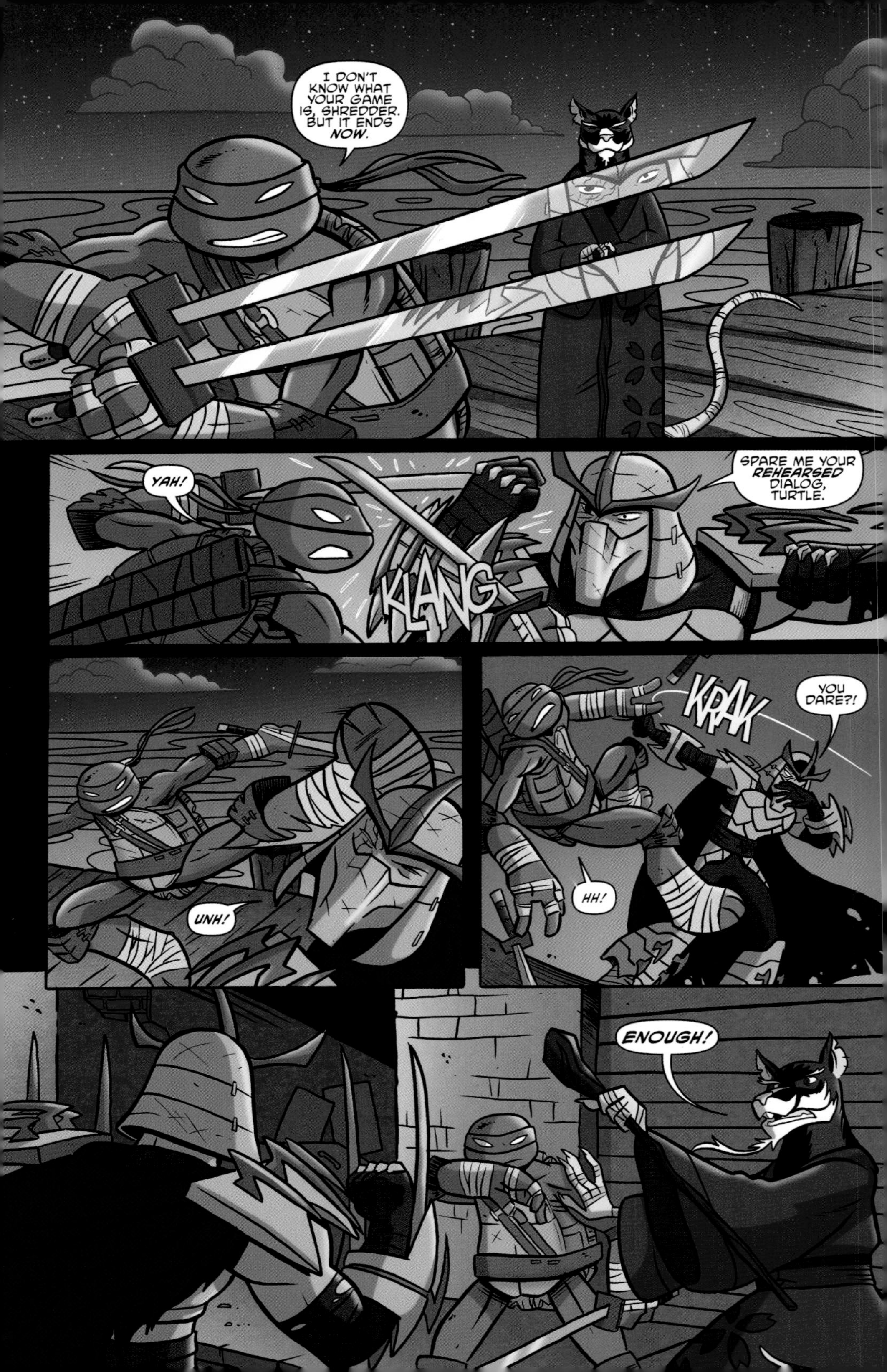
I DON'T KNOW WHAT YOUR GAME IS, SHREDDER. BUT IT ENDS NOW.
YAH!
KLANG
SPARE ME YOUR REHEARSED DIALOG, TURTLE.
UNH!
KRAK
YOU DARE?!
HH!
ENOUGH!

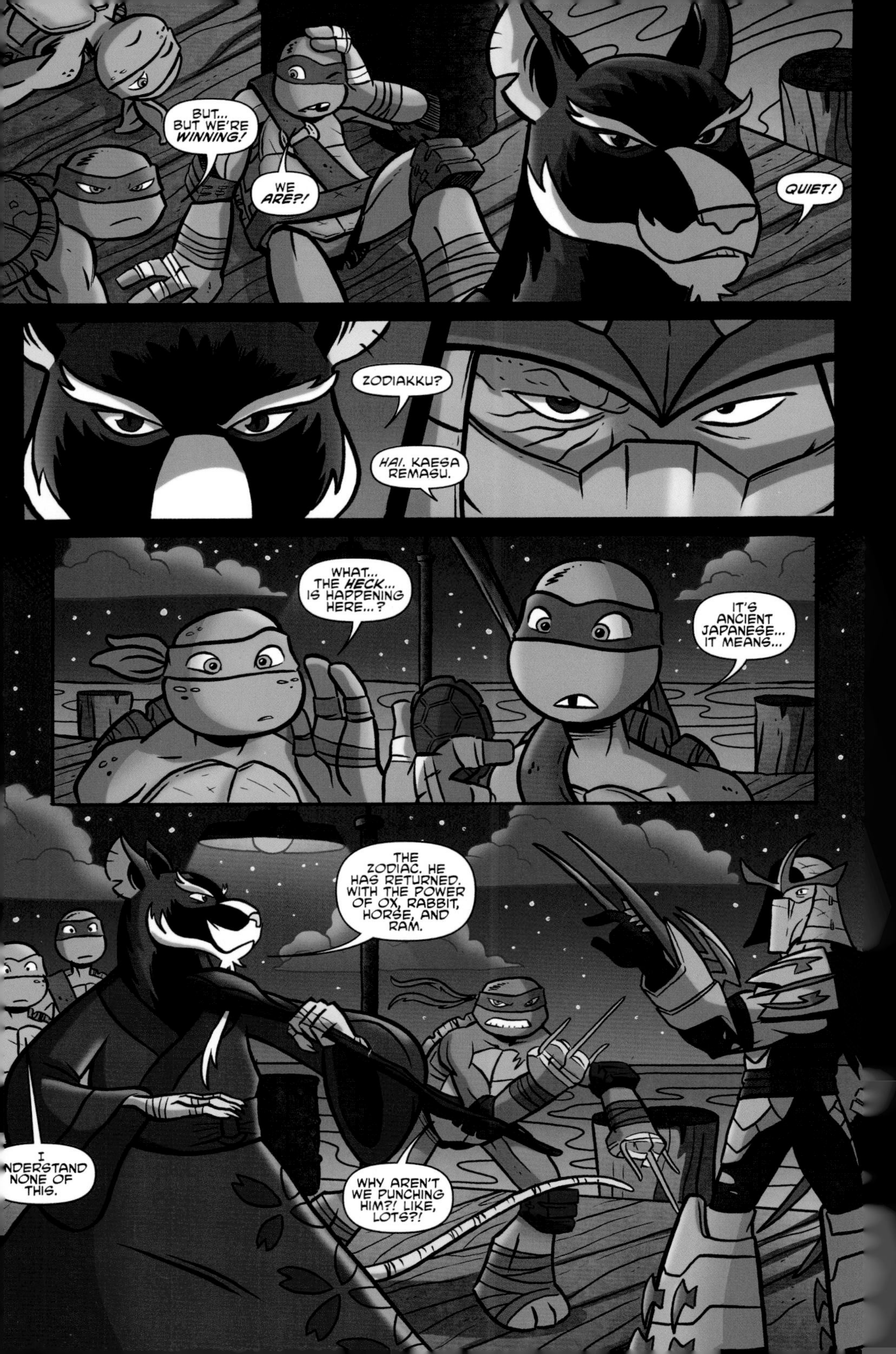

BUT... BUT WE'RE WINNING!
WE ARE?!
QUIET!
ZODIAKKU?
HAI. KAESA REMASU.
WHAT... THE HECK... IS HAPPENING HERE...?
IT'S ANCIENT JAPANESE... IT MEANS...
THE ZODIAC. HE HAS RETURNED. WITH THE POWER OF OX, RABBIT, HORSE, AND RAM.
I NDERSTAND NONE OF THIS.
WHY AREN'T WE PUNCHING HIM?! LIKE, LOTS?!

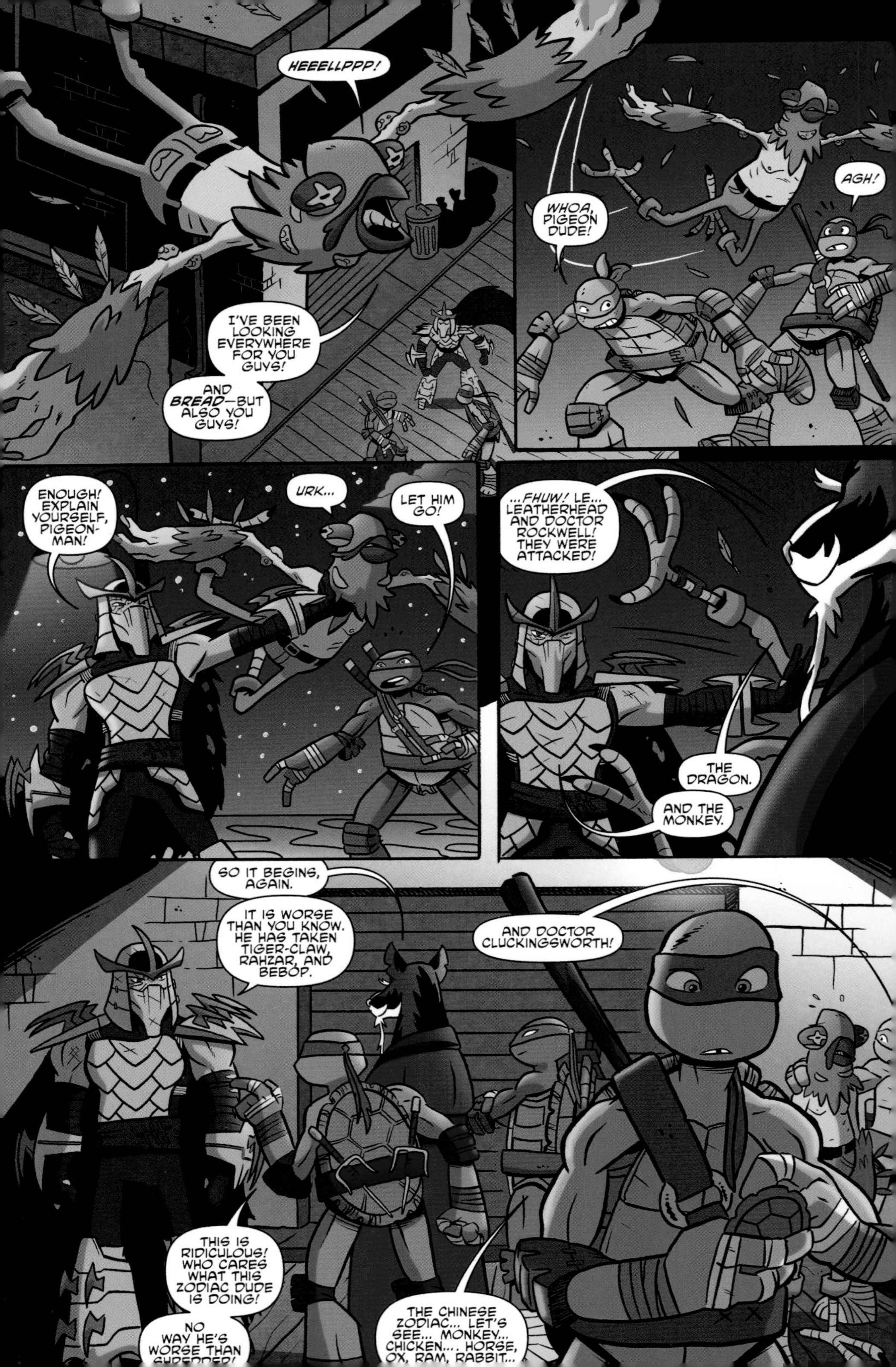
HEEELLPPP!
I'VE BEEN LOOKING EVERYWHERE FOR YOU GUYS!
AND BREAD—BUT ALSO YOU GUYS!
WHOA, PIGEON DUDE!
AGH!
ENOUGH! EXPLAIN YOURSELF, PIGEON-MAN!
URK...
LET HIM GO!
...FHUW! LE... LEATHERHEAD AND DOCTOR ROCKWELL! THEY WERE ATTACKED!
THE DRAGON.
AND THE MONKEY.
SO IT BEGINS, AGAIN.
IT IS WORSE THAN YOU KNOW. HE HAS TAKEN TIGER-CLAW, RAHZAR, AND BEBOP.
AND DOCTOR CLUCKINGSWORTH!
THIS IS RIDICULOUS! WHO CARES WHAT THIS ZODIAC DUDE IS DOING!
NO WAY HE'S WORSE THAN
THE CHINESE ZODIAC... LET'S SEE... MONKEY... CHICKEN... HORSE, OX, RAM, RABBIT...

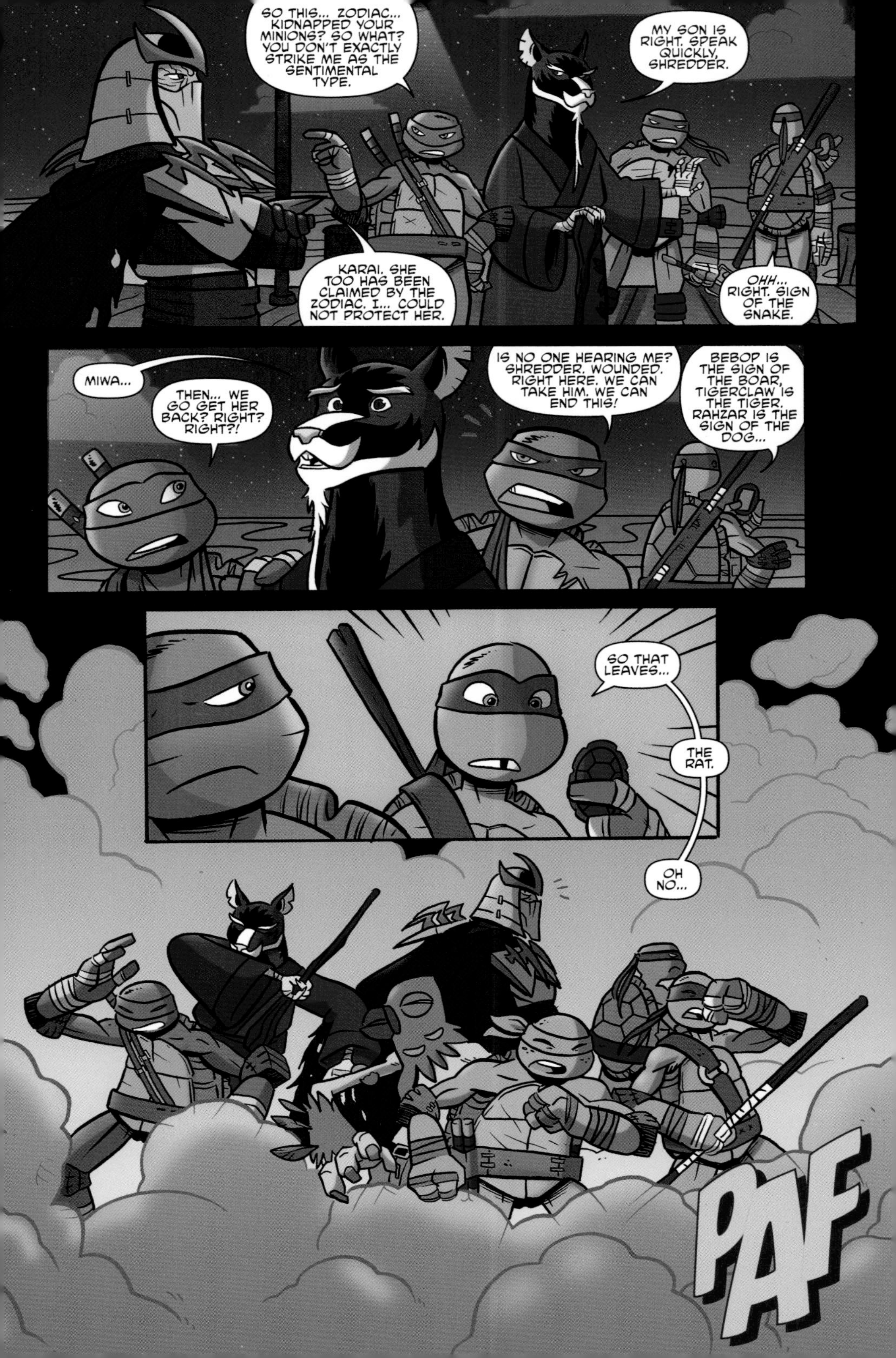
SO THIS... ZODIAC... KIDNAPPED YOUR MINIONS? SO WHAT? YOU DON'T EXACTLY STRIKE ME AS THE SENTIMENTAL TYPE.
MY SON IS RIGHT. SPEAK QUICKLY, SHREDDER.
KARAI. SHE TOO HAS BEEN CLAIMED BY THE ZODIAC. I... COULD NOT PROTECT HER.
OHH... RIGHT. SIGN OF THE SNAKE.
MIWA...
THEN... WE GO GET HER BACK? RIGHT? RIGHT?!
IS NO ONE HEARING ME? SHREDDER. WOUNDED. RIGHT HERE. WE CAN TAKE HIM. WE CAN END THIS!
BEBOP IS THE SIGN OF THE BOAR, TIGERCLAW IS THE TIGER. RAHZAR IS THE SIGN OF THE DOG...
SO THAT LEAVES...
THE RAT.
OH NO...
PAF

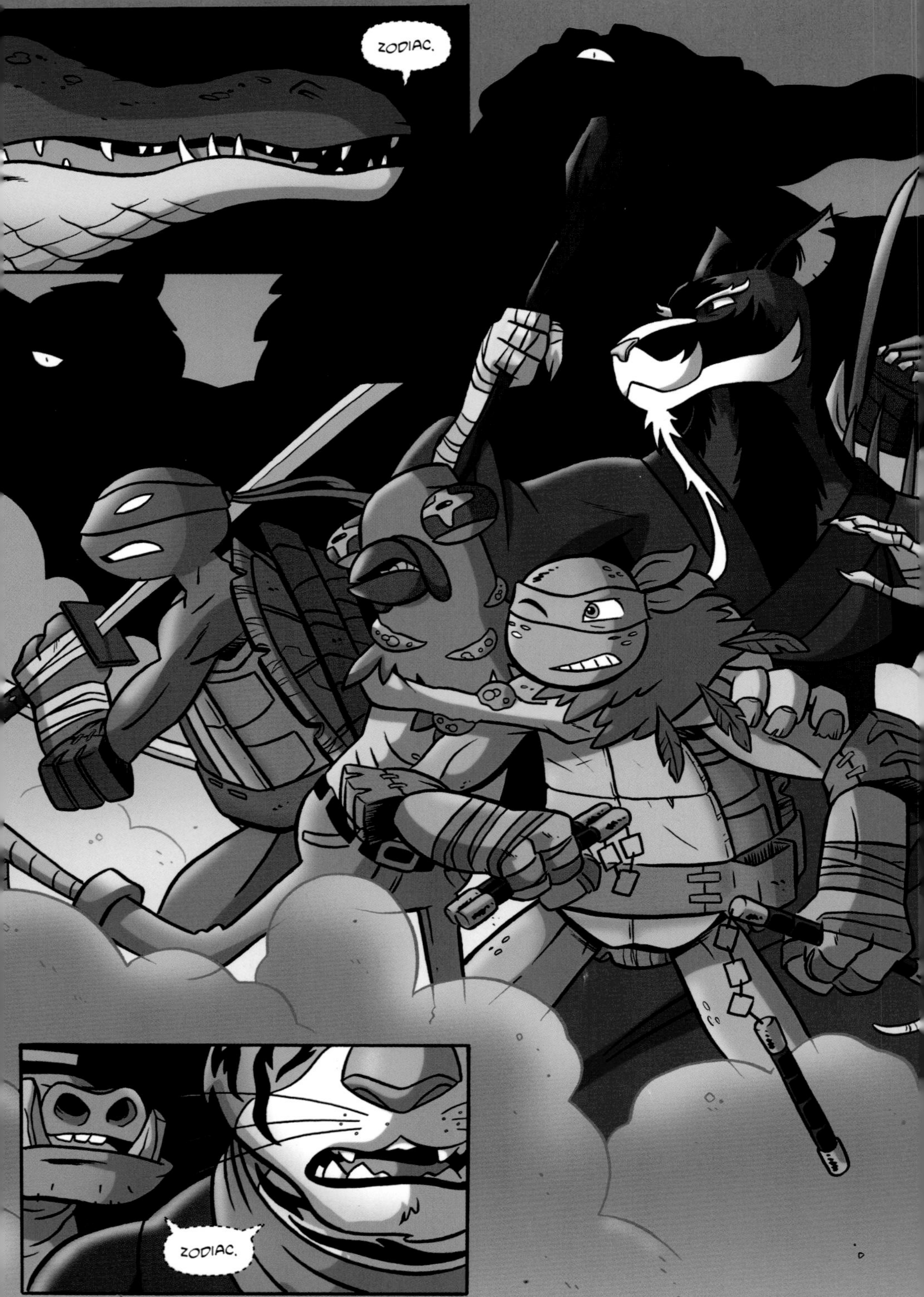
ZODIAC.
ZODIAC.

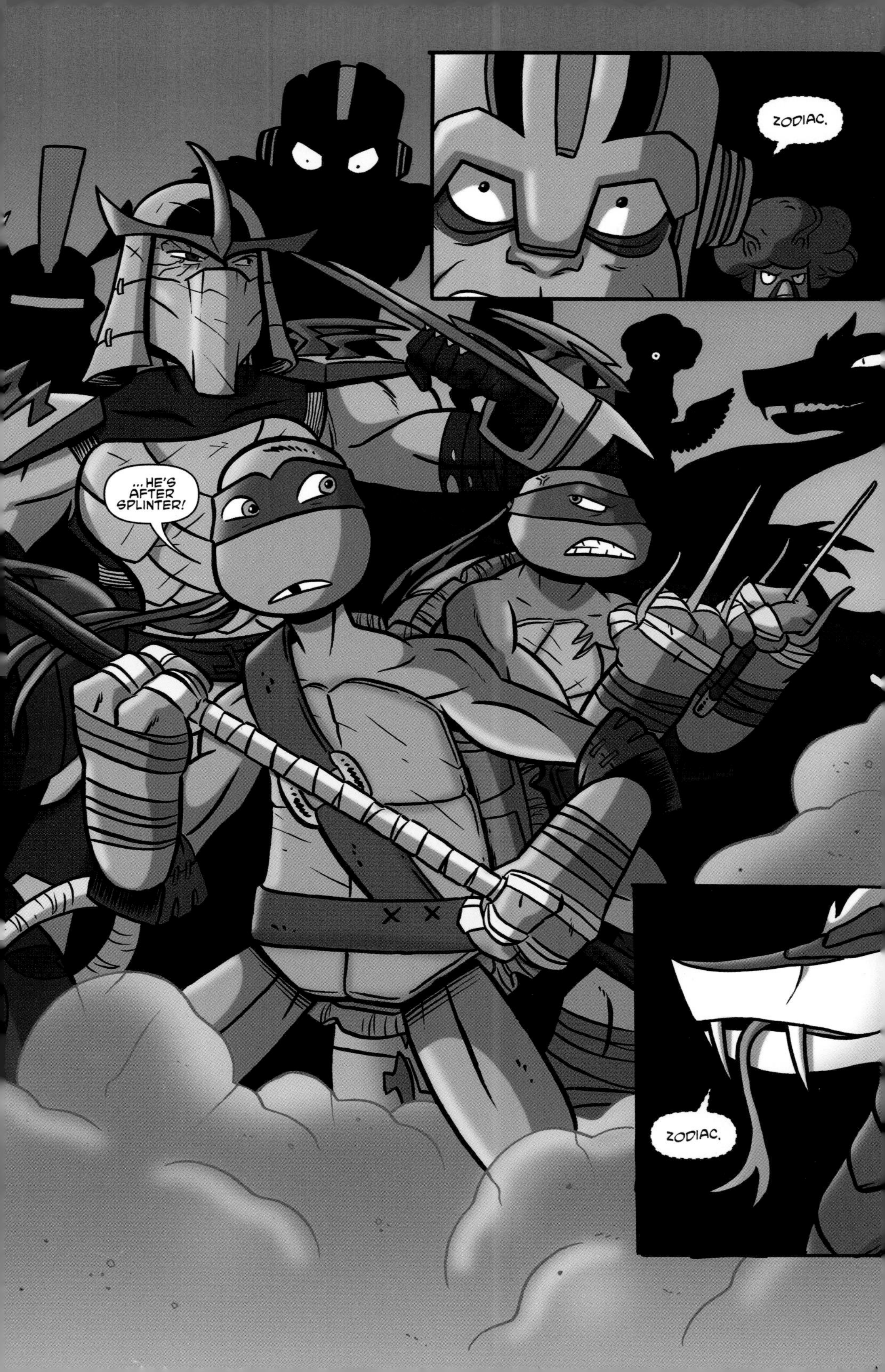
ZODIAC.
...HE'S AFTER SPLINTER!
ZODIAC.

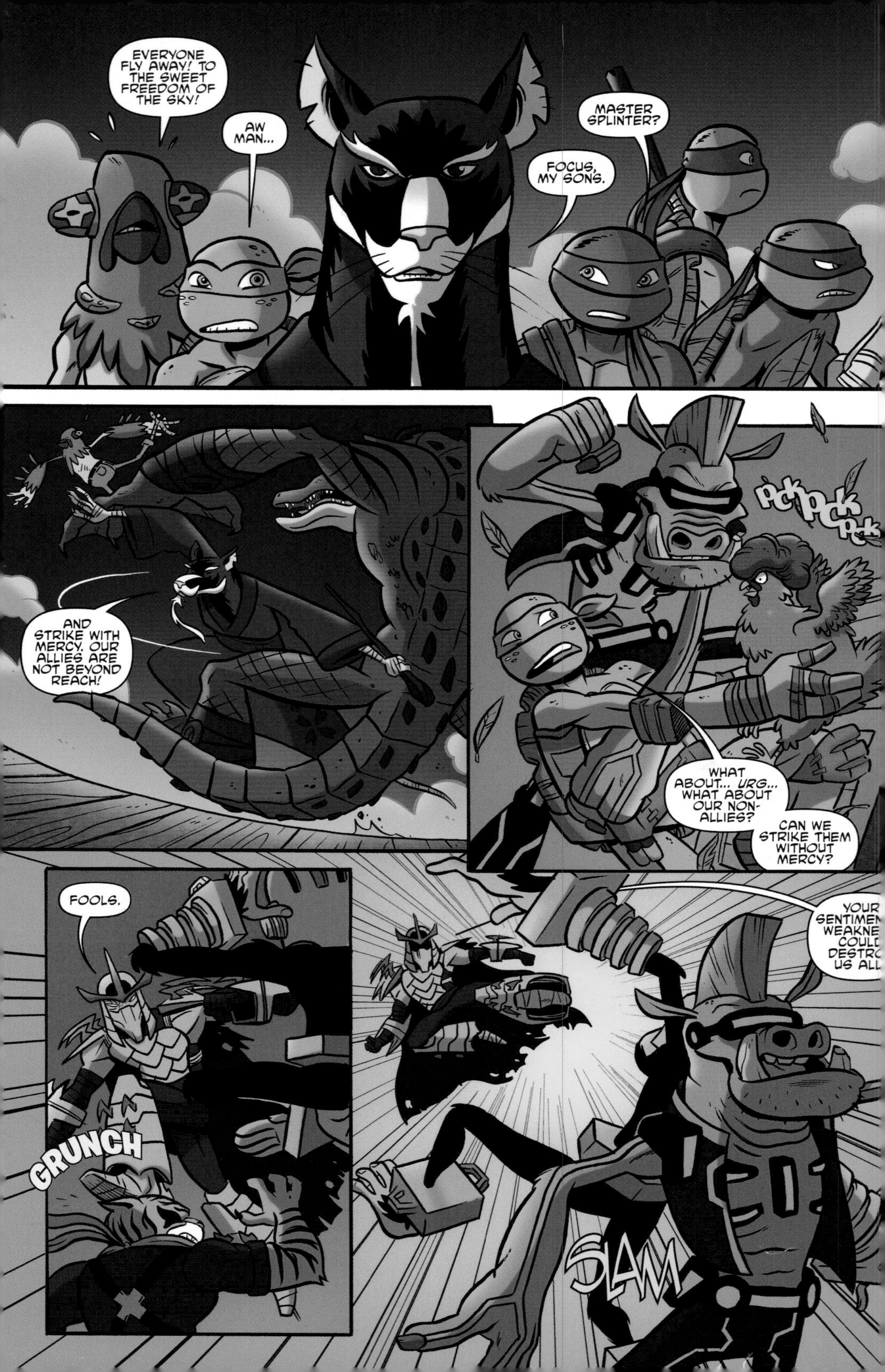
EVERYONE FLY AWAY! TO THE SWEET FREEDOM OF THE SKY!
AW MAN...
MASTER SPLINTER?
FOCUS, MY SONS.
AND STRIKE WITH MERCY. OUR ALLIES ARE NOT BEYOND REACH!
PCKPCK PCKPCK
WHAT ABOUT... URG... WHAT ABOUT OUR NON-ALLIES?
CAN WE STRIKE THEM WITHOUT MERCY?
FOOLS.
GRUNCH
SLAM

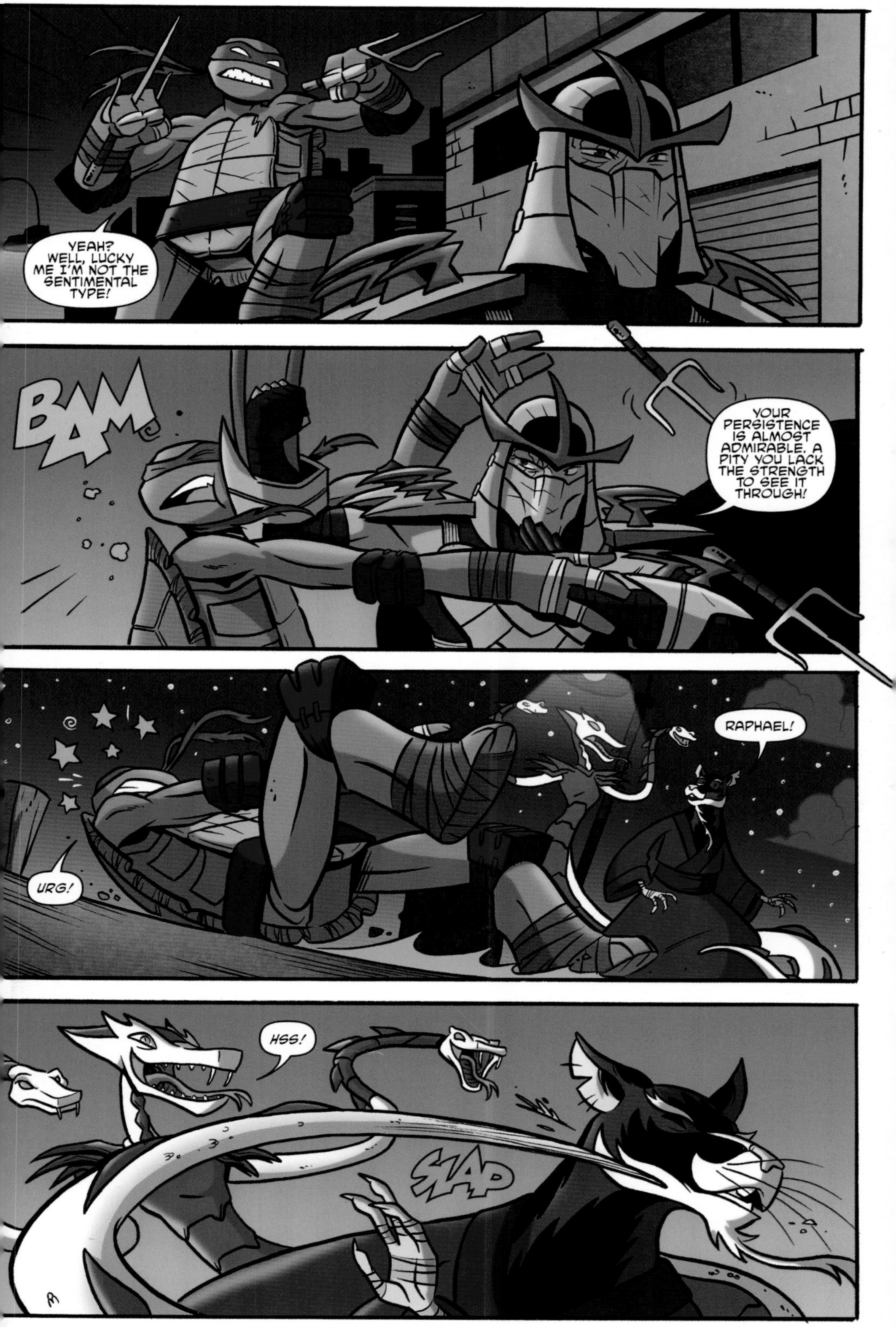
YEAH? WELL, LUCKY ME I'M NOT THE SENTIMENTAL TYPE!
BAM
YOUR PERSISTENCE IS ALMOST ADMIRABLE. A PITY YOU LACK THE STRENGTH TO SEE IT THROUGH!
RAPHAEL!
URG!
HSS!
SLAP

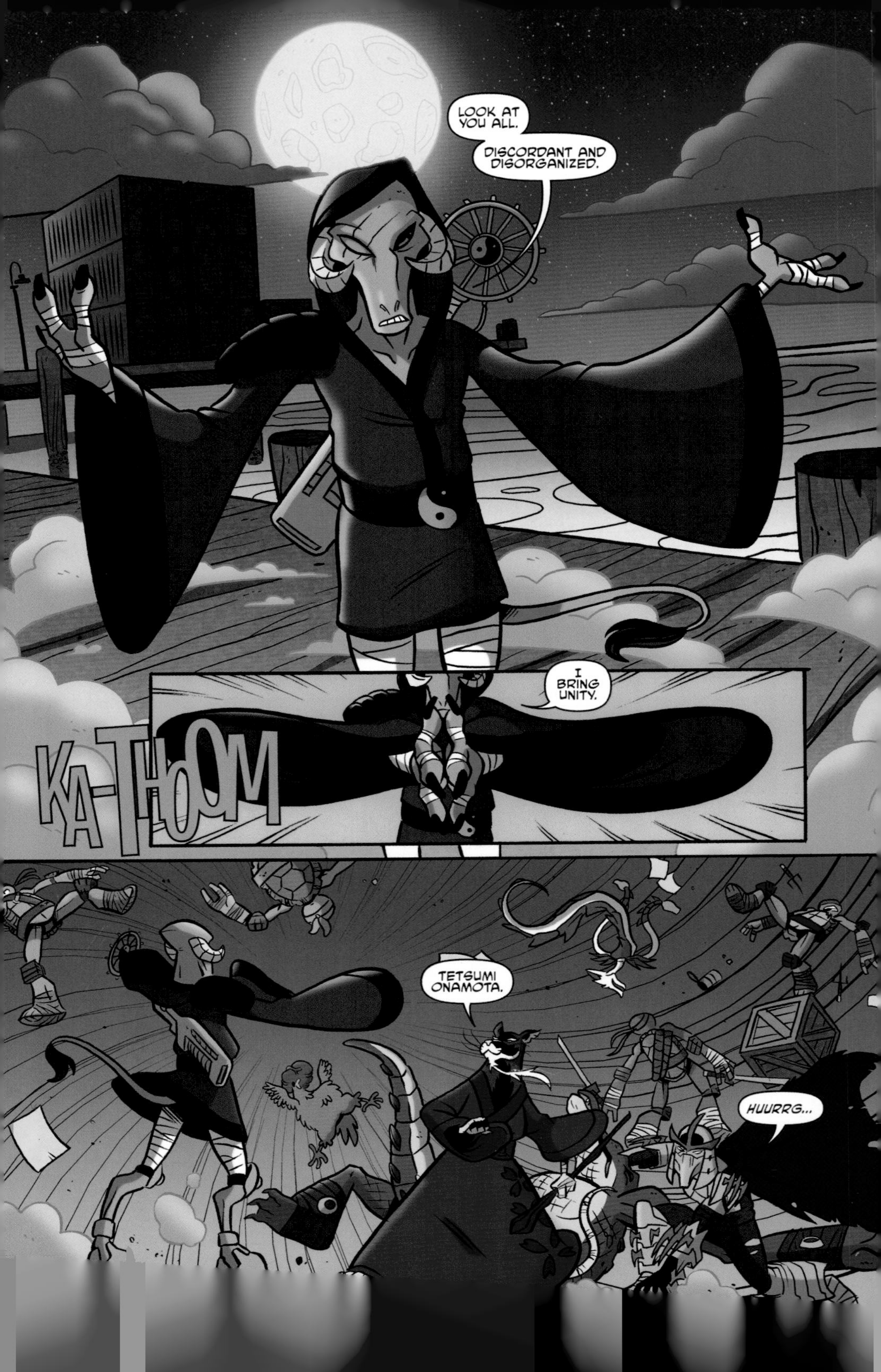
LOOK AT YOU ALL.
DISCORDANT AND DISORGANIZED.
I BRING UNITY.
KA-THOOM
TETSUMI ONAMOTA.
HUURRG...

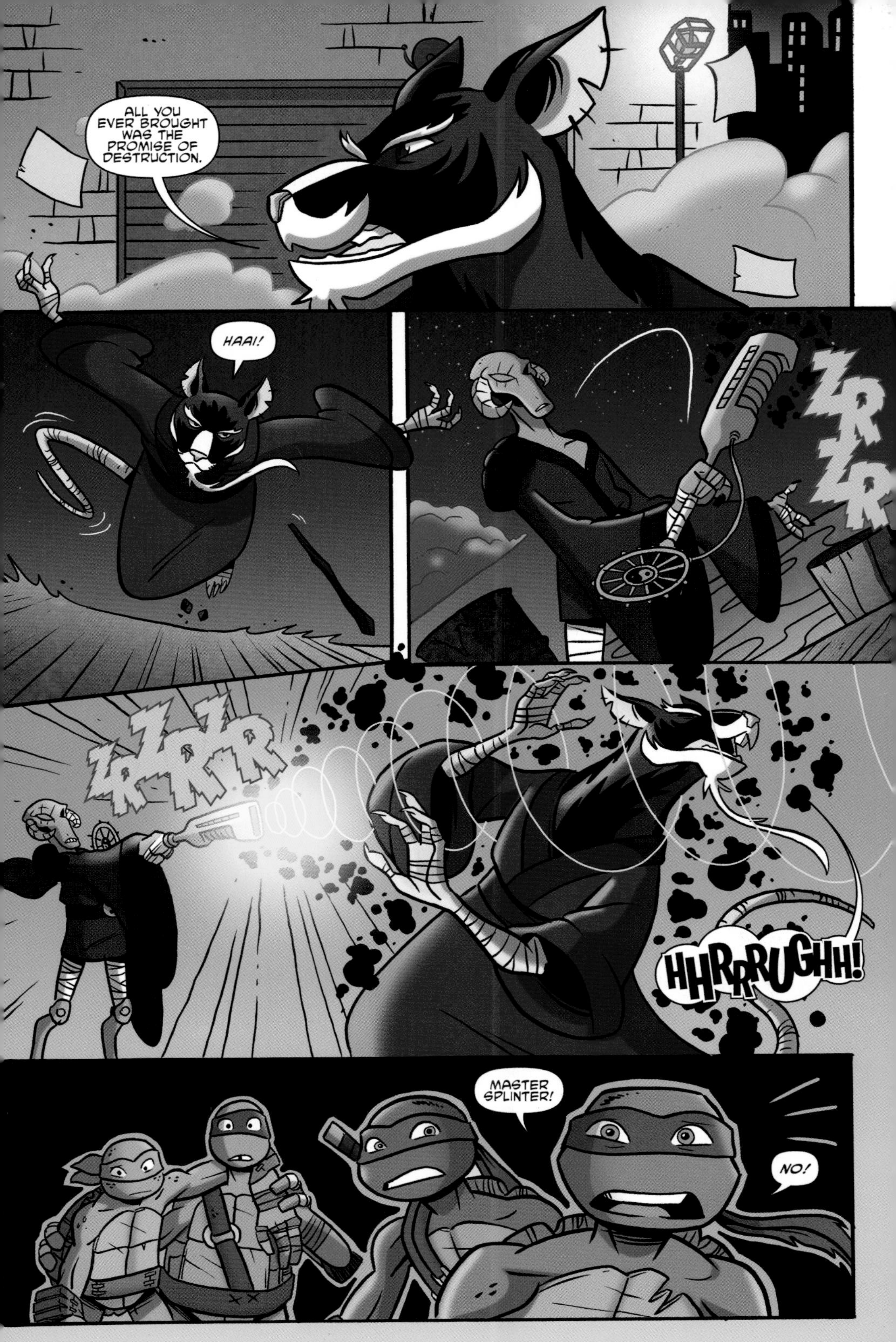

ALL YOU EVER BROUGHT WAS THE PROMISE OF DESTRUCTION.
HAAI!
ZRZR
ZRZRZRZR
HHHRRRUGHH!
MASTER SPLINTER!
NO!

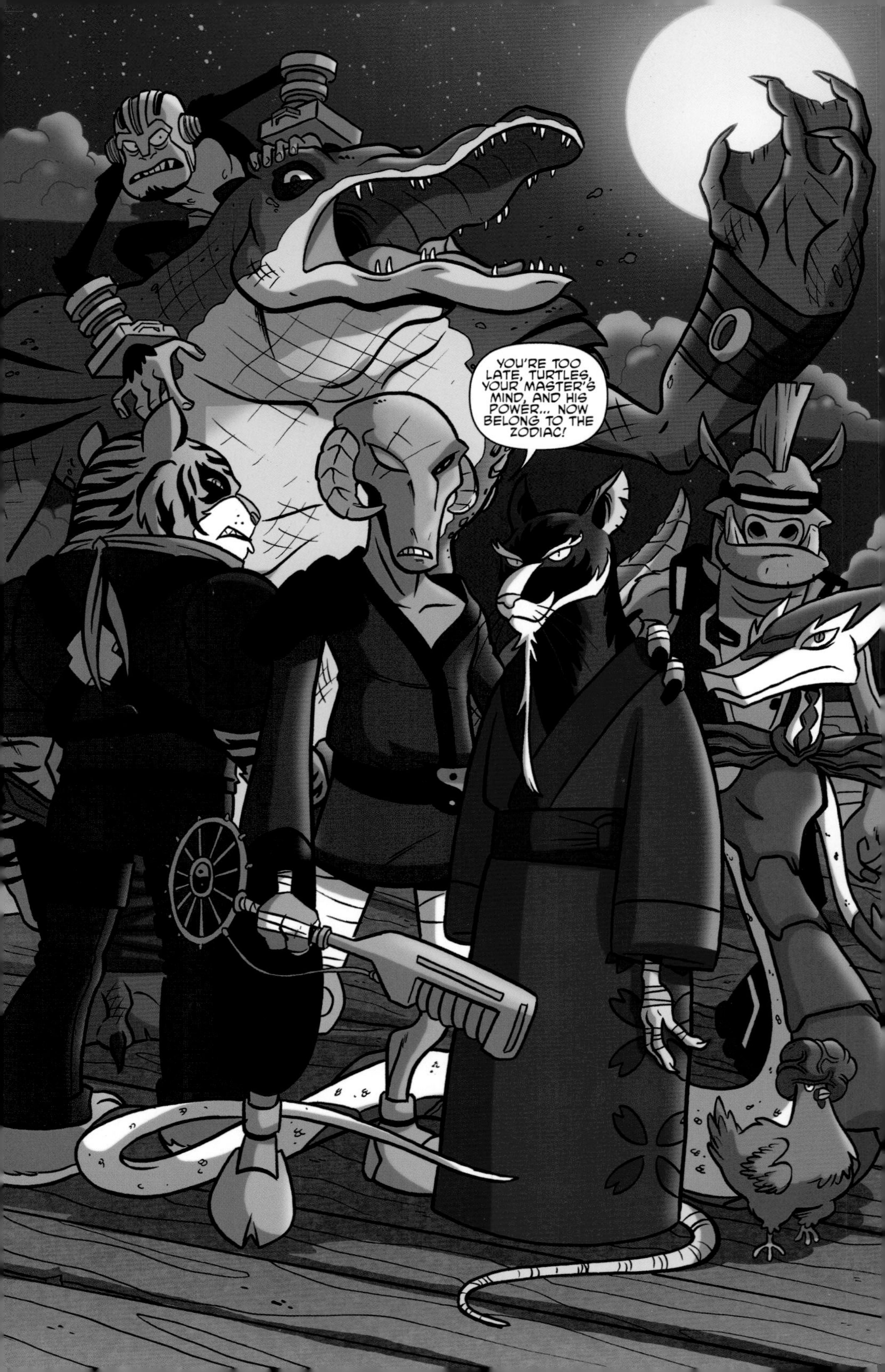
YOU'RE TOO LATE, TURTLES. YOUR MASTER'S MIND, AND HIS POWER... NOW BELONG TO THE ZODIAC!

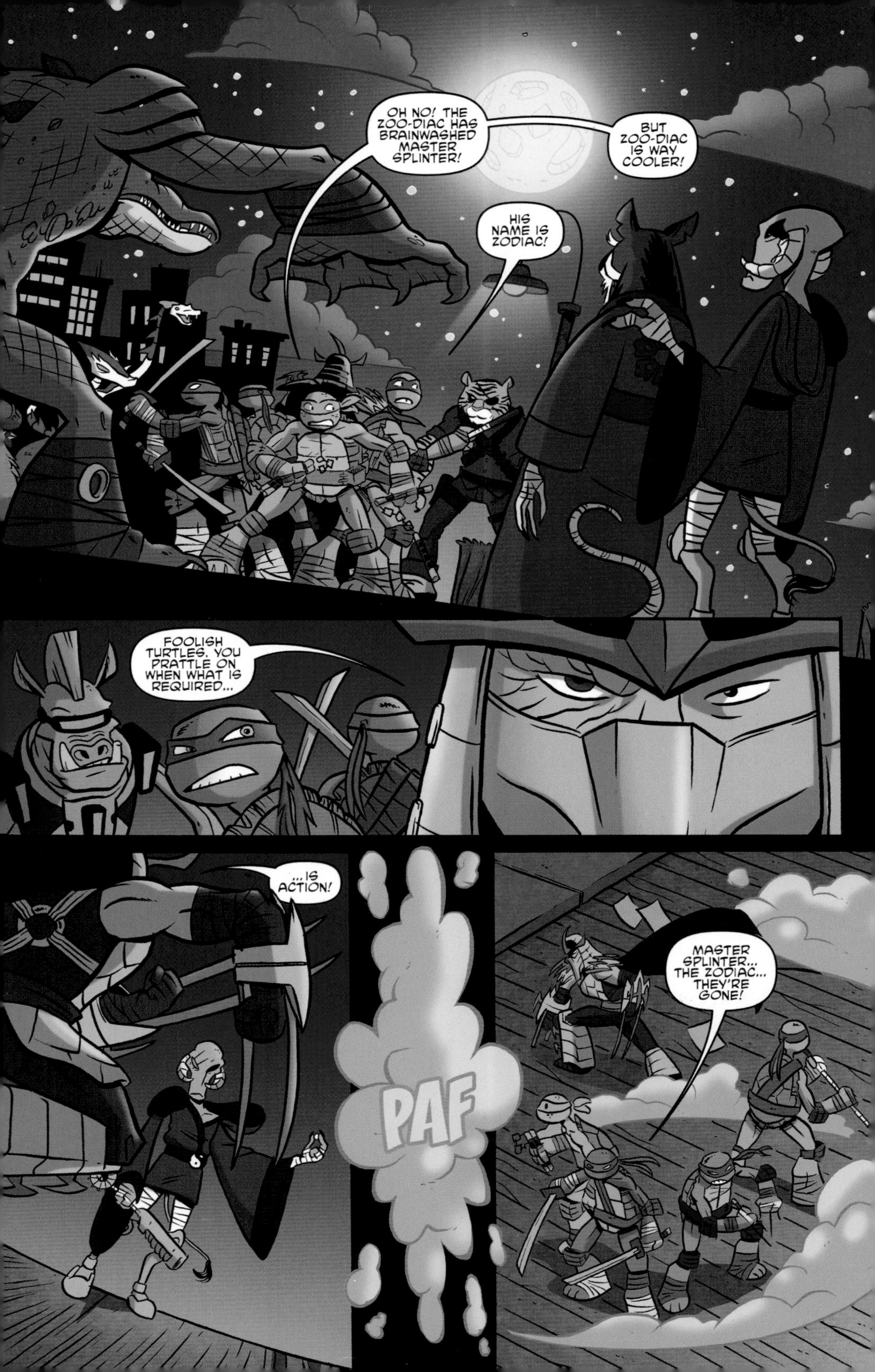
OH NO! THE ZOO-DIAC HAS BRAINWASHED MASTER SPLINTER!
BUT ZOO-DIAC IS WAY COOLER!
HIS NAME IS ZODIAC!
FOOLISH TURTLES. YOU PRATTLE ON WHEN WHAT IS REQUIRED...
...IS ACTION!
PAF
MASTER SPLINTER... THE ZODIAC... THEY'RE GONE!

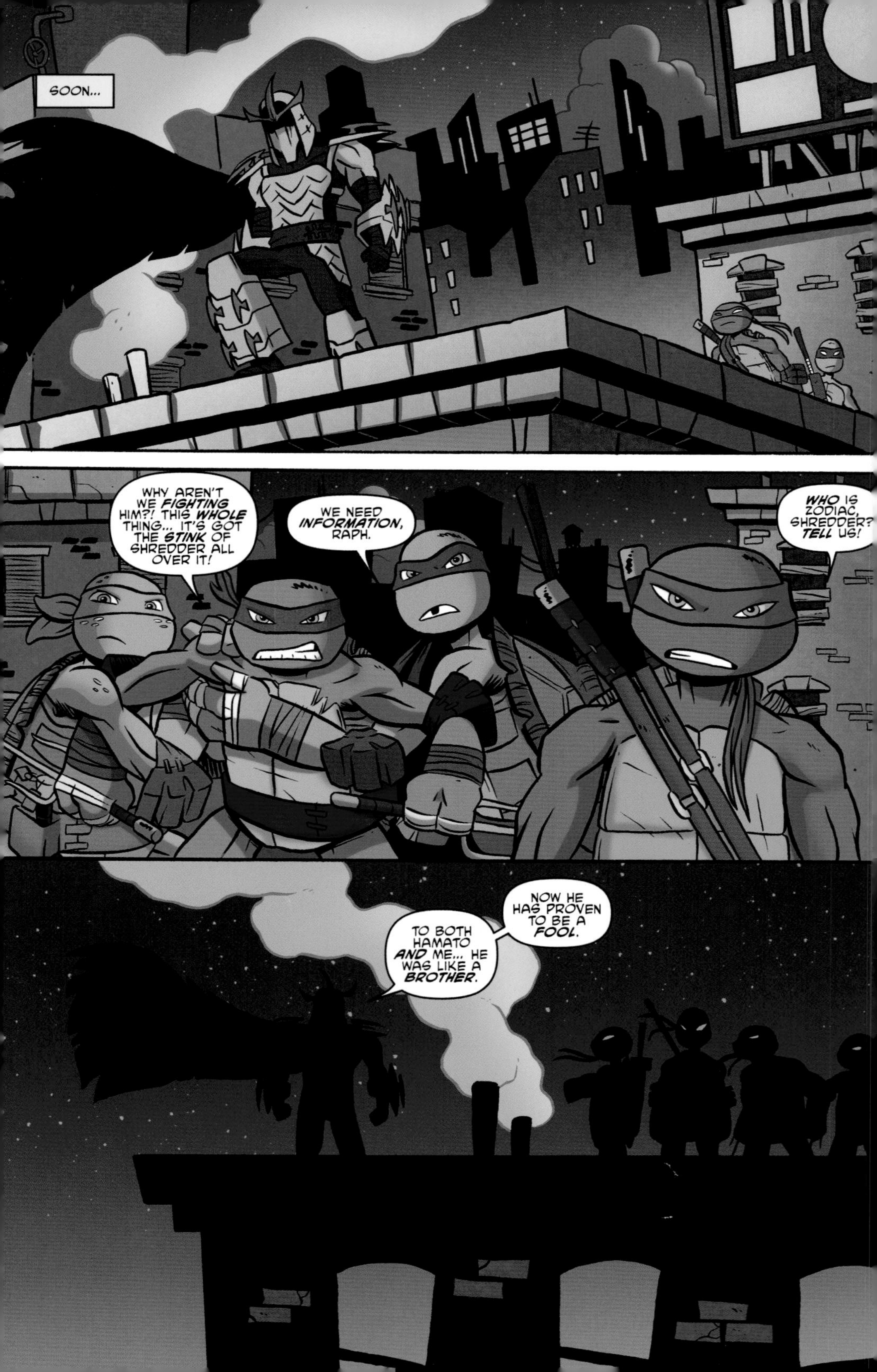
SOON...
WHY AREN'T WE FIGHTING HIM?! THIS WHOLE THING... IT'S GOT THE STINK OF SHREDDER ALL OVER IT!
WE NEED INFORMATION, RAPH.
WHO IS ZODIAC, SHREDDER? TELL US!
NOW HE HAS PROVEN TO BE A FOOL.
TO BOTH HAMATO AND ME... HE WAS LIKE A BROTHER.

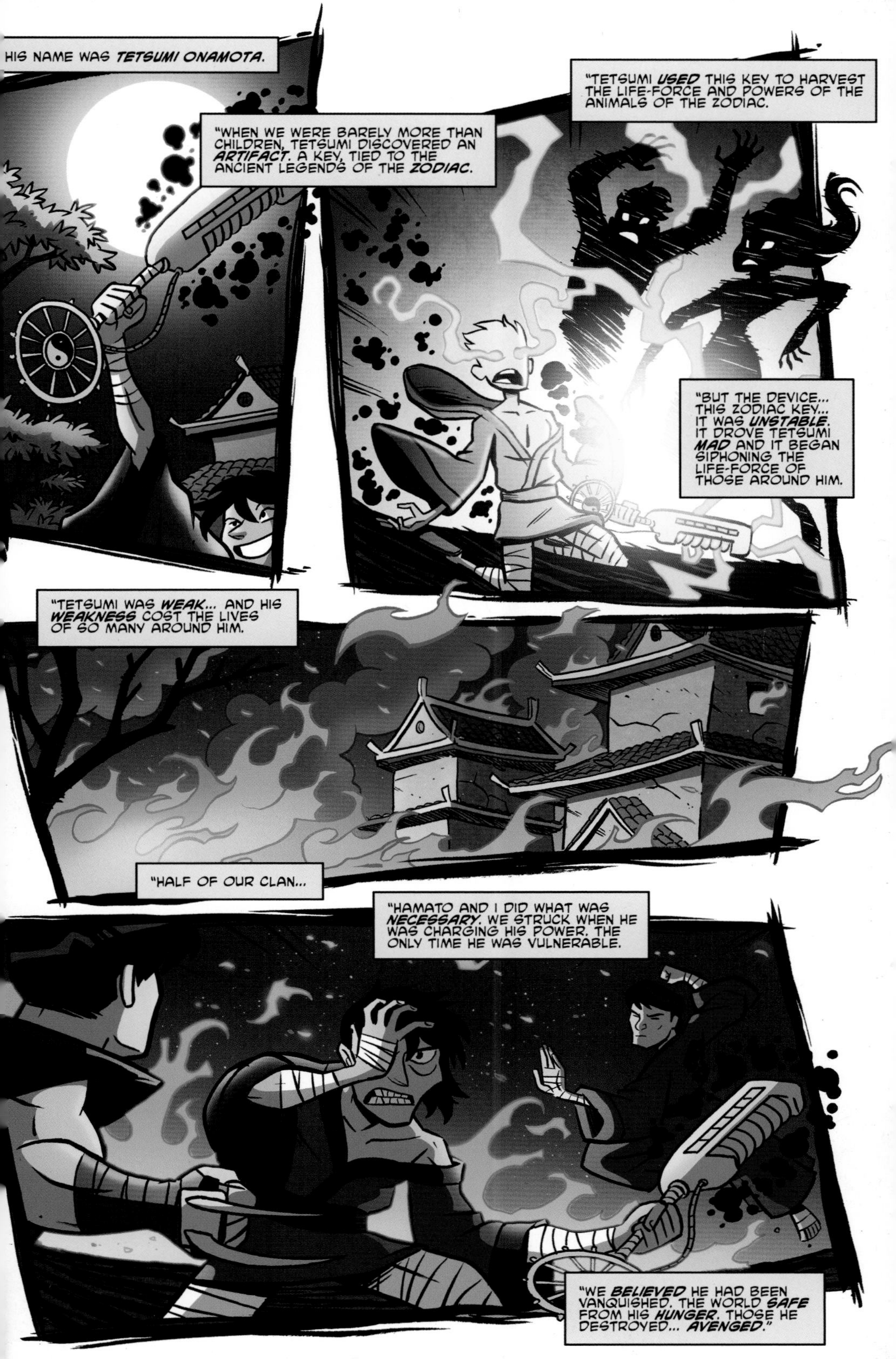
HIS NAME WAS TETSUMI ONAMOTA.
"WHEN WE WERE BARELY MORE THAN CHILDREN, TETSUMI DISCOVERED AN ARTIFACT. A KEY, TIED TO THE ANCIENT LEGENDS OF THE ZODIAC.
"TETSUMI USED THIS KEY TO HARVEST THE LIFE-FORCE AND POWERS OF THE ANIMALS OF THE ZODIAC.
"BUT THE DEVICE... THIS ZODIAC KEY... IT WAS UNSTABLE. IT DROVE TETSUMI MAD AND IT BEGAN SIPHONING THE LIFE-FORCE OF THOSE AROUND HIM.
"TETSUMI WAS WEAK... AND HIS WEAKNESS COST THE LIVES OF SO MANY AROUND HIM.
"HALF OF OUR CLAN...
"HAMATO AND I DID WHAT WAS NECESSARY. WE STRUCK WHEN HE WAS CHARGING HIS POWER. THE ONLY TIME HE WAS VULNERABLE.
"WE BELIEVED HE HAD BEEN VANQUISHED. THE WORLD SAFE FROM HIS HUNGER. THOSE HE DESTROYED... AVENGED."

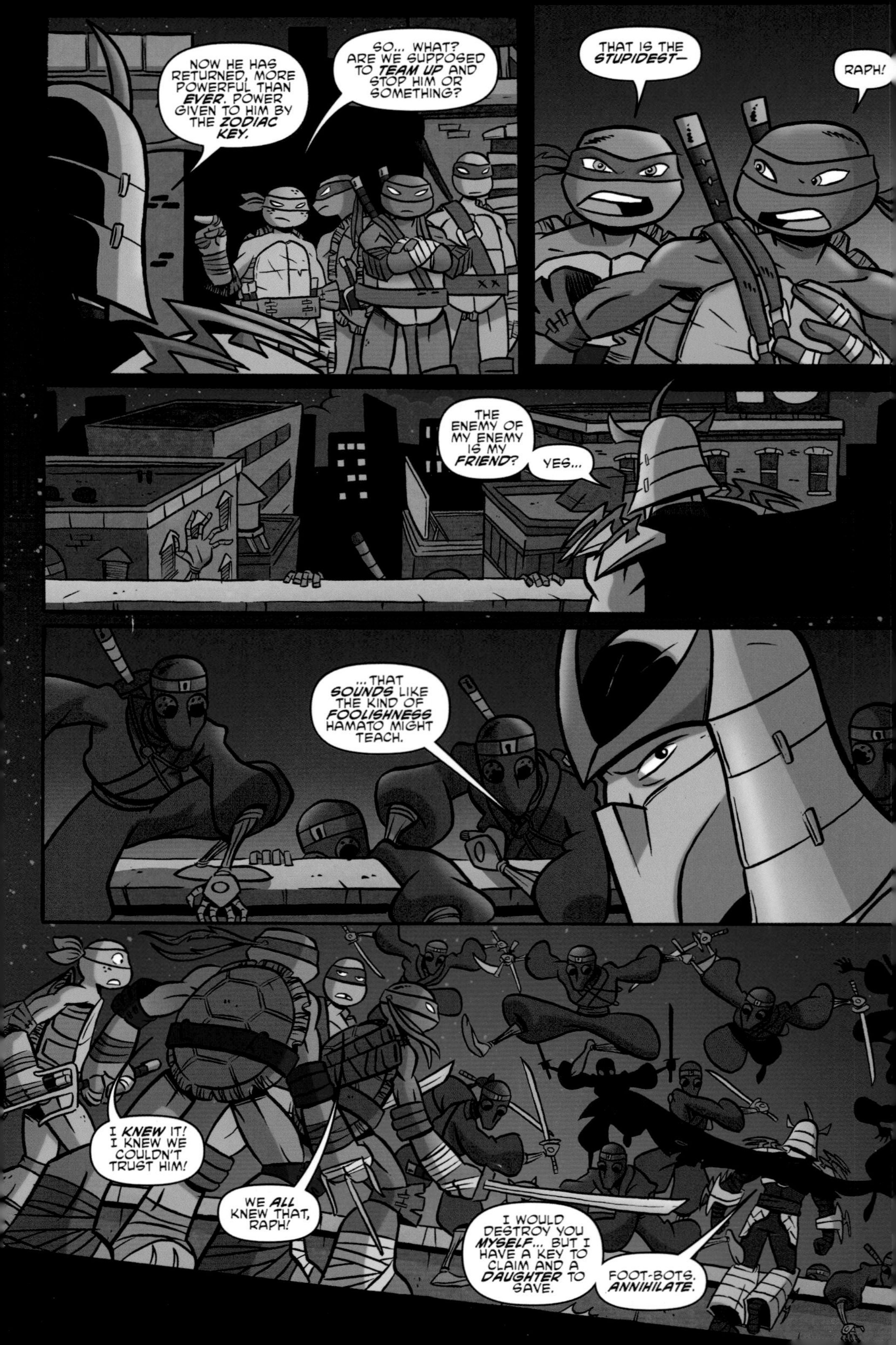
NOW HE HAS RETURNED, MORE POWERFUL THAN EVER. POWER GIVEN TO HIM BY THE ZODIAC KEY.
SO... WHAT? ARE WE SUPPOSED TO TEAM UP AND STOP HIM OR SOMETHING?
THAT IS THE STUPIDEST—
RAPH!
THE ENEMY OF MY ENEMY IS MY FRIEND?
YES...
...THAT SOUNDS LIKE THE KIND OF FOOLISHNESS HAMATO MIGHT TEACH.
I KNEW IT! I KNEW WE COULDN'T TRUST HIM!
WE ALL KNEW THAT, RAPH!
I WOULD DESTROY YOU MYSELF... BUT I HAVE A KEY TO CLAIM AND A DAUGHTER TO SAVE.
FOOT-BOTS. ANNIHILATE.

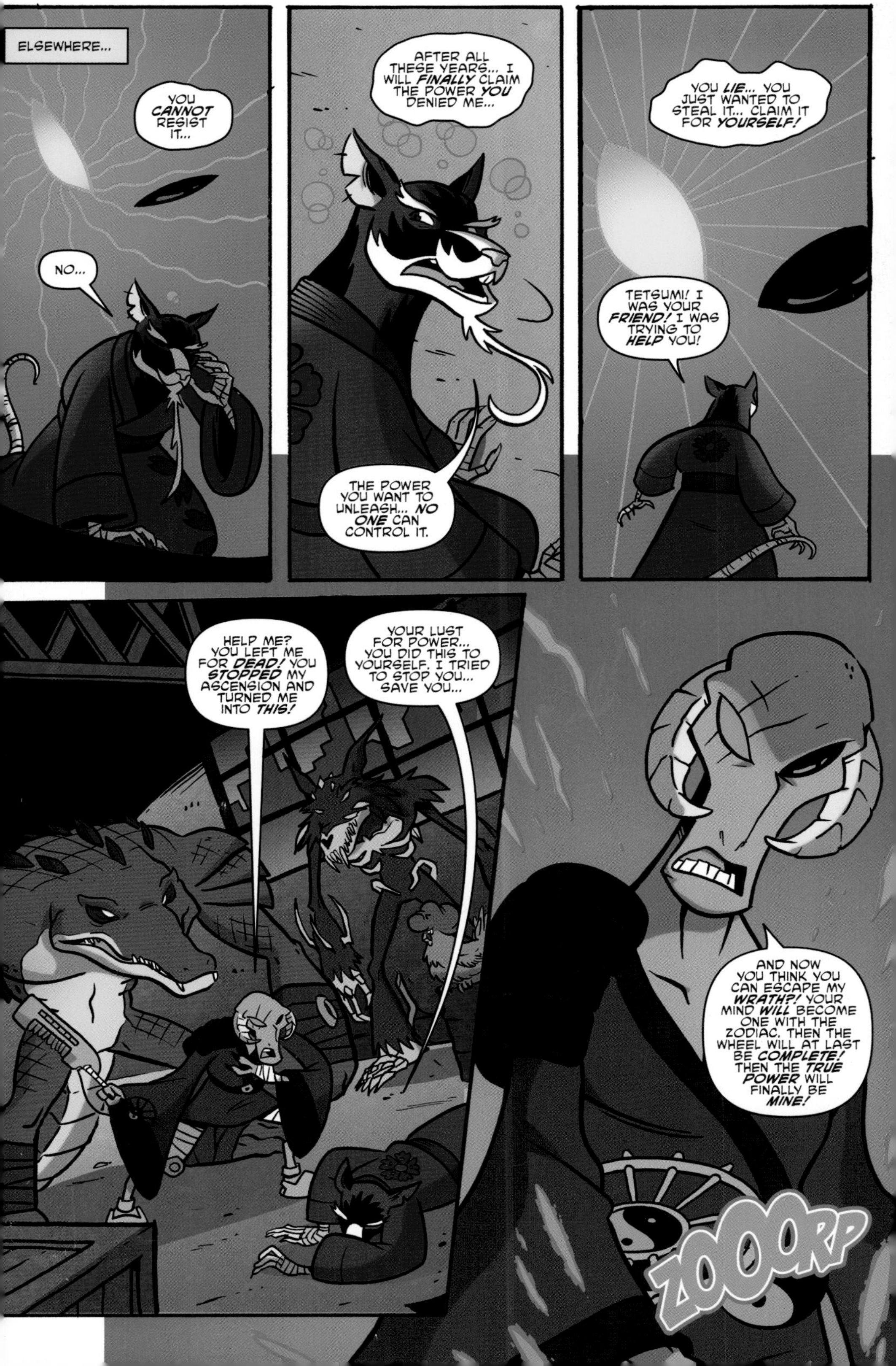
ELSEWHERE...
YOU CANNOT RESIST IT...
NO...
AFTER ALL THESE YEARS... I WILL FINALLY CLAIM THE POWER YOU DENIED ME...
THE POWER YOU WANT TO UNLEASH... NO ONE CAN CONTROL IT.
YOU LIE... YOU JUST WANTED TO STEAL IT... CLAIM IT FOR YOURSELF!
TETSUMI! I WAS YOUR FRIEND! I WAS TRYING TO HELP YOU!
HELP ME? YOU LEFT ME FOR DEAD! YOU STOPPED MY ASCENSION AND TURNED ME INTO THIS!
YOUR LUST FOR POWER... YOU DID THIS TO YOURSELF. I TRIED TO STOP YOU... SAVE YOU...
AND NOW YOU THINK YOU CAN ESCAPE MY WRATH?! YOUR MIND WILL BECOME ONE WITH THE ZODIAC. THEN THE WHEEL WILL AT LAST BE COMPLETE! THEN THE TRUE POWER WILL FINALLY BE MINE!
ZOOORP

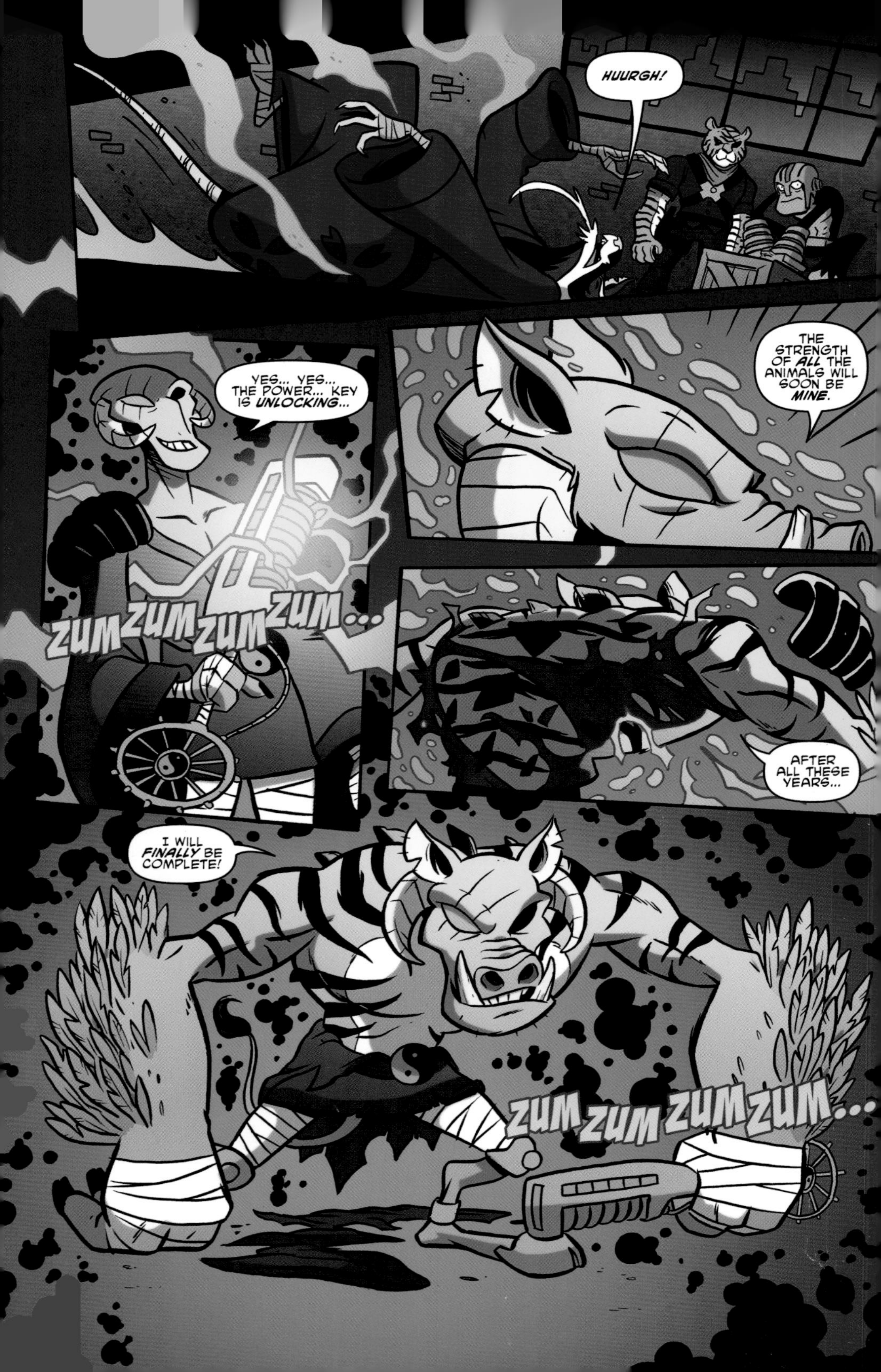

HUURGH!
YES... YES... THE POWER... KEY IS UNLOCKING...
ZUMZUMZUMZUM...
THE STRENGTH OF ALL THE ANIMALS WILL SOON BE MINE.
AFTER ALL THESE YEARS...
I WILL FINALLY BE COMPLETE!
ZUMZUMZUMZUM...

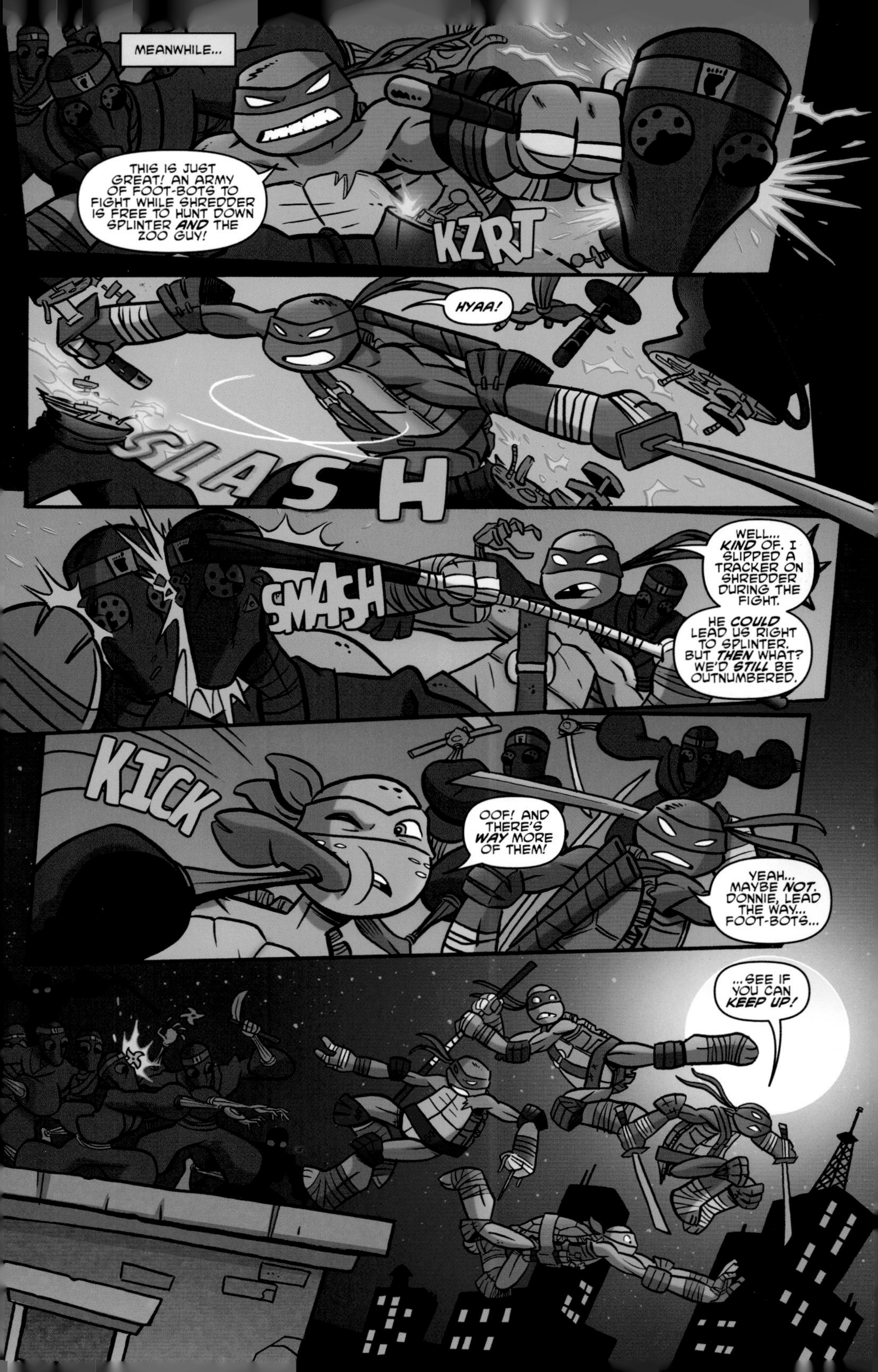
MEANWHILE...
THIS IS JUST GREAT! AN ARMY OF FOOT-BOTS TO FIGHT WHILE SHREDDER IS FREE TO HUNT DOWN SPLINTER AND THE ZOO GUY!
KZRT
HYAA!
SLASH
SMASH
WELL... KIND OF. I SLIPPED A TRACKER ON SHREDDER DURING THE FIGHT.
HE COULD LEAD US RIGHT TO SPLINTER. BUT THEN WHAT? WE'D STILL BE OUTNUMBERED.
KICK
OOF! AND THERE'S WAY MORE OF THEM!
YEAH... MAYBE NOT. DONNIE, LEAD THE WAY... FOOT-BOTS...
...SEE IF YOU CAN KEEP UP!

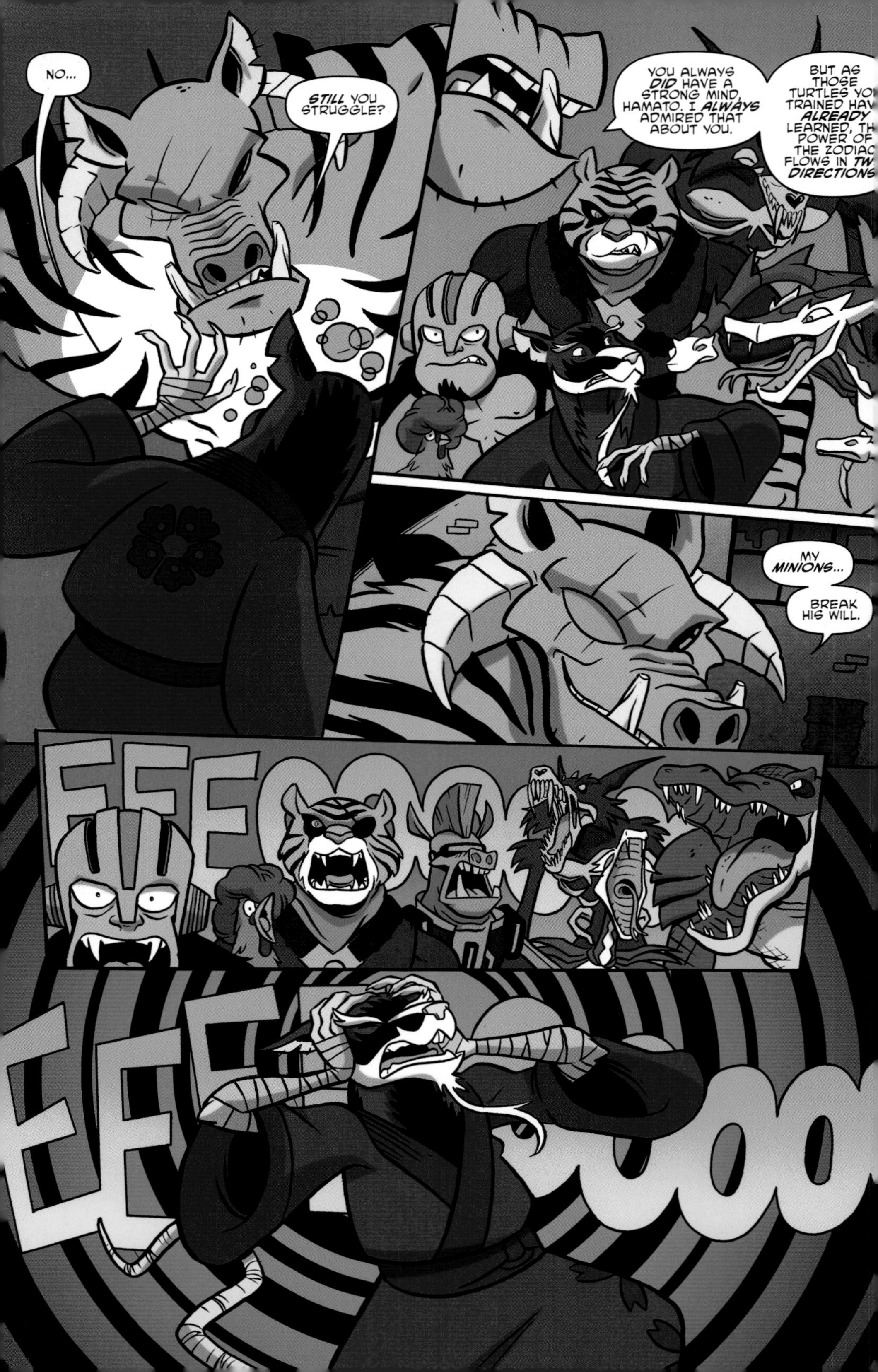
NO...
STILL YOU STRUGGLE?
YOU ALWAYS DID HAVE A STRONG MIND, HAMATO. I ALWAYS ADMIRED THAT ABOUT YOU.
BUT AS THOSE TURTLES YO TRAINED HAV ALREADY LEARNED, TH POWER OF THE ZODIAC FLOWS IN TW DIRECTIONS
MY MINIONS...
BREAK HIS WILL.
EEEOOOO
EEEOOOO

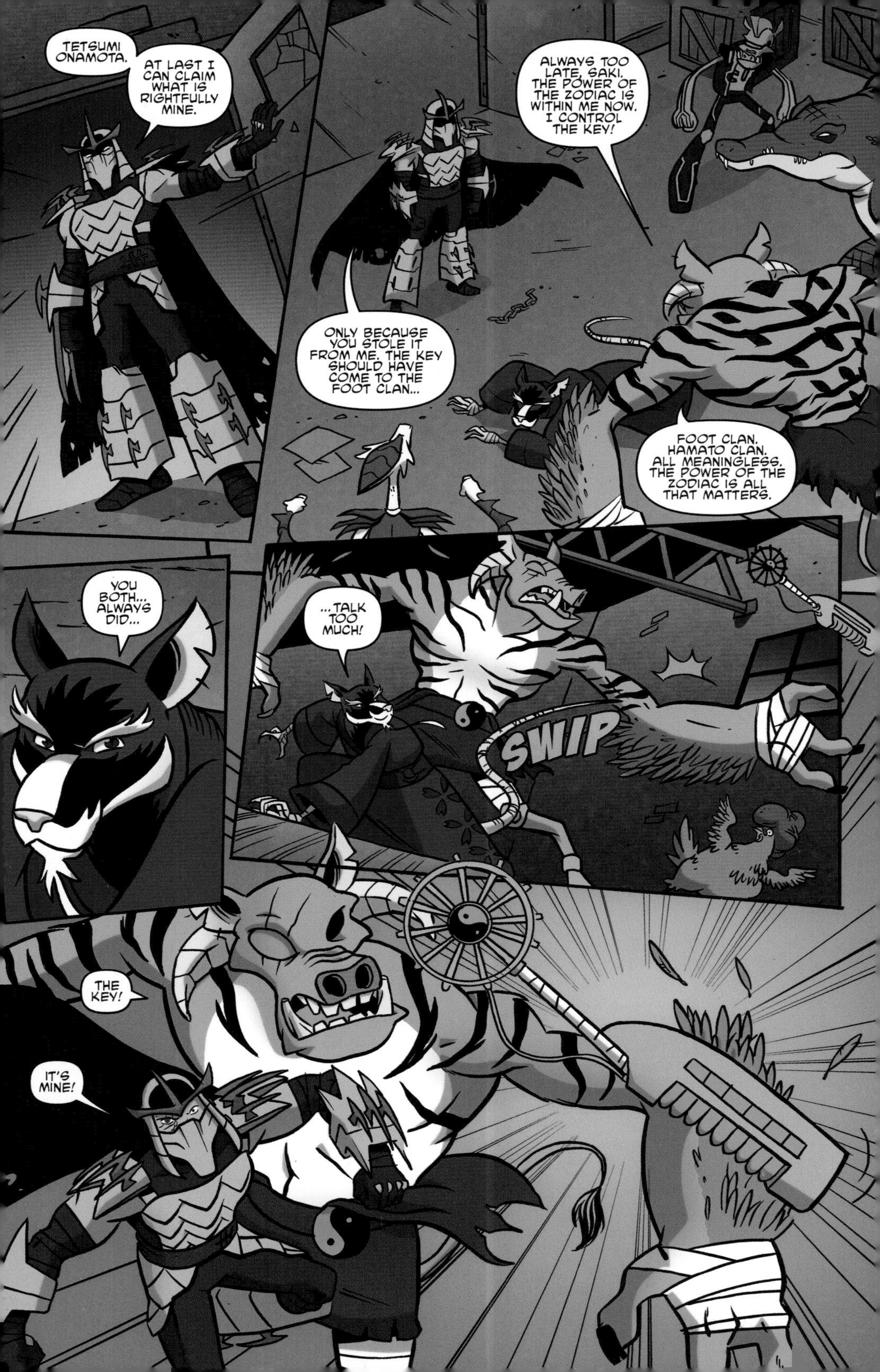
TETSUMI ONAMOTA.
AT LAST I CAN CLAIM WHAT IS RIGHTFULLY MINE.
ALWAYS TOO LATE, SAKI. THE POWER OF THE ZODIAC IS WITHIN ME NOW. I CONTROL THE KEY!
ONLY BECAUSE YOU STOLE IT FROM ME. THE KEY SHOULD HAVE COME TO THE FOOT CLAN...
FOOT CLAN. HAMATO CLAN. ALL MEANINGLESS. THE POWER OF THE ZODIAC IS ALL THAT MATTERS.
YOU BOTH... ALWAYS DID...
...TALK TOO MUCH!
SWIP
THE KEY!
IT'S MINE!

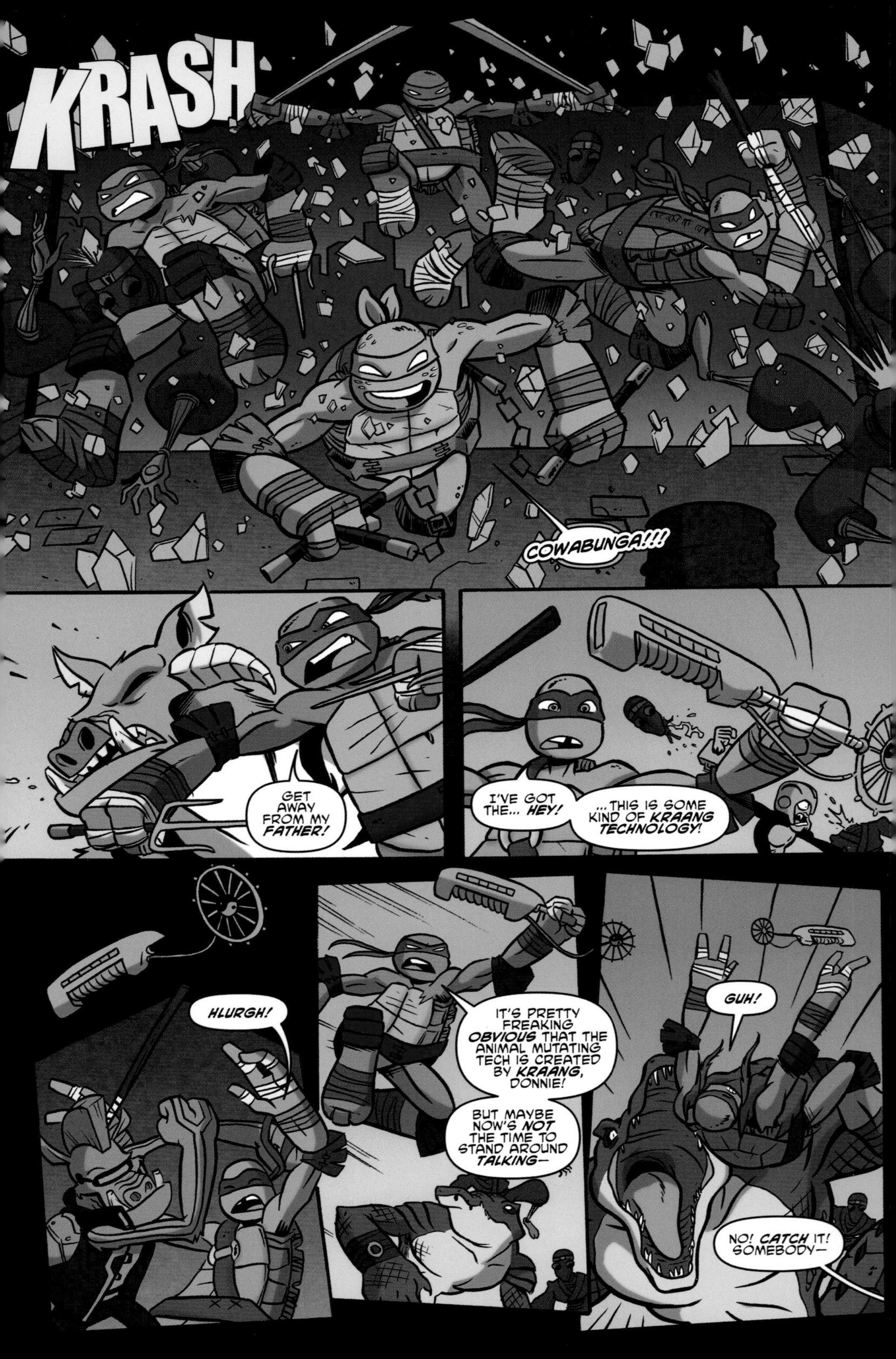
KRASH
COWABUNGA!!!
GET AWAY FROM MY FATHER!
I'VE GOT THE... HEY!
...THIS IS SOME KIND OF KRAANG TECHNOLOGY!
HLURGH!
IT'S PRETTY FREAKING OBVIOUS THAT THE ANIMAL MUTATING TECH IS CREATED BY KRAANG, DONNIE!
BUT MAYBE NOW'S NOT THE TIME TO STAND AROUND TALKING—
GUH!
NO! CATCH IT! SOMEBODY—

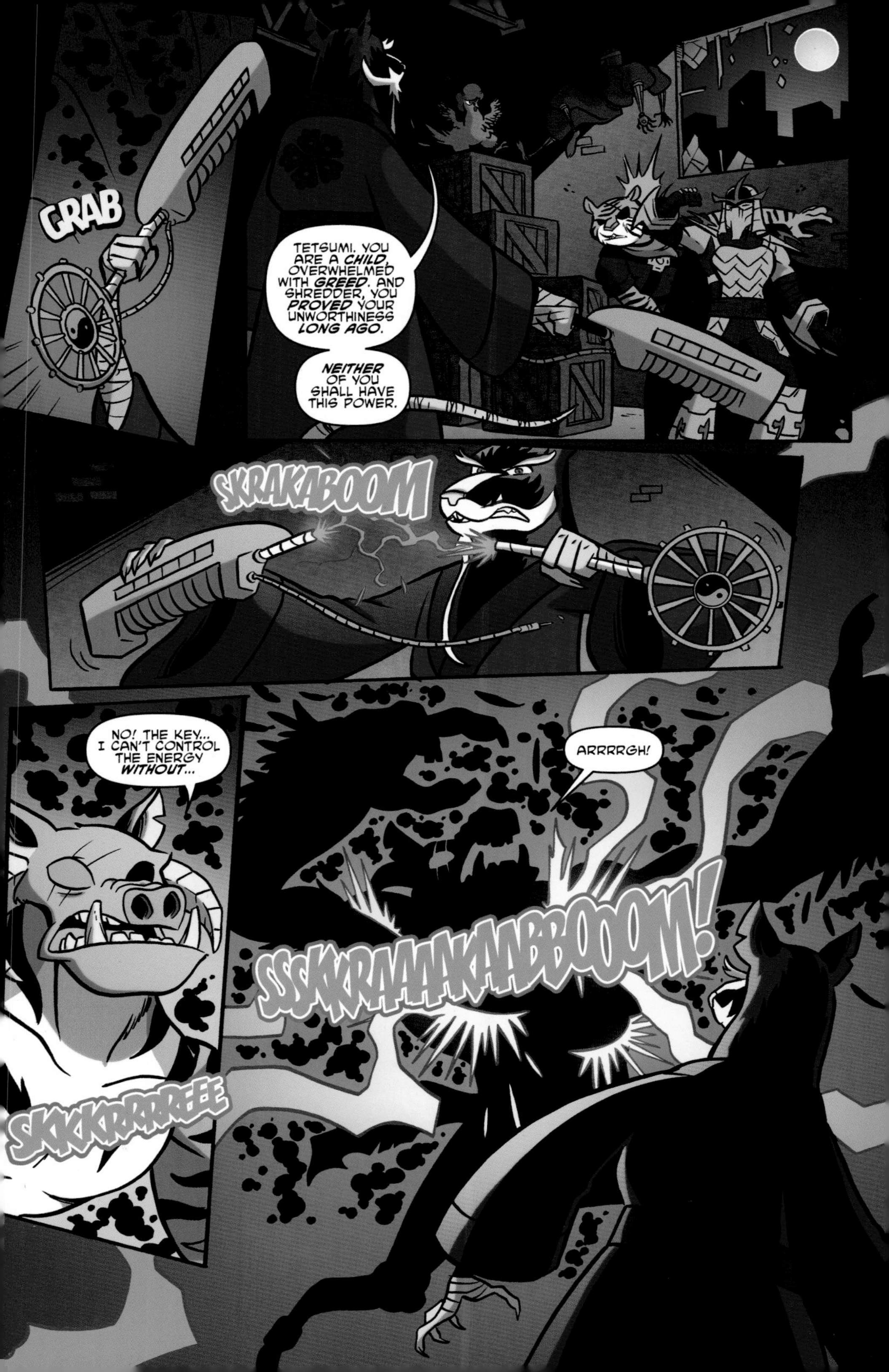
GRAB
TETSUMI. YOU ARE A CHILD, OVERWHELMED WITH GREED. AND SHREDDER, YOU PROVED YOUR UNWORTHINESS LONG AGO.
NEITHER OF YOU SHALL HAVE THIS POWER.
SKRAKABOOM
NO! THE KEY... I CAN'T CONTROL THE ENERGY WITHOUT...
ARRRRGH!
SSSKKRAAAAKAABBOOOM!
SKKKRRRRREEE

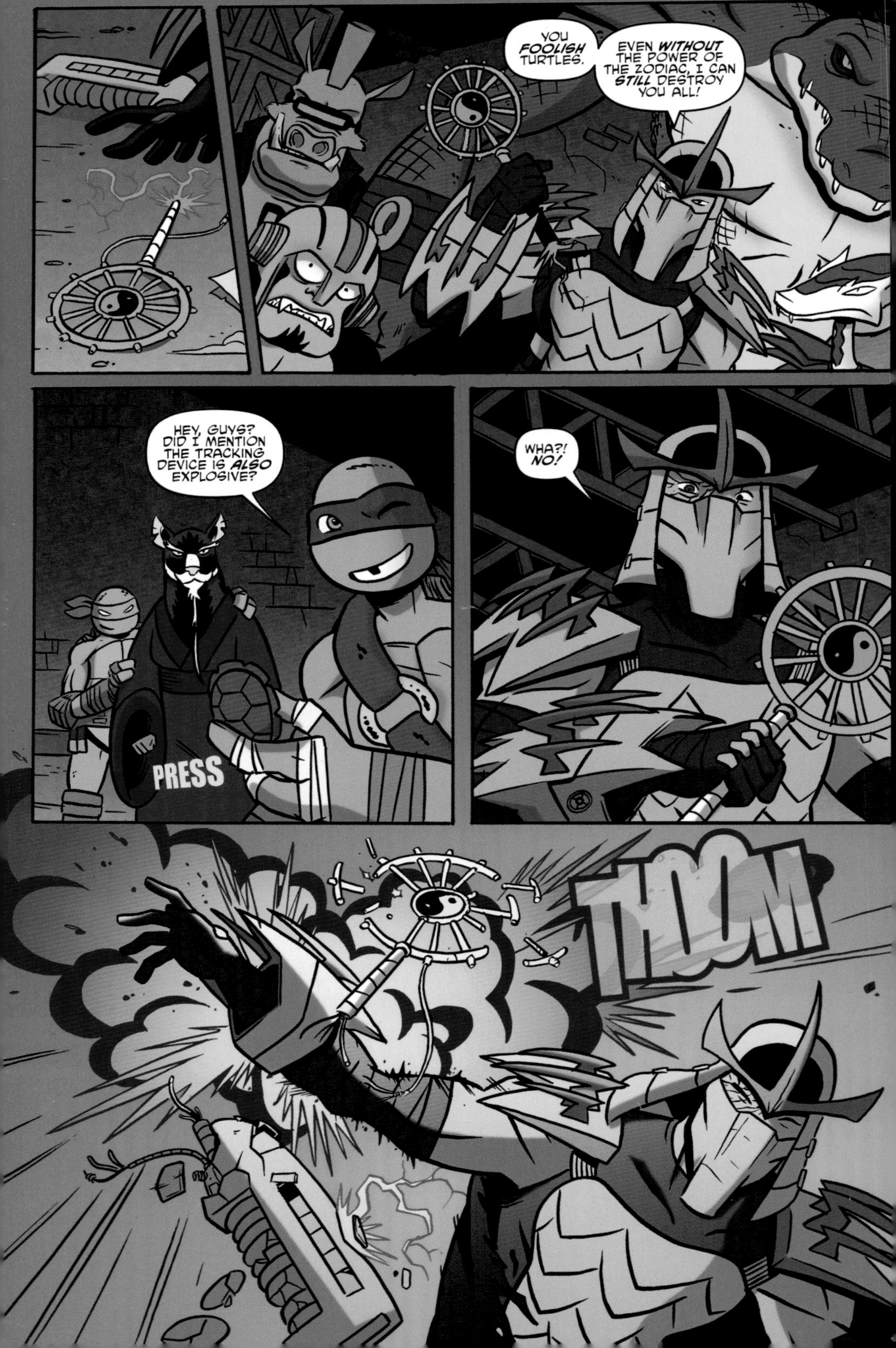

YOU FOOLISH TURTLES.
EVEN WITHOUT THE POWER OF THE ZODIAC, I CAN STILL DESTROY YOU ALL!
HEY, GUYS? DID I MENTION THE TRACKING DEVICE IS ALSO EXPLOSIVE?
PRESS
WHA?! NO!
THOOM

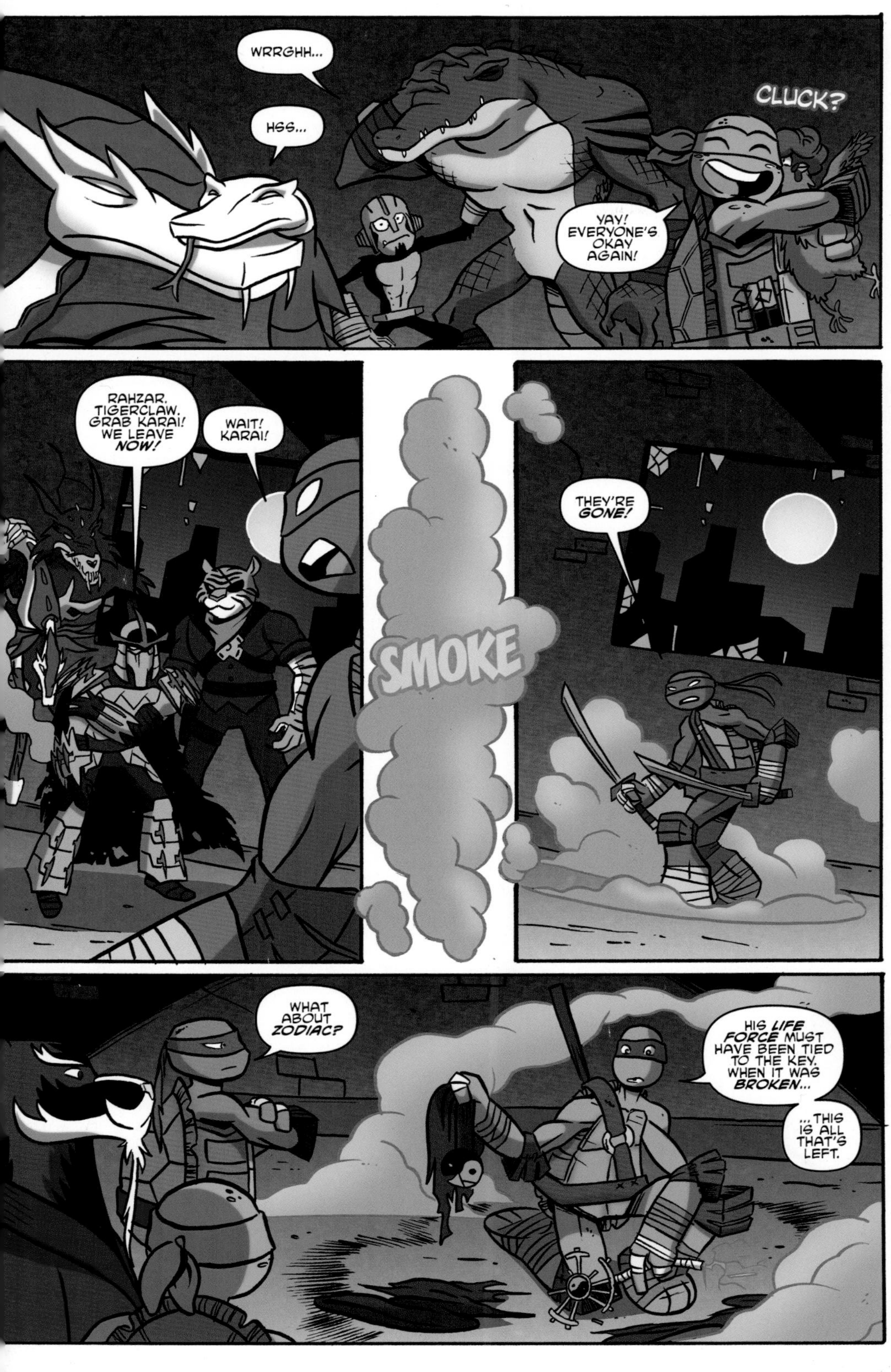
WRRGHH...
HSS...
CLUCK?
YAY! EVERYONE'S OKAY AGAIN!
RAHZAR. TIGERCLAW. GRAB KARAI! WE LEAVE NOW!
WAIT! KARAI!
SMOKE
THEY'RE GONE!
WHAT ABOUT ZODIAC?
HIS LIFE FORCE MUST HAVE BEEN TIED TO THE KEY. WHEN IT WAS BROKEN...
...THIS IS ALL THAT'S LEFT.

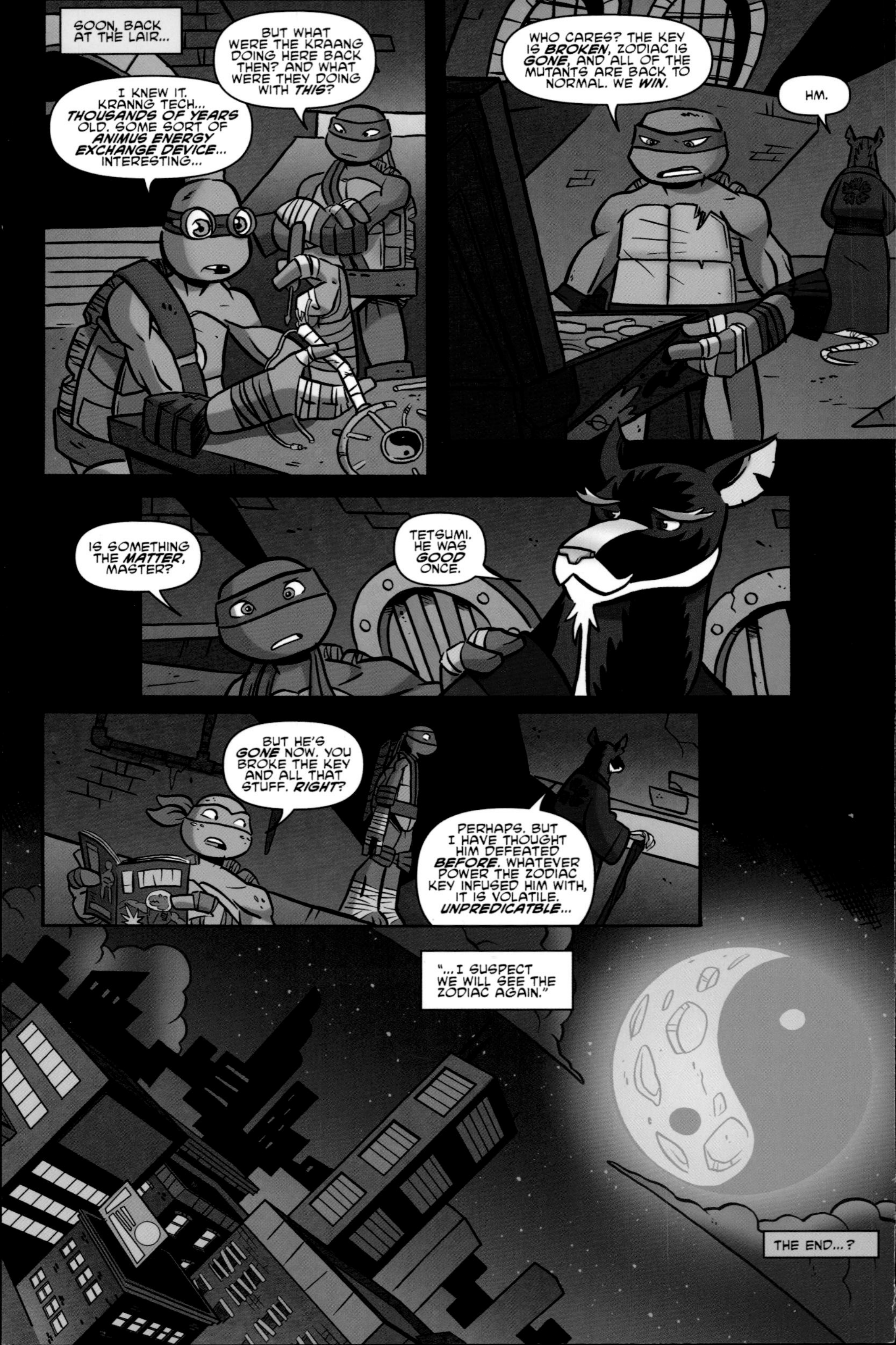
SOON, BACK AT THE LAIR...
BUT WHAT WERE THE KRAANG DOING HERE BACK THEN? AND WHAT WERE THEY DOING WITH *THIS*?
I KNEW IT. KRANNG TECH... *THOUSANDS OF YEARS* OLD. SOME SORT OF *ANIMUS ENERGY EXCHANGE DEVICE*... INTERESTING...
WHO CARES? THE KEY IS *BROKEN*, ZODIAC IS *GONE*, AND ALL OF THE MUTANTS ARE BACK TO NORMAL. WE *WIN*.
HM.
IS SOMETHING THE *MATTER*, MASTER?
TETSUMI. HE WAS *GOOD* ONCE.
BUT HE'S *GONE* NOW. YOU BROKE THE KEY AND ALL THAT STUFF. *RIGHT*?
PERHAPS. BUT I HAVE THOUGHT HIM DEFEATED *BEFORE*. WHATEVER POWER THE ZODIAC KEY INFUSED HIM WITH, IT IS VOLATILE. *UNPREDICATBLE*...
"...I SUSPECT WE WILL SEE THE ZODIAC AGAIN."
THE END...?

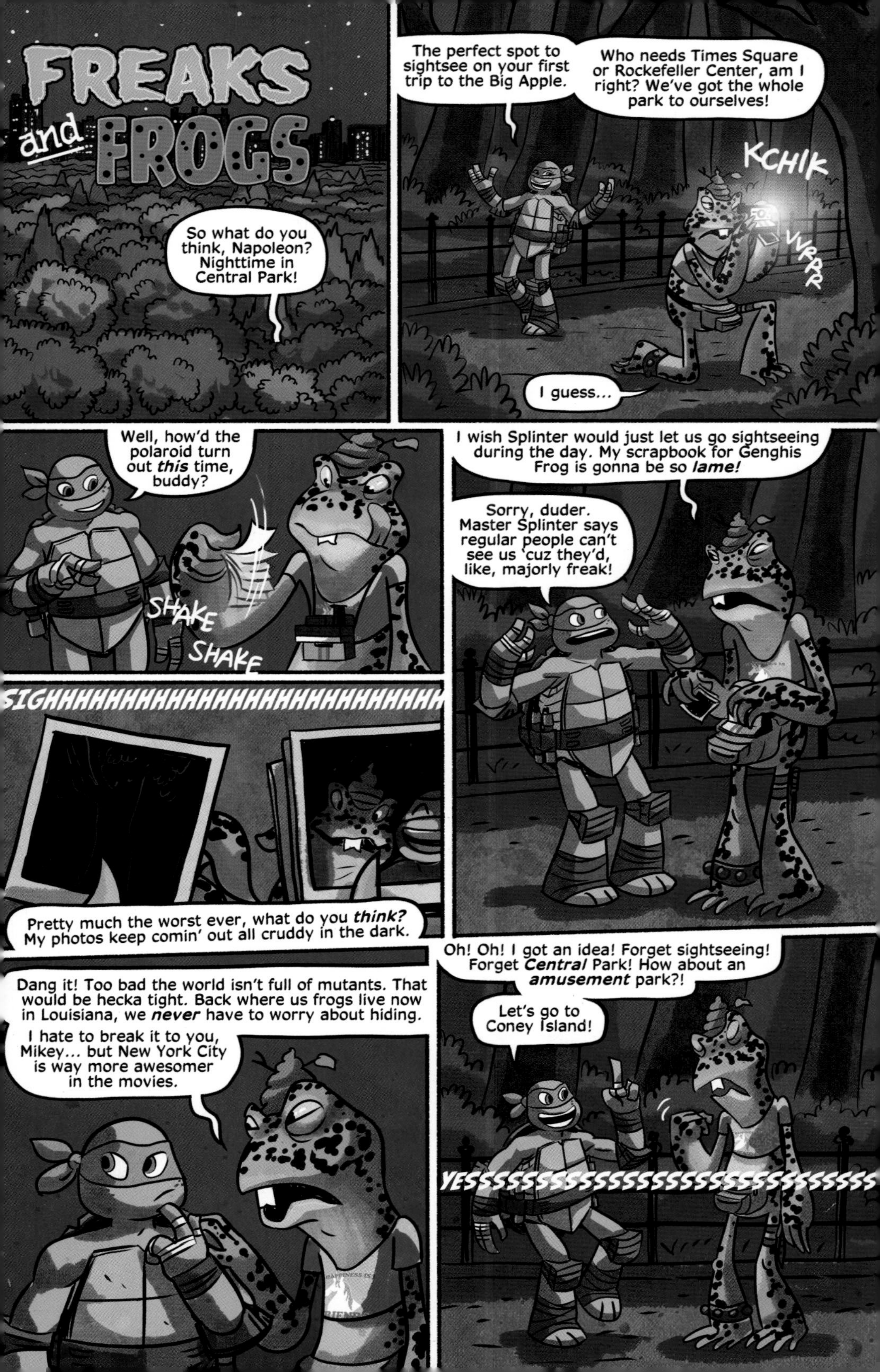
FREAKS and FROGS
So what do you think, Napoleon? Nighttime in Central Park!
The perfect spot to sightsee on your first trip to the Big Apple.
Who needs Times Square or Rockefeller Center, am I right? We've got the whole park to ourselves!
KCHIK
VVRRR
I guess...
Well, how'd the polaroid turn out *this* time, buddy?
SHAKE
SHAKE
SIGHHHHHHHHHHHHHHHHHHHHHHHHHHHHH
Pretty much the worst ever, what do you *think?* My photos keep comin' out all cruddy in the dark.
I wish Splinter would just let us go sightseeing during the day. My scrapbook for Genghis Frog is gonna be so *lame!*
Sorry, duder. Master Splinter says regular people can't see us 'cuz they'd, like, majorly freak!
Dang it! Too bad the world isn't full of mutants. That would be hecka tight. Back where us frogs live now in Louisiana, we *never* have to worry about hiding.
I hate to break it to you, Mikey... but New York City is way more awesomer in the movies.
Oh! Oh! I got an idea! Forget sightseeing! Forget *Central* Park! How about an *amusement* park?!
Let's go to Coney Island!
YESSSSSSSSSSSSSSSSSSSSSSSSSSSSSS

We're gonna have so much fun! Rides, games, ice cream, candy!

Flippin' sweet!

But how can we have any fun if we've gotta skulk in the shadows like a couple of dweebs?

Uh--'cuz I'm totally a *ninja* that's how!

Luckyyyyyyyy.

Oh yeah...? I'll *see* your "don't let go or they'll be scrapin' frog pizza off the pavement," and *raise* you a "hold on with one hand as we yell, 'Ninja skills rule, non-ninja skills drool'."

...

Can I just take a moment to bask in the glory of your genius, sir?

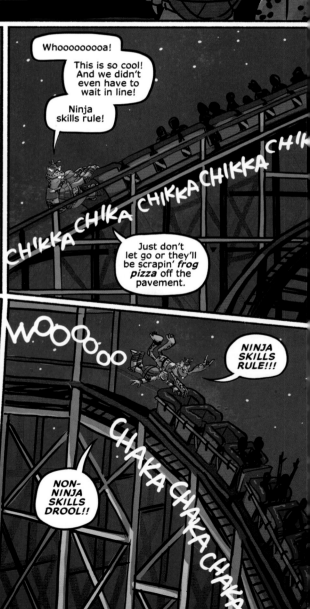

Whoooooooooa!

This is so cool! And we didn't even have to wait in line!

Ninja skills rule!

CH'IKKA CHIKA CHIKKA CHIKKA CHIK

Just don't let go or they'll be scrapin' *frog pizza* off the pavement.

WOOOOOOO

NINJA SKILLS RULE!!!

NON-NINJA SKILLS DROOL!!

CHAKA CHAKA CHAKA

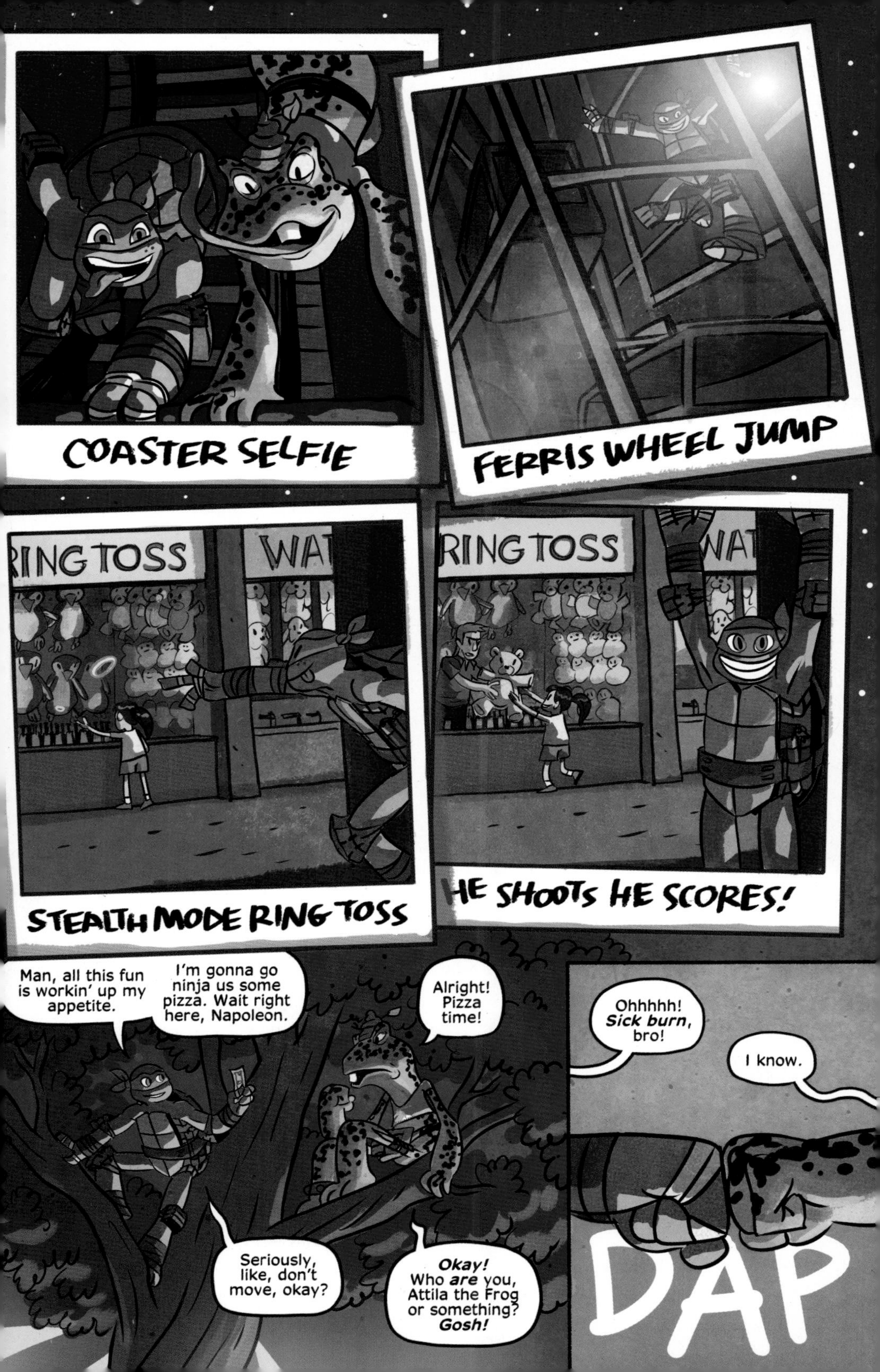

COASTER SELFIE
FERRIS WHEEL JUMP
RING TOSS
WAT
STEALTH MODE RING TOSS
RING TOSS
WAT
HE SHOOTS HE SCORES!
Man, all this fun is workin' up my appetite.
I'm gonna go ninja us some pizza. Wait right here, Napoleon.
Alright! Pizza time!
Seriously, like, don't move, okay?
Okay! Who *are* you, Attila the Frog or something? *Gosh!*
Ohhhhh! *Sick burn*, bro!
I know.
DAP

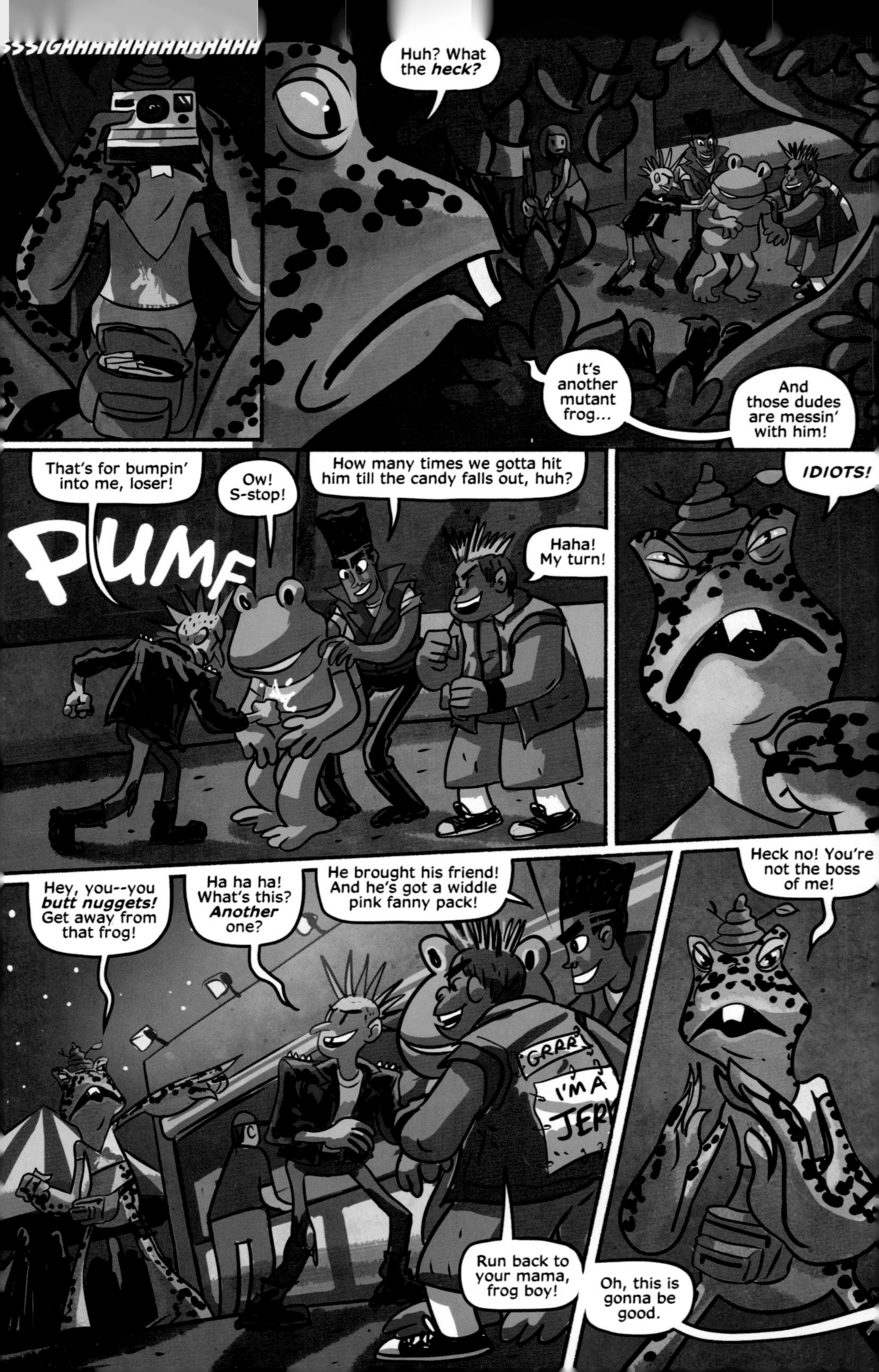

SSSIGHHHHHHHHHHHHHH
Huh? What the heck?
It's another mutant frog...
And those dudes are messin' with him!
That's for bumpin' into me, loser!
Ow! S-stop!
How many times we gotta hit him till the candy falls out, huh?
PUMF
Haha! My turn!
IDIOTS!
Hey, you--you butt nuggets! Get away from that frog!
Ha ha ha! What's this? Another one?
He brought his friend! And he's got a widdle pink fanny pack!
GRRR
I'M A JERK
Run back to your mama, frog boy!
Heck no! You're not the boss of me!
Oh, this is gonna be good.

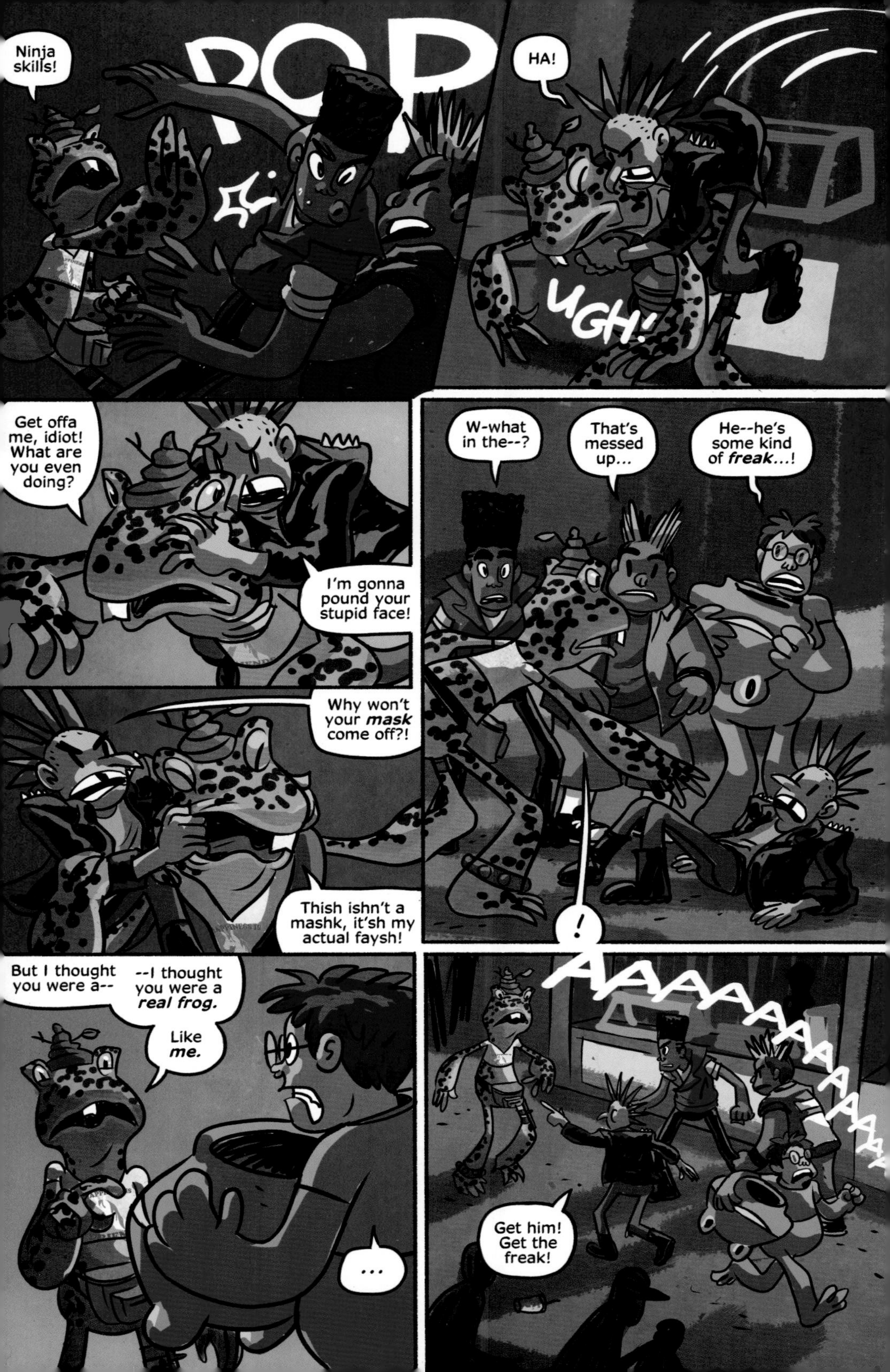
Ninja skills!
POP
HA!
UGH!
Get offa me, idiot! What are you even doing?
I'm gonna pound your stupid face!
Why won't your *mask* come off?!
Thish ishn't a mashk, it'sh my actual faysh!
W-what in the--?
That's messed up...
He--he's some kind of *freak*...!
!
But I thought you were a--
--I thought you were a *real frog.*
Like *me.*
...
AAAAAAAAAAAA
Get him! Get the freak!

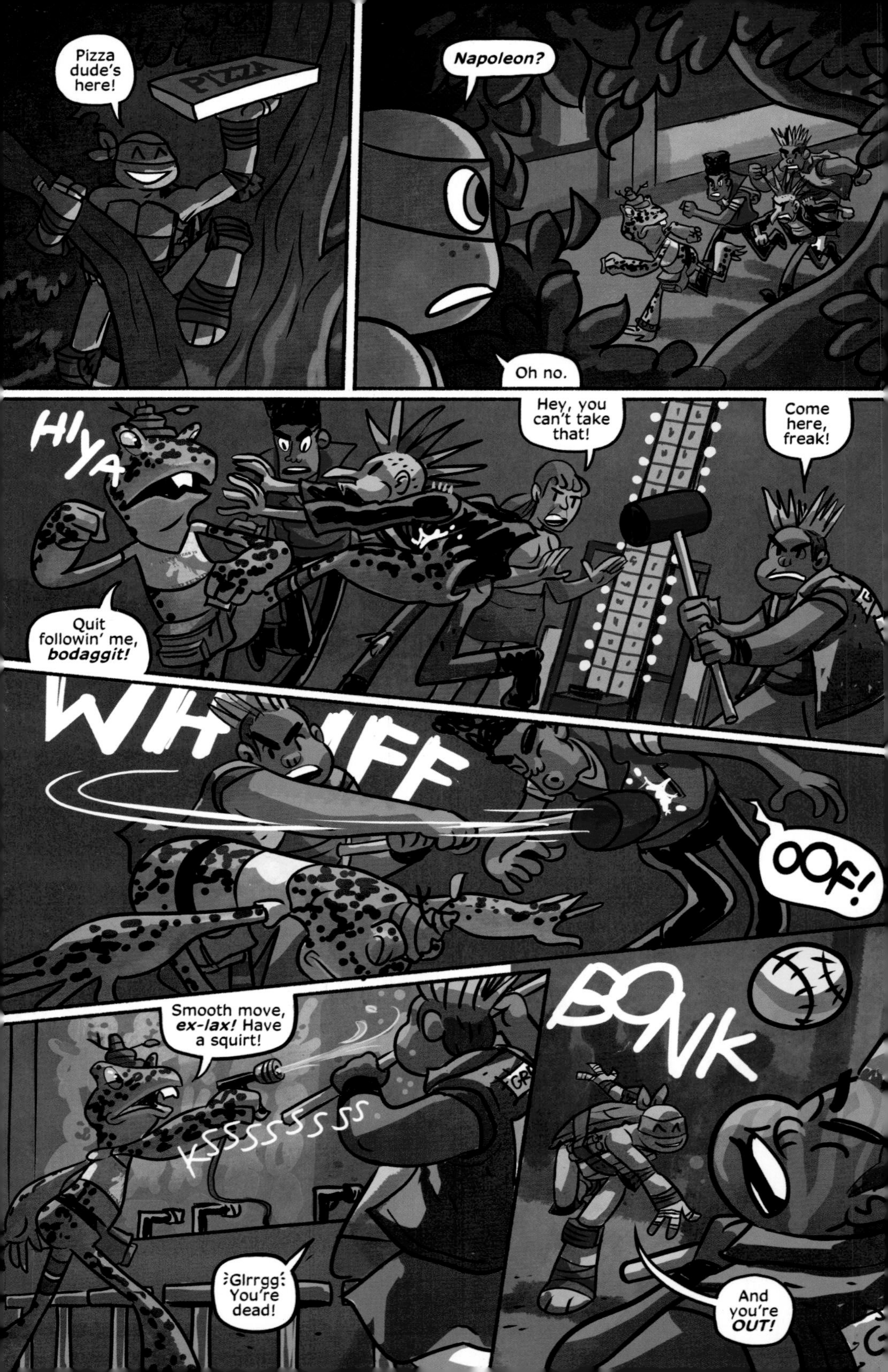
Pizza dude's here!
PIZZA
Napoleon?
Oh no.
HIYA
Quit followin' me, *bodaggit!*
Hey, you can't take that!
Come here, freak!
WHIFF
OOF!
Smooth move, *ex-lax!* Have a squirt!
KSSSSSSSS
Glrrgg You're dead!
BONK
And you're *OUT!*

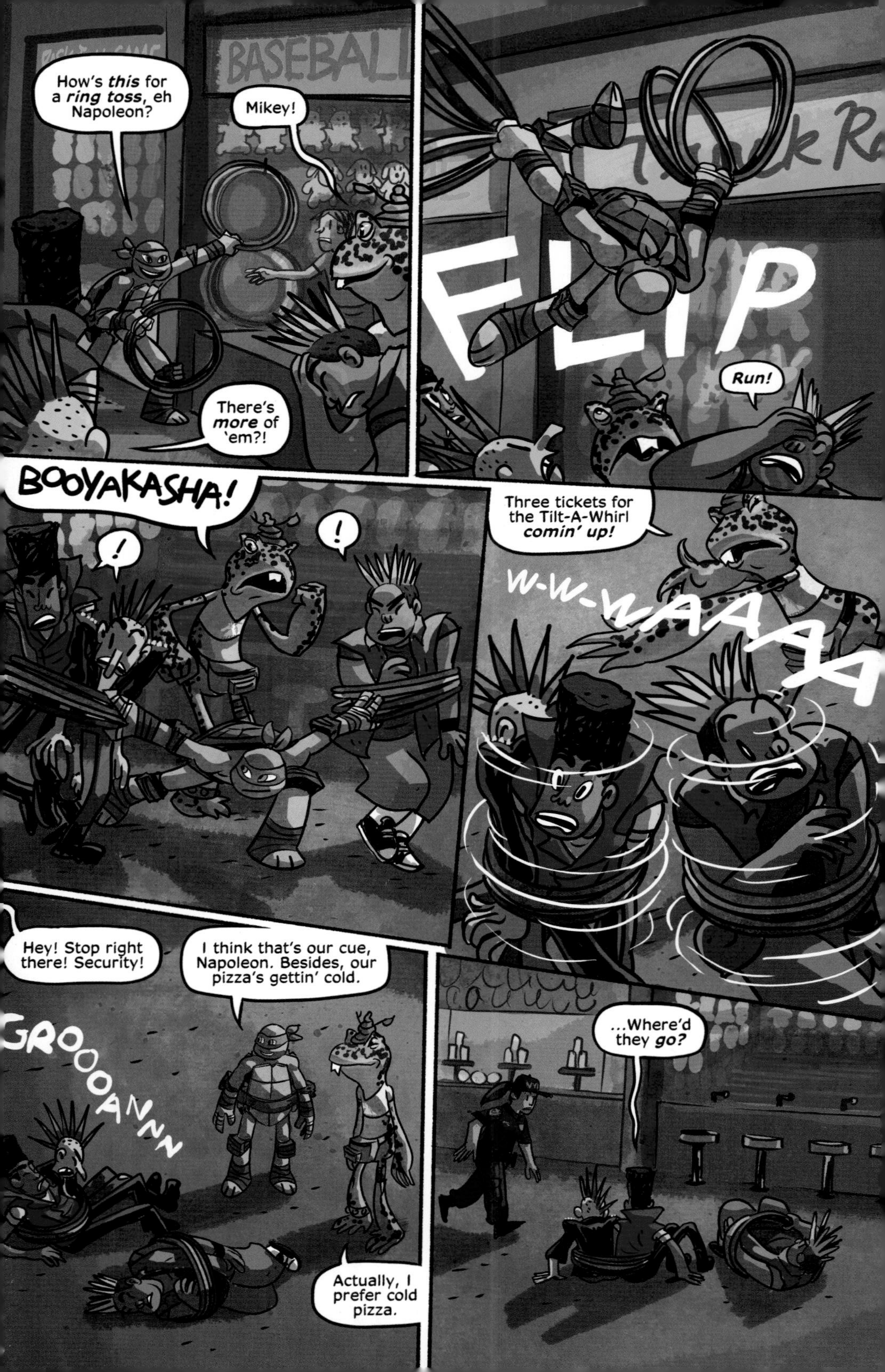
How's *this* for a *ring toss*, eh Napoleon?
Mikey!
There's *more* of 'em?!
FLIP
Run!
BOOYAKASHA!
!
!
Three tickets for the Tilt-A-Whirl *comin' up!*
W-W-WAAAAA
Hey! Stop right there! Security!
I think that's our cue, Napoleon. Besides, our pizza's gettin' cold.
GROOOANNN
Actually, I prefer cold pizza.
...Where'd they *go?*

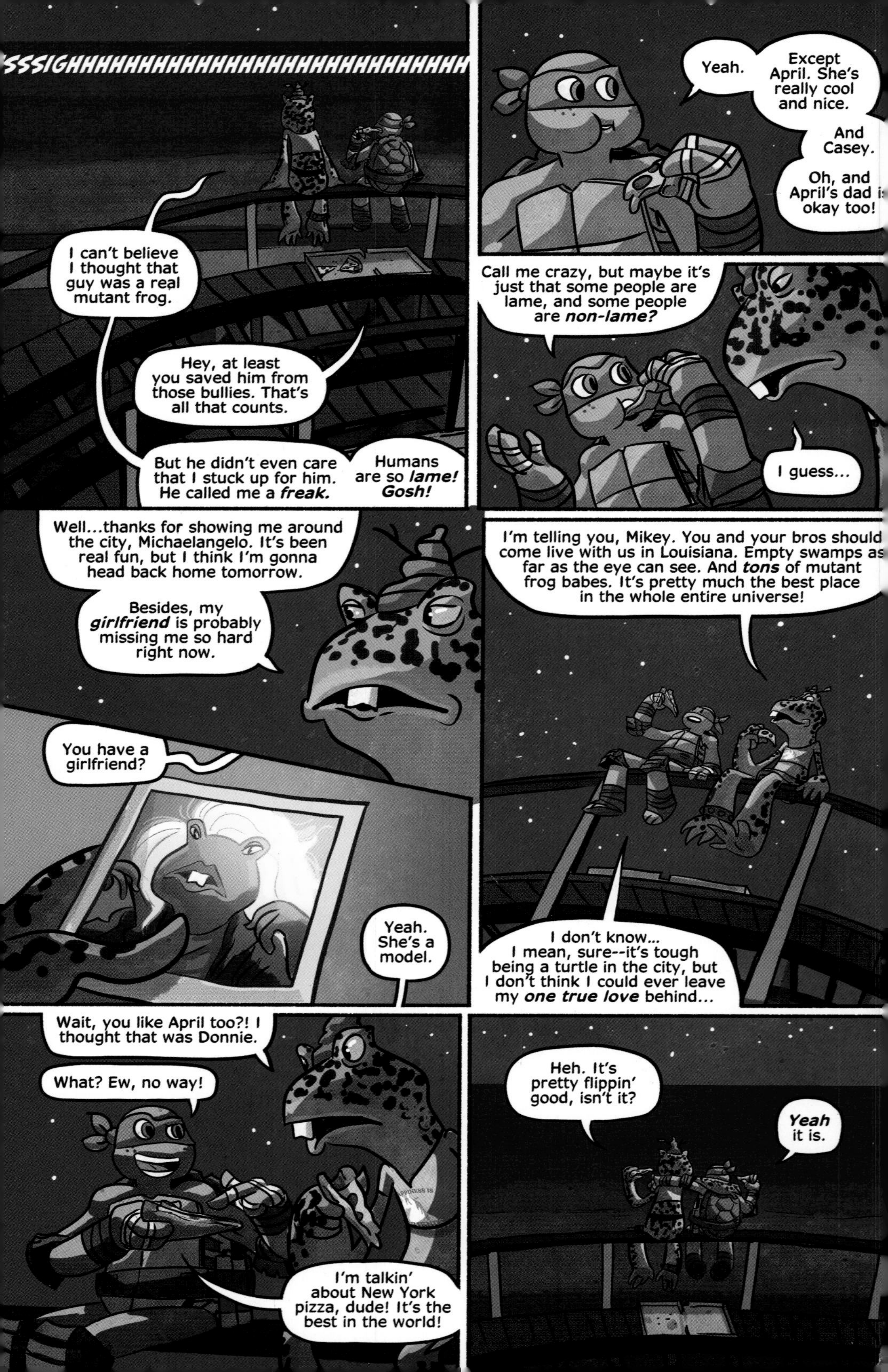
SSSIGHHHHHHHHHHHHHHHHHHHHHHHHHHHHHHHH
I can't believe I thought that guy was a real mutant frog.
Hey, at least you saved him from those bullies. That's all that counts.
But he didn't even care that I stuck up for him. He called me a *freak.*
Humans are so *lame! Gosh!*
Yeah.
Except April. She's really cool and nice.
And Casey.
Oh, and April's dad is okay too!
Call me crazy, but maybe it's just that some people are lame, and some people are *non-lame?*
I guess...
Well...thanks for showing me around the city, Michaelangelo. It's been real fun, but I think I'm gonna head back home tomorrow.
Besides, my *girlfriend* is probably missing me so hard right now.
You have a girlfriend?
Yeah. She's a model.
I'm telling you, Mikey. You and your bros should come live with us in Louisiana. Empty swamps as far as the eye can see. And *tons* of mutant frog babes. It's pretty much the best place in the whole entire universe!
I don't know... I mean, sure--it's tough being a turtle in the city, but I don't think I could ever leave my *one true love* behind...
Wait, you like April too?! I thought that was Donnie.
What? Ew, no way!
I'm talkin' about New York pizza, dude! It's the best in the world!
Heh. It's pretty flippin' good, isn't it?
Yeah it is.

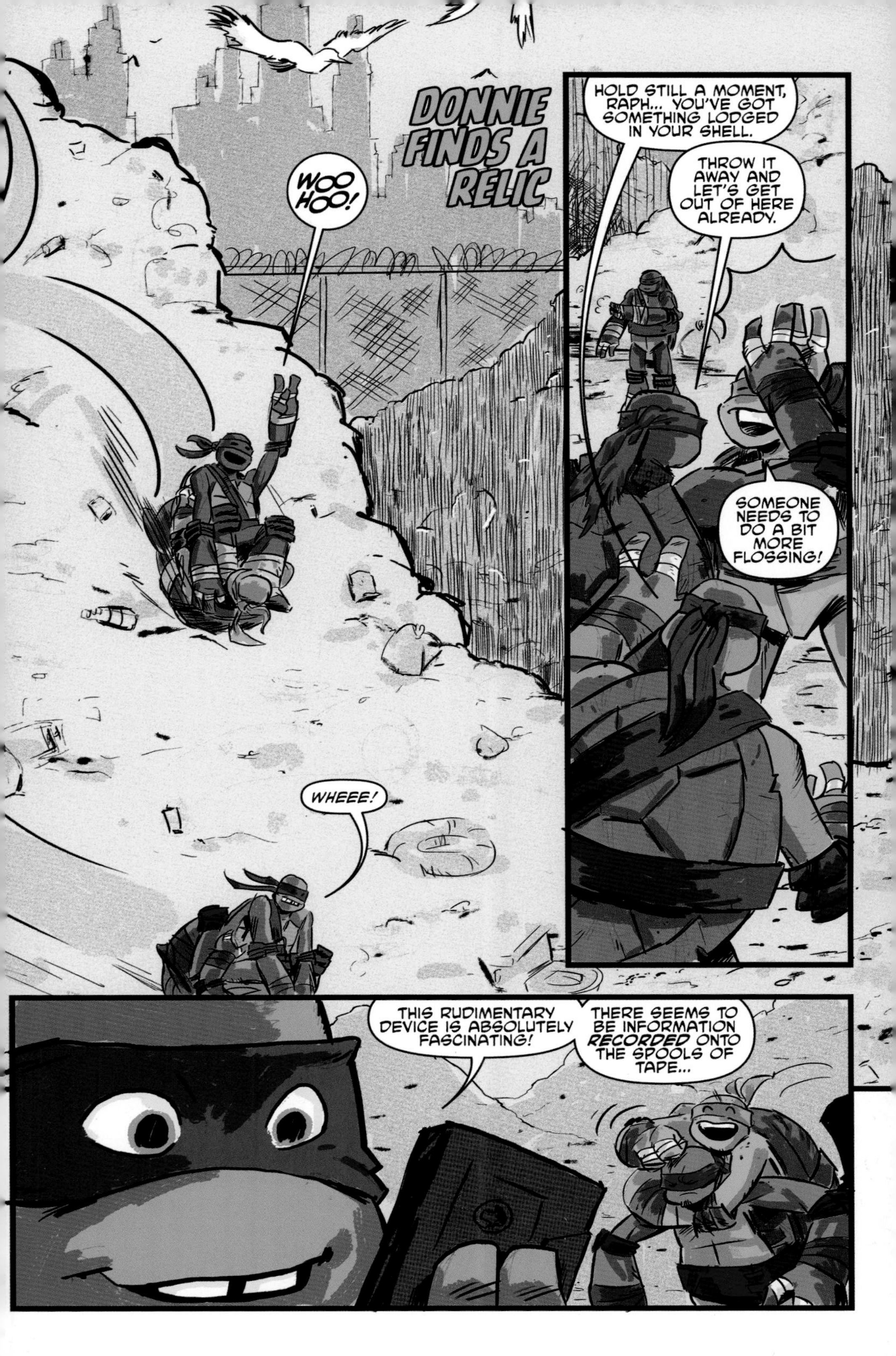
DONNIE FINDS A RELIC
WOO HOO!
WHEEE!
HOLD STILL A MOMENT, RAPH... YOU'VE GOT SOMETHING LODGED IN YOUR SHELL.
THROW IT AWAY AND LET'S GET OUT OF HERE ALREADY.
SOMEONE NEEDS TO DO A BIT MORE FLOSSING!
THIS RUDIMENTARY DEVICE IS ABSOLUTELY FASCINATING!
THERE SEEMS TO BE INFORMATION *RECORDED* ONTO THE SPOOLS OF TAPE...

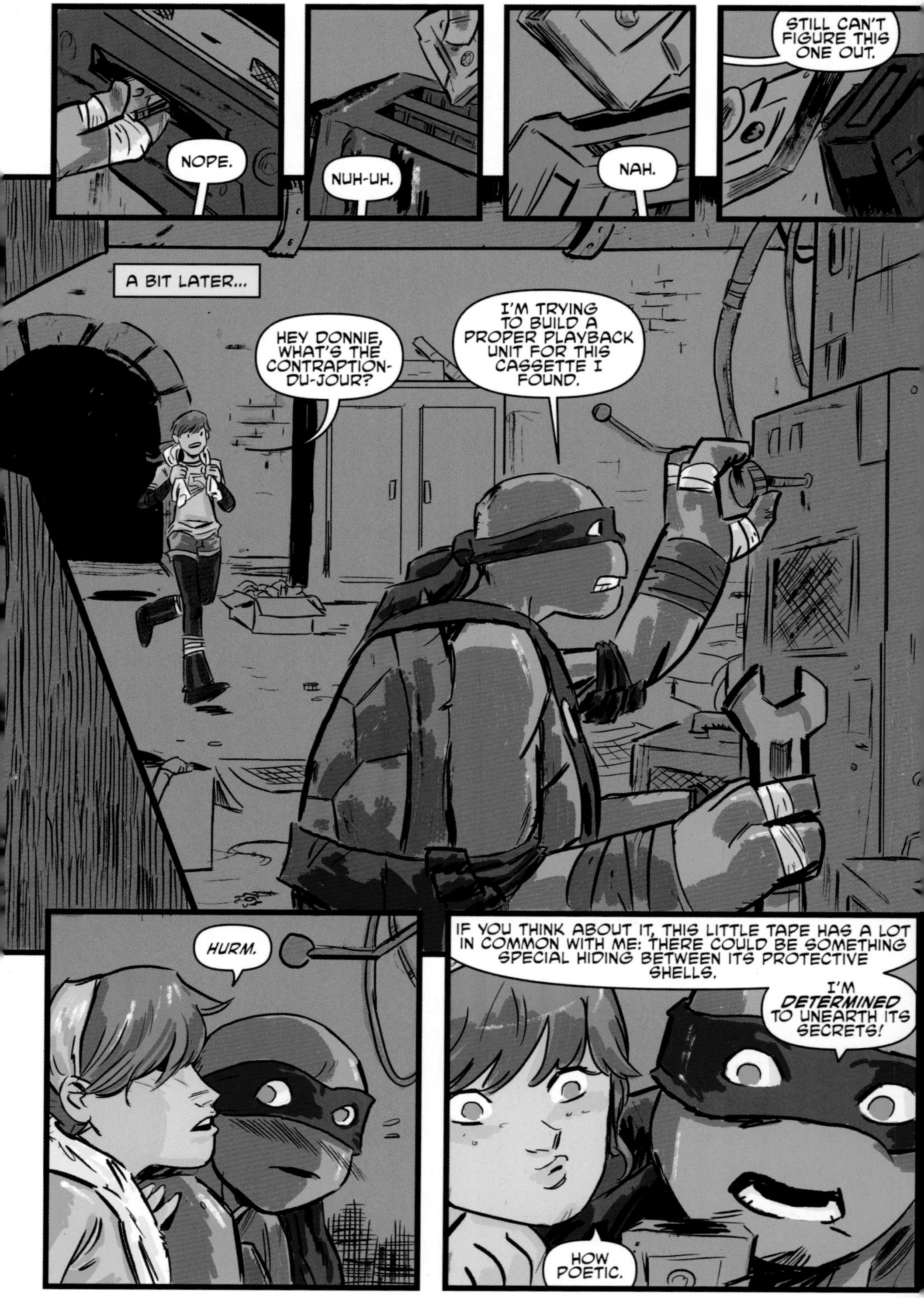
NOPE.
NUH-UH.
NAH.
STILL CAN'T FIGURE THIS ONE OUT.
A BIT LATER...
HEY DONNIE, WHAT'S THE CONTRAPTION-DU-JOUR?
I'M TRYING TO BUILD A PROPER PLAYBACK UNIT FOR THIS CASSETTE I FOUND.
HURM.
IF YOU THINK ABOUT IT, THIS LITTLE TAPE HAS A LOT IN COMMON WITH ME: THERE COULD BE SOMETHING SPECIAL HIDING BETWEEN ITS PROTECTIVE SHELLS.
I'M *DETERMINED* TO UNEARTH ITS SECRETS!
HOW POETIC.

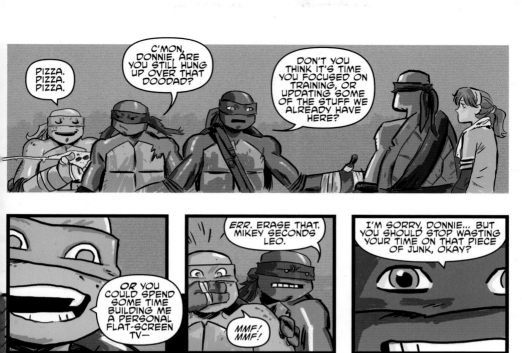

PIZZA. PIZZA. PIZZA.

C'MON, DONNIE, ARE YOU STILL HUNG UP OVER THAT DOODAD?

DON'T YOU THINK IT'S TIME YOU FOCUSED ON TRAINING, OR UPDATING SOME OF THE STUFF WE ALREADY HAVE HERE?

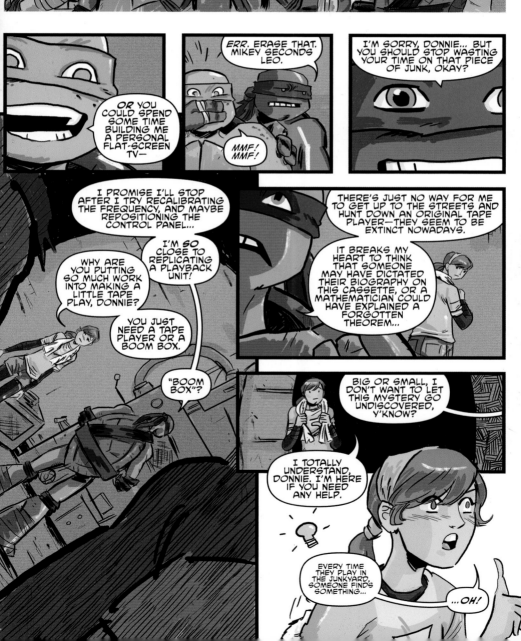

ERR. ERASE THAT. MIKEY SECONDS LEO.

OR YOU COULD SPEND SOME TIME BUILDING ME A PERSONAL FLAT-SCREEN TV—

MMF! MMF!

I'M SORRY, DONNIE... BUT YOU SHOULD STOP WASTING YOUR TIME ON THAT PIECE OF JUNK, OKAY?

I PROMISE I'LL STOP AFTER I TRY RECALIBRATING THE FREQUENCY, AND MAYBE REPOSITIONING THE CONTROL PANEL...

I'M SO CLOSE TO REPLICATING A PLAYBACK UNIT!

WHY ARE YOU PUTTING SO MUCH WORK INTO MAKING A LITTLE TAPE PLAY, DONNIE?

YOU JUST NEED A TAPE PLAYER OR A BOOM BOX.

"BOOM BOX"?

THERE'S JUST NO WAY FOR ME TO GET UP TO THE STREETS AND HUNT DOWN AN ORIGINAL TAPE PLAYER—THEY SEEM TO BE EXTINCT NOWADAYS.

IT BREAKS MY HEART TO THINK THAT SOMEONE MAY HAVE DICTATED THEIR BIOGRAPHY ON THIS CASSETTE, OR A MATHEMATICIAN COULD HAVE EXPLAINED A FORGOTTEN THEOREM...

BIG OR SMALL, I DON'T WANT TO LET THIS MYSTERY GO UNDISCOVERED, Y'KNOW?

I TOTALLY UNDERSTAND, DONNIE. I'M HERE IF YOU NEED ANY HELP.

EVERY TIME THEY PLAY IN THE JUNKYARD, SOMEONE FINDS SOMETHING...

...OH!

THAT EVENING...

GET IN AND GET OUT, APRIL.

KEEP YOUR HEAD DOWN, DON'T MAKE EYE CONTACT WITH ANYONE... YOU'LL BE BACK BEFORE SPLINTER EVEN NOTICES.

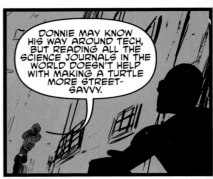

DONNIE MAY KNOW HIS WAY AROUND TECH, BUT READING ALL THE SCIENCE JOURNALS IN THE WORLD DOESN'T HELP WITH MAKING A TURTLE MORE STREET-SAVVY.

IF I KNOW ANYTHING ABOUT THIS NEIGHBORHOOD...

...IT'S THAT *VINTAGE* IS ALWAYS IN STYLE!

OOOOOH!

THERE IT IS!

YIKES! WHO KNEW A PIECE OF JUNK— ERR— *HISTORY,* WOULD COST SO MUCH?!

I DON'T SUPPOSE YOU GIVE STUDENT DISCOUNTS, DO YOU?

NO DISCOUNTS. CASH, CREDIT, OR EXCHANGE ONLY.

EXCHANGE, *HUH?*

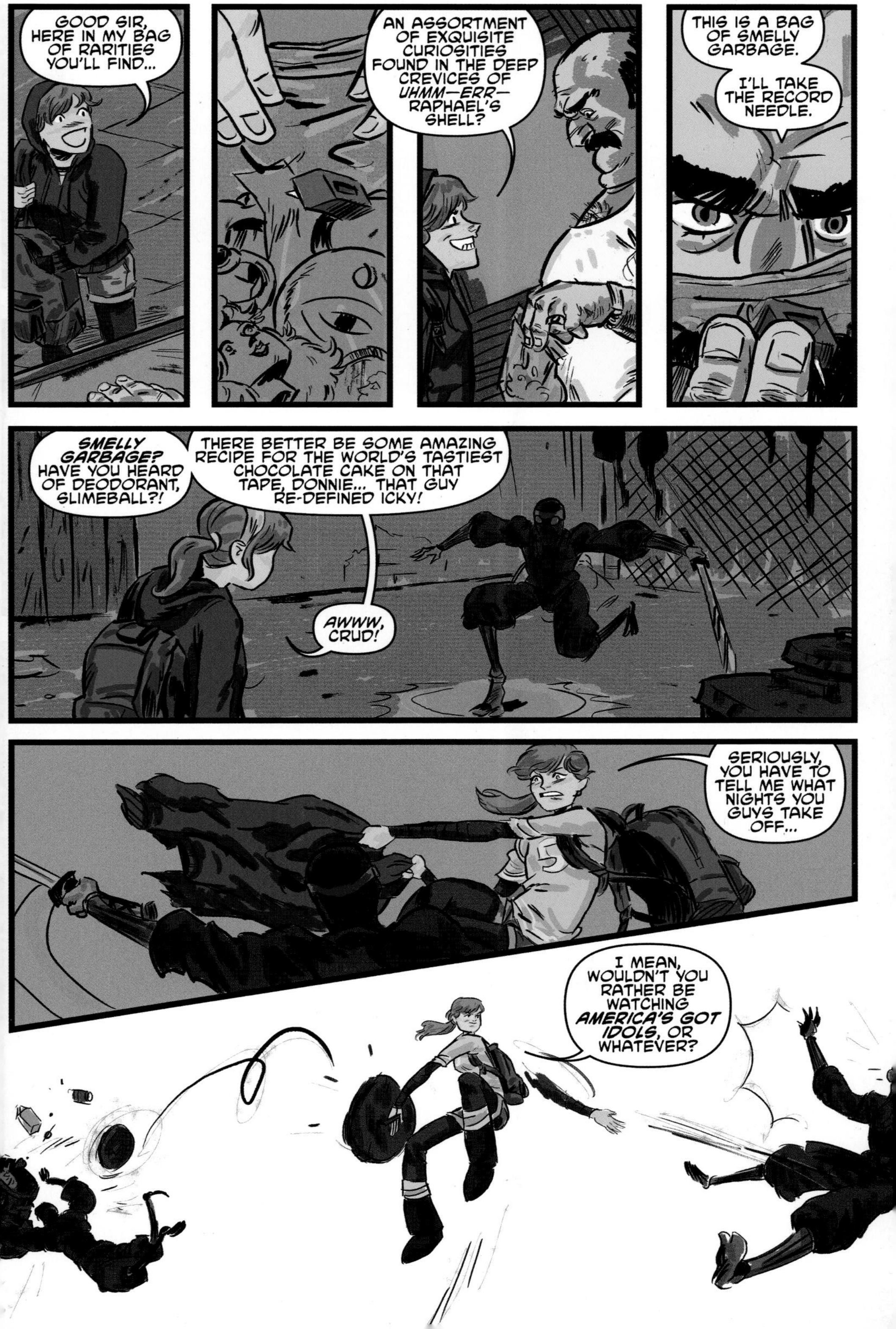

GOOD SIR, HERE IN MY BAG OF RARITIES YOU'LL FIND...
AN ASSORTMENT OF EXQUISITE CURIOSITIES FOUND IN THE DEEP CREVICES OF *UHMM—ERR—* RAPHAEL'S SHELL?
THIS IS A BAG OF SMELLY GARBAGE.
I'LL TAKE THE RECORD NEEDLE.
SMELLY GARBAGE? HAVE YOU HEARD OF DEODORANT, SLIMEBALL?!
THERE BETTER BE SOME AMAZING RECIPE FOR THE WORLD'S TASTIEST CHOCOLATE CAKE ON THAT TAPE, DONNIE... THAT GUY RE-DEFINED ICKY!
AWWW, CRUD!
SERIOUSLY, YOU HAVE TO TELL ME WHAT NIGHTS YOU GUYS TAKE OFF...
I MEAN, WOULDN'T YOU RATHER BE WATCHING ***AMERICA'S GOT IDOLS***, OR WHATEVER?

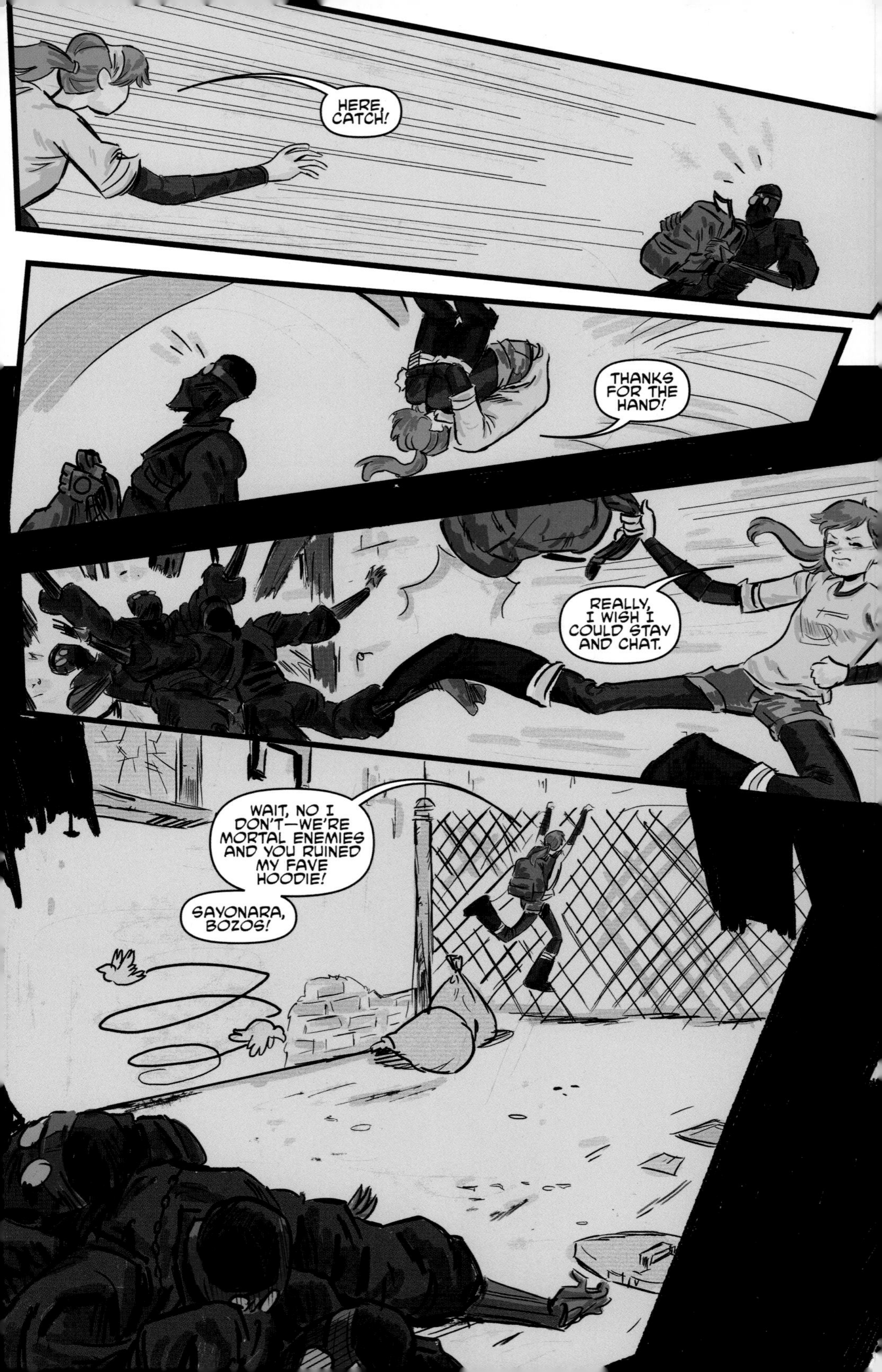
HERE, CATCH!
THANKS FOR THE HAND!
REALLY, I WISH I COULD STAY AND CHAT.
WAIT, NO I DON'T—WE'RE MORTAL ENEMIES AND YOU RUINED MY FAVE HOODIE!
SAYONARA, BOZOS!

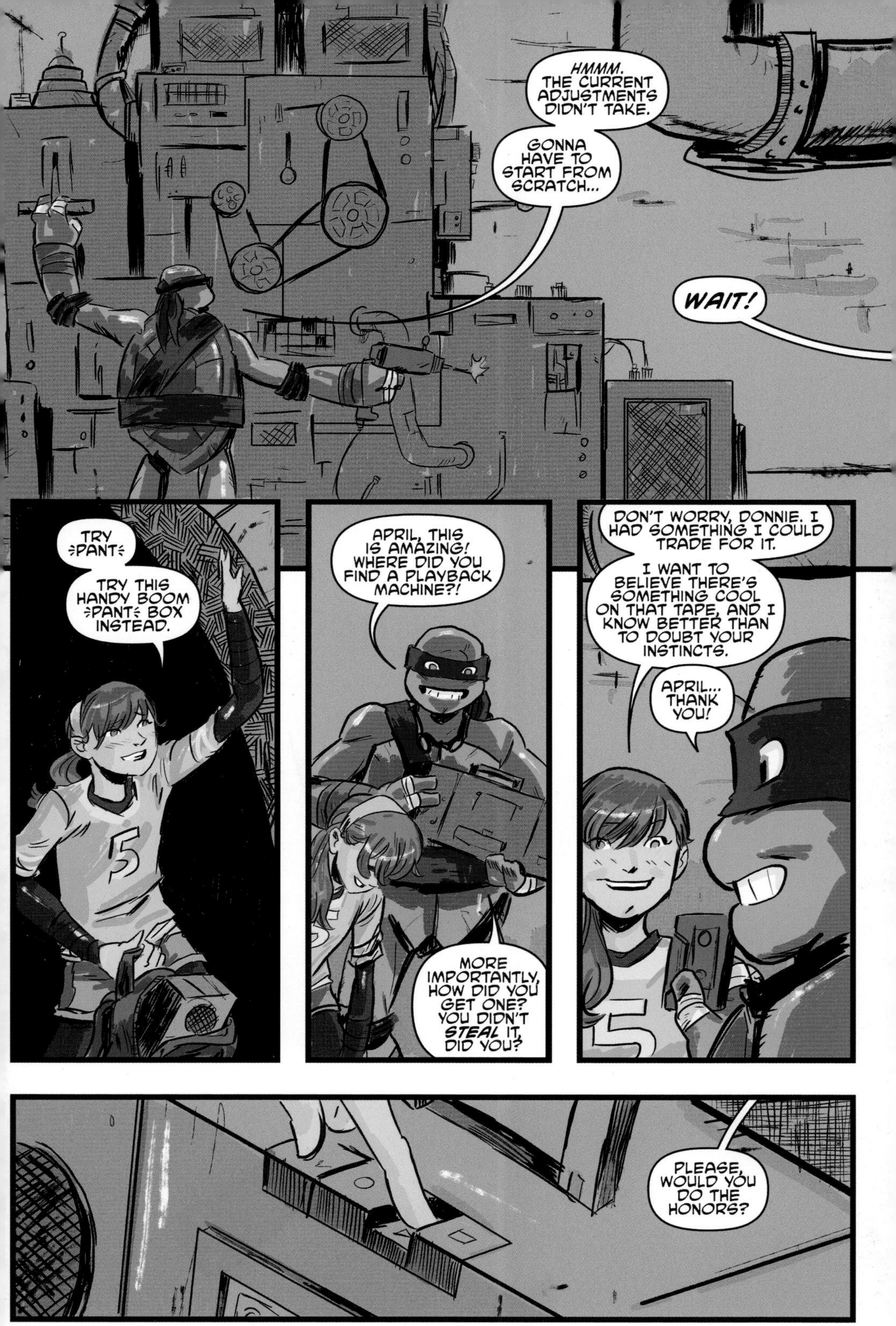
HMMM. THE CURRENT ADJUSTMENTS DIDN'T TAKE.
GONNA HAVE TO START FROM SCRATCH...
WAIT!
TRY ≑PANT≑
TRY THIS HANDY BOOM ≑PANT≑ BOX INSTEAD.
APRIL, THIS IS AMAZING! WHERE DID YOU FIND A PLAYBACK MACHINE?!
MORE IMPORTANTLY, HOW DID YOU GET ONE? YOU DIDN'T STEAL IT, DID YOU?
DON'T WORRY, DONNIE. I HAD SOMETHING I COULD TRADE FOR IT.
I WANT TO BELIEVE THERE'S SOMETHING COOL ON THAT TAPE, AND I KNOW BETTER THAN TO DOUBT YOUR INSTINCTS.
APRIL... THANK YOU!
PLEASE, WOULD YOU DO THE HONORS?

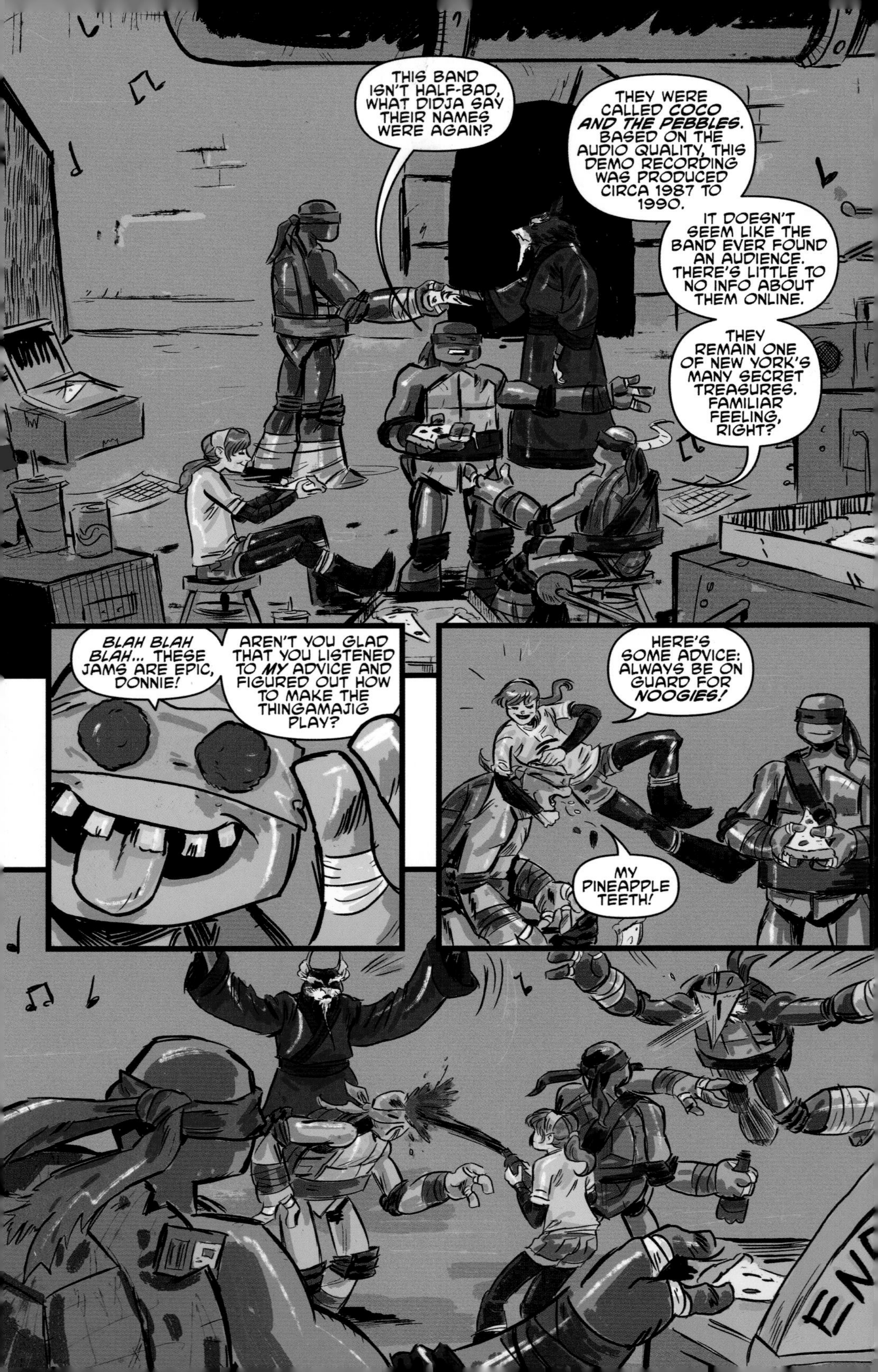
THIS BAND ISN'T HALF-BAD, WHAT DIDJA SAY THEIR NAMES WERE AGAIN?
THEY WERE CALLED COCO AND THE PEBBLES. BASED ON THE AUDIO QUALITY, THIS DEMO RECORDING WAS PRODUCED CIRCA 1987 TO 1990.
IT DOESN'T SEEM LIKE THE BAND EVER FOUND AN AUDIENCE. THERE'S LITTLE TO NO INFO ABOUT THEM ONLINE.
THEY REMAIN ONE OF NEW YORK'S MANY SECRET TREASURES. FAMILIAR FEELING, RIGHT?
BLAH BLAH BLAH... THESE JAMS ARE EPIC, DONNIE!
AREN'T YOU GLAD THAT YOU LISTENED TO MY ADVICE AND FIGURED OUT HOW TO MAKE THE THINGAMAJIG PLAY?
HERE'S SOME ADVICE: ALWAYS BE ON GUARD FOR NOOGIES!
MY PINEAPPLE TEETH!
END

Art by **Jon Sommariva**

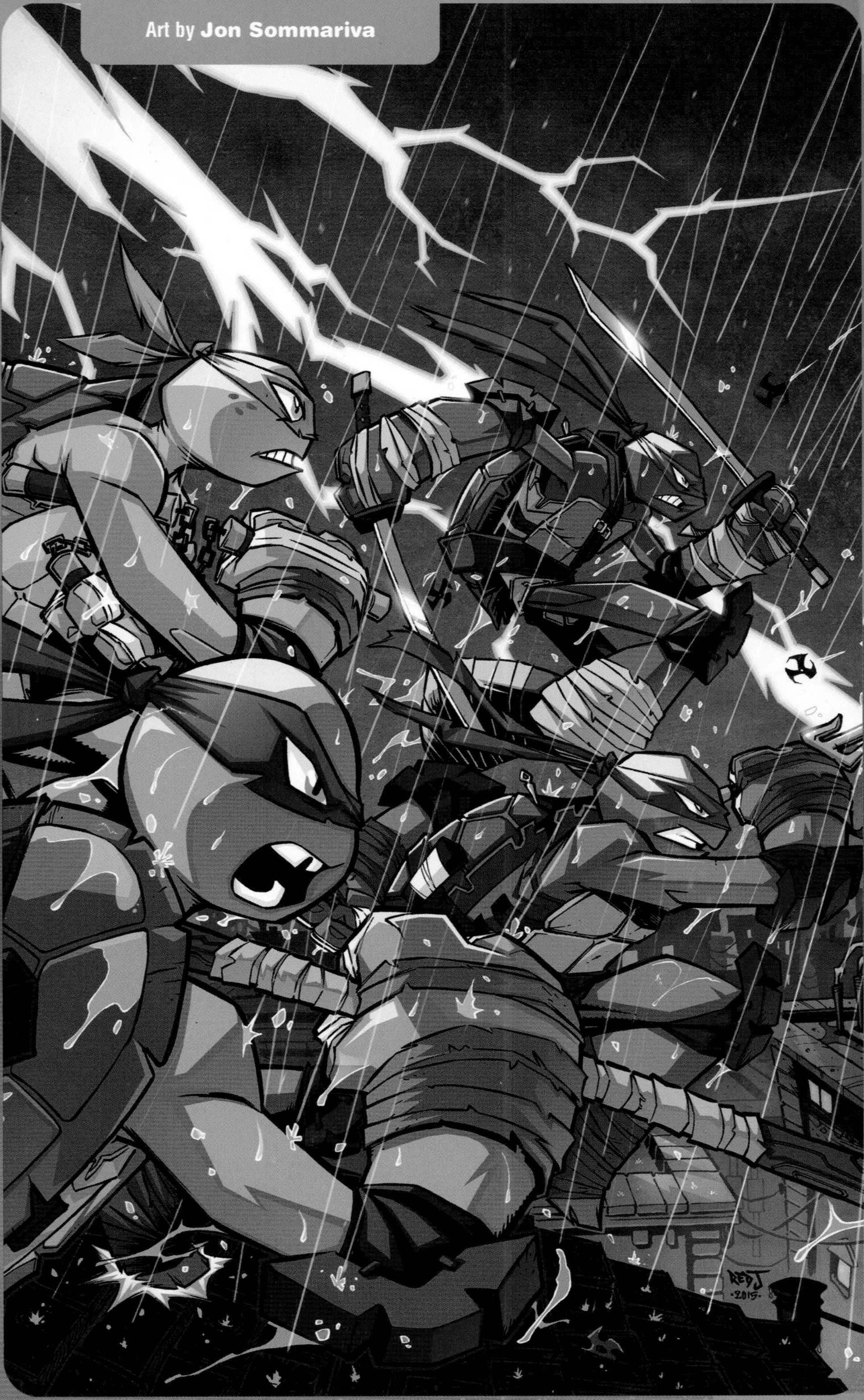

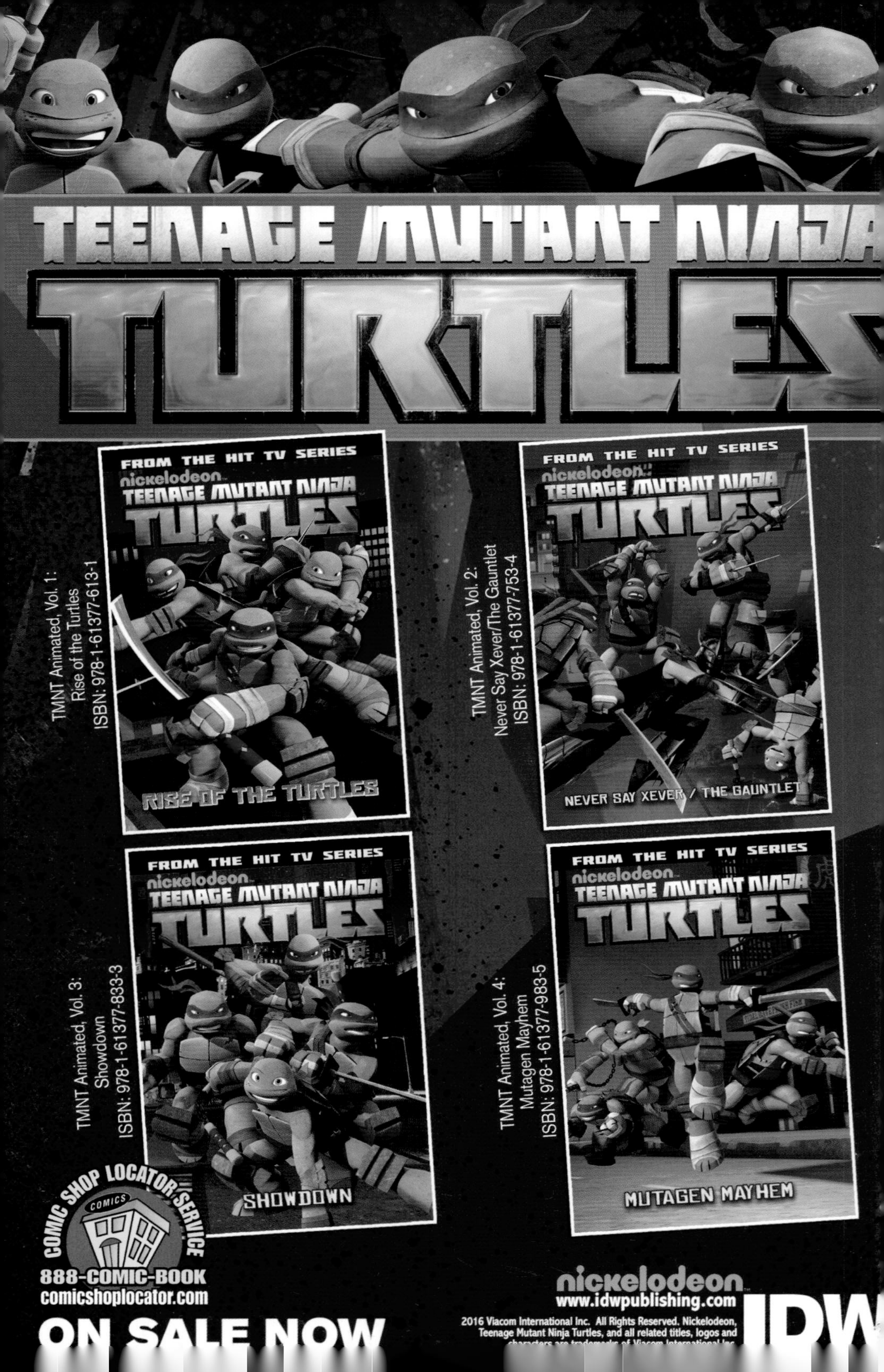
TEENAGE MUTANT NINJA TURTLES
FROM THE HIT TV SERIES
nickelodeon
TEENAGE MUTANT NINJA TURTLES
RISE OF THE TURTLES
TMNT Animated, Vol. 1:
Rise of the Turtles
ISBN: 978-1-61377-613-1
FROM THE HIT TV SERIES
nickelodeon
TEENAGE MUTANT NINJA TURTLES
NEVER SAY XEVER / THE GAUNTLET
TMNT Animated, Vol. 2:
Never Say Xever/The Gauntlet
ISBN: 978-1-61377-753-4
FROM THE HIT TV SERIES
nickelodeon
TEENAGE MUTANT NINJA TURTLES
SHOWDOWN
TMNT Animated, Vol. 3:
Showdown
ISBN: 978-1-61377-833-3
FROM THE HIT TV SERIES
nickelodeon
TEENAGE MUTANT NINJA TURTLES
MUTAGEN MAYHEM
TMNT Animated, Vol. 4:
Mutagen Mayhem
ISBN: 978-1-61377-983-5
COMIC SHOP LOCATOR SERVICE
COMICS
888-COMIC-BOOK
comicshoplocator.com
ON SALE NOW
nickelodeon
www.idwpublishing.com
2016 Viacom International Inc. All Rights Reserved. Nickelodeon,
Teenage Mutant Ninja Turtles, and all related titles, logos and
IDW